I0721402

Jersey Devils

or

An Account of Curious Goings On in the Pine Barrens

By R.E. Sohl

Dedications

I'd like to thank Dennis Cronin for his enthusiasm about this project,

Brenda Lynn for sharing her Jersey Devil encounter,

and my fellow Barnegat expatiate Tim Castelluccio for his recollections of local folklore.

Prelude: In a Forest

The woods were vast, dense and knotted with secrets. Dark secrets, and it knew how to hide them.

Usually.

Yet every so often these ugly truths, deemed too gruesome for the carefully ordered world of straight lines, sidewalks and strip malls that humanity had fashioned for itself on the edge of this wilderness, could no longer be contained. The chaos of the untamed forest would break through, like a demon clawing its way back up from the deepest pits of hell to challenge our very notion of sanity. In these terrible moments, the illusion of our mastery and understanding of the world is shattered. We are stripped of any comfort, left to shudder in the cold light of a new reality: the dark things of the world are real and always hovering somewhere on the edge of our awareness, ever poised to strike.

The woman who went by the unlikely name of Agent Method tried to shut out grim thoughts such as these. It was difficult to do in the face of the mass of gibbering, pulsating fury that snapped and snarled impotently at her from the other side of the transparent barrier. The beast clawed at the obstruction, gnashing its blackened teeth in rage, hurling itself bodily against it. It was too dumb to understand that there was no way to get to Agent Method and her colleagues. All it saw was a meal. All it knew was a boundless, elemental hunger that could never be satiated.

Agent Method reached inside her black dress jacket and nervously placed her hand on the silver handle of the sidearm nestled in her holster. She'd read the file on this abomination. She knew that if somehow the *thing* before her escaped from the wall of emerald energy which ensnared it, even weapons as fantastic as the ones she'd been entrusted with wouldn't stop it. The best she could hope for was to slow it down. Yet she still couldn't help but play with the pistol's grip. Even though she'd seen many unbelievable things in her line of work, somehow none of that had prepared her for the mind-shattering reality which now confronted her.

Her companion, Agent Fresh, was relatively new to this line of work and it showed. He already had his weapon drawn and pointed at the horrible thing that was thrashing and crashing about, frenzied at the prospect of fresh meat mere feet away from it. He was trying his best not to let his hands tremble as he kept his gleaming gun trained on the beast, but he was failing. Agent Method rolled her eyes at his nervousness. She was afraid too, but she wouldn't, *couldn't* let that affect her performance. That's when mistakes were made, and mistakes are what got people killed.

There'd already been enough deaths in these woods lately, and she'd be damned if there'd be any more on her watch.

Agent Method couldn't bear to continue looking upon the stinking mass of bubbling flesh wildly scratching at the barrier. Nor could she stand to watch the newbie agent she'd been saddled with teeter on the edge of a disappointingly unprofessional panic. Instead she glanced over her shoulder, refocusing her attention on the other member of her party - her superior, Agent Ember. Good old Agent Ember. The older woman had worked with her for years. At least she knew she could depend on Ember to have her back if things suddenly went south. Agent Ember also had the advantage of being a particularly powerful witch. In fact, it was her magically generated barrier which now contained the monster.

The barrier was strong enough to keep the thing at bay, but it wouldn't last forever.

Method's eyes widened in alarm behind her Ray-Ban sunglasses. Less than five minutes were left! She knew this from the heads-up display projected onto her sunglasses by a highly efficient mini computer strapped to her wrist. The computer was currently counting down the time remaining before the spell that protected them from the raging creature would expire and need to be recast.

The spell was a fairly basic one and wouldn't take long to recast, but during that brief window of opportunity, they'd be completely vulnerable. The slobbering beast that wanted nothing more in the whole world than to tear their throats out and feast upon their flesh was incredibly fast for such a misshapen monstrosity. It only needed a moment to rend them to pieces. She said nothing, stepping back a few feet to draw her weapon. Agent Fresh caught her movement and moved back with her so they would still be standing shoulder to shoulder on the sandy trail.

Agent Method risked another look behind her to check on Agent Ember's progress and breathed a sigh of relief as she watched her boss levitating the last of the heavy stones into place. It lowered gently to rest atop the other two rough hewn columns of rock which loomed over the edges of the trail. The resulting structure reminded Method of a part of Stonehenge or some other mysterious megalithic monument. It was one of several such collections of standing stones scattered throughout this remote stretch of New Jersey's Pine Barrens. Together, they helped create an invisible fence that the beast could not cross. Or at least they did so long as the stones remained intact. A recent archaeological expedition had disturbed the stones and paid the ultimate price for it. It was their mission to make sure that never happened again. Signs had been posted, trail cameras and motion sensors installed. If any more civilians got too close to this area, her organization would be alerted immediately.

Method silently cursed at her own hands, shaking as they pointed her silver ray-gun of a weapon towards the monster. She chalked this crack in her carefully cultivated demeanor of cool detachment to another power of the stone structure; it was generating a deep sense of unease which now seized her mind. This profoundly unpleasant feeling was designed to further dissuade hapless travelers from wandering into the creature's domain. With some effort, Method pushed down these emotions. She concentrated instead on the fact that now that the stones were back in place, the creature couldn't possibly hurt them so long as they stayed on the other side. To this end, she began backing towards the structure, passing under its gate-like shadow and stopping on the other side. The gut wrenching feeling of *wrongness* immediately dissipated, leaving only her revulsion at the monster that still howled and snarled at them. Agent Fresh joined her, his face betraying his sense of relief.

"I still don't understand why we don't just kill that thing!" Agent Fresh griped.

Method frowned. This was all covered in the dossier. Hadn't Fresh bothered to read any of it?

"Because it cannot be killed," Ember explained patiently in her whispery voice.

Agent Method couldn't help but raise a skeptical eyebrow at this. She'd been trained that true bodily immortality was impossible, even with the help of magic. Then again, the thing before them was a product of dark, forbidden spells. Furthermore, if what she'd read about it was accurate, then technically it was stuck in a kind of constant state of flux between life and death.

"Then why not just zap it into another dimension or something? Or at least lock it up someplace where we don't have to worry about civilians running into it?" Fresh continued to complain, only confirming Agent Method's conclusion that the rookie had completely ignored all the briefing materials they'd been hastily provided.

"It has a deep connection to this land. It cannot be removed from it, the consequences of doing so would be catastrophic," Ember answered gravely.

Suddenly, the glowing green shield that had kept the beast at bay vanished. The alarm on Method's wrist computer wailed, only to be joined by the equally shrill cries of the monster as it surged forth like an unstoppable wave of wrath.

Agent Fresh yelped in shock. He squeezed the trigger of his pistol, sending sizzling bolts of brilliant blue plasma barreling into the beast. The wretched thing cried out with a mixture of outrage and pain. They all watched in amazement as the monster kept on sprinting forward, only to come to an abrupt halt as it ran into the unseen wall created by the enchanted stones. The still smoking holes in its hide closed up as the skin around them rippled and crawled to cover them. Method fought down the urge to vomit.

"That was unnecessary! It can't hurt us unless we pass the stones!" Agent Method exclaimed angrily.

Agent Fresh laughed in derision. "Is that compassion you're showing? For this *monster*? Don't you remember all the people it's killed?"

Method shook her head, her shoulder length strawberry blonde hair swaying as she did so. "I haven't forgotten, but I don't hate it for being what it is. I can't forget that it was once human. All it knows now is endless hunger. It will do what it must to try to satisfy that hunger. It can't control itself, but *we* can control how we respond to it. So I ask you: who is the real monster in this situation?"

Fresh grimaced at her admonition, placing his weapon back in the hidden holster under his black dress suit jacket. He then pulled a small cylinder out of his breast pocket and sprayed it into his mouth, nervously modeling the origin of his peculiar code-name.

"Let's get out of here," Ember said in a tone that brokered no further argument. With that, she turned on her heel, her long black hair and equally inky dress swirling as she did so.

Her two subordinates wordlessly followed her up the trail and towards the sleek black Cadillac that awaited them. Agent Method took one last fleeting look behind her, where the thing still watched them, its eyes burning with mania as it repeatedly tried and failed to breach the barrier. She wondered how long it would continue to try and get at them before it finally lost interest.

Were they really doing the right thing, leaving it out here where someone could cross into its territory? Why not at least put up a real fence around it? She knew that her superiors must have their reasons, and she knew better than to question them. Supposedly, it had lived like this for decades before the recent troubles with relatively few incidents. She tried to trust in the wisdom of her leaders, but she couldn't shake the feeling that this wasn't the end of their problems with this thing.

The deep well of chaos that churned in the dark and secret heart of the world couldn't be held back forever. It always found a way of bubbling over and crawling into the deceptively safe world of streetlights and neat rows of houses. For now, it had been pushed back to where it could do little but seep into our collective nightmares. She feared it was only a matter of time before the awful, physical reality of it found a way out again. All she knew was that she was relieved to be away from it - from the terrible sight which offended her fundamental sense of reality.

Chapter One: A Meeting of Friends

Athena Arden beamed at her dining room table in pride. It wasn't set out with any meal, or at least nothing resembling a healthy one, but it was ready to serve its purpose for tonight. It was laid out with snack bowls full of various treats: party mix, Doritos (in both cool ranch *and* spicy nacho), popcorn, and her husband Dennis' personal favorite, Herr's brand sour cream and onion potato chips. There was even a bowl of plain ridged chips and dip for those who preferred to do it the old-fashioned way, like her brother Mark. A pair of 2 liter bottles, one Coke and one Pepsi, sat beside each other in the center of the table, peacefully unaware of the ongoing war raging between their corporate creators. Beside them was a neat stack of red Solo cups.

She deemed that the junk food tableau before her should be sufficient to satisfy her guests - the other members of the Jersey Shore Paranormal Society (or JSPS for short). She felt confident that she had properly catered to the individual tastes of each of the members of her team. After nearly twenty-two years of chasing everything that goes bump in the night together, she had developed an expert knowledge of what they liked.

Her best friend, Miranda "Mira" Robbins entered the room, a small stack of books cradled in the crook of her arms. Even in her early fifties Mira was still an attractive woman, with short cropped dirty blonde hair and a thin physique that Athena envied. Miranda had been there right from the beginning of the JSPS during the sweltering summer of '94. The JSPS' first case had involved investigating Miranda's childhood home, where her own father had murdered her mother before taking his own life. The ghosts of both of her parents had still been trapped there, but the JSPS had gotten them to move on with the help of an eccentric local mystic by the unlikely name of Clark Kismet. The whole episode had cemented their friendship and helped Miranda get over her childhood trauma. Well, as much as anyone can ever really "get over" something as horrific as their parents' murder-suicide. Athena knew that her friend sometimes still fretted that she'd inherited some of her father's darkness. It was an idea that always struck Athena as ludicrous. Her friend was one of the most friendly and positive people she'd ever known. Miranda was all rainbows and cuddly puppies as opposed to Athena's perpetual Wednesday Addams impression.

Athena decided that she looked like an idiot, grinning away at a table full of things that would've given the Surgeon General of the United States a heart attack as if she'd just cooked a gourmet meal, and quickly adopted a more neutral expression.

"These are the ones you wanted?" Miranda asked as she set the books down on a vacant corner of the table.

Athena appraised the small stack, scanning the titles spelled out on their spines. "Well done! I'll make a librarian out of you yet!"

This was high praise indeed from the head librarian of the Barnegat branch of the Ocean County Library. It was a role she'd fallen into more out of a fear of change than a wealth of ambition. Athena had simply existed so long in her role that when her old boss retired it was obvious to everyone that she was the most experienced and qualified person for the position. However, Athena knew that a new career in Library Science was the last thing Miranda wanted; she was quite content making a killing as a real estate agent. In that capacity, she often found new allegedly haunted houses for the team to probe. It was quite a convenient arrangement.

"It wasn't hard. I couldn't remember all those titles you gave me, so I just picked out the nonfiction ones that had 'Jersey Devil' somewhere in the title."

"Some of those fiction ones are real stinkers, but that doesn't seem to stop Dennis from picking them up," Athena noted with a sigh. Her husband's enthusiasm for New Jersey's resident cryptid was something she didn't normally share.

"Or collecting all that Jersey Devils merchandise!" Most of the people in their part of Jersey who bothered to follow professional hockey were fans of the Philadelphia Flyers rather than their state's own team. For that reason, Miranda had always found it slightly peculiar that Dennis had so many things emblazoned with the Jersey Devils logo lying around.

"Tell me about it!" Athena laughed, "he doesn't even watch any sports! He's such a poseur! All you have to do is write 'Jersey Devil' on something and he'll buy it! Like we don't have enough useless collectibles littering up the damn place!"

She waved her hand around the room, indicating the carefully posed action figures cavorting on the shelves of the heavy, dark wood antique sideboard that dominated the wall behind her. It was a family heirloom inherited from Dennis' side of the family.

Most people would've used such a fine piece of furniture to display their good china, but instead it had been transformed by Dennis into a battleground for the conflict between the Galactic Empire and the Rebel Alliance from Star Wars. It was part of the compromise they'd agreed to when they first moved in together: she would put up with his display cases filled with his various collections and he would put up with her numerous shelves bursting with books. Indeed, as a result much of their house resembled a cross between a comic book shop and a decidedly less tidy version of her workplace.

"Speak of the devil, here he comes!" Miranda pointed towards the large bay window in the living room, visible from the dining room where they stood. Through its glass they could see Dennis' work van pull into the driveway. Dennis owned his own small HVAC repair and installation business. Fortunately, he kept most of the clutter from that enterprise confined to the garage. It was so crammed with his work-related paraphernalia that they couldn't actually use it for parking their cars anymore. Oh well, as Athena often remarked, it beat the hell out of having to rent a storage space.

"Oh shit!" Athena swore. She frantically cast about the table before her for something, *anything* to cover up the books. She'd been trying to keep the subject of tonight's meeting a secret from her husband for the past week or so. This was no easy task, with him constantly trying to guess what she was up to. He'd even correctly figured it out once, putting her poker face to the ultimate test. She'd been surprised to find that it was up to the task. She despised phoniness and so often thought herself terrible at the fine art of deception - it was good to know that she could rise (or was that sink?) to the occasion when required. Athena quickly covered the short stack of books with a half empty bag of party mix that was lingering nearby. Then she realized that she could've simply set the books on the seat of the chair in front of her. So that's exactly what she did next, scrambling to move the books down there and pushing the chair up against the table with hardly any time to spare. Scarcely a moment later Dennis came sauntering in through the front door, a large plastic cup in one hand and a crumpled up paper bag in the other.

Athena regarded her husband as he entered the living room, forcing what she hoped was an innocent look onto her face. Even after 19 years of marriage and virtually a lifetime of knowing each other, she still found the sparkling blue eyes which were easily his best physical feature quite sexy. His once-thick, sandy blonde hair was significantly both thinner and darker now than it had been when they were younger, but there was still enough of it left to warrant hanging onto in her opinion, although he sometimes threatened to shave it all off. He was a thickly built fellow, he always had been. Yet despite his lack of muscular definition he was as strong as an ox - another thing about him that turned her on. He made her feel safe, and he made her laugh. What more could you ask for?

Athena felt that she couldn't be too critical about his weight without being a hypocrite. She was afraid that she'd "let herself go" quite a while ago and was currently doing fuck all about it. Dennis, thankfully, didn't seem to mind. He always told her that she got more beautiful every year, and she had no reason to doubt his sincerity, but despite his sweet reassurances, she didn't *feel* beautiful. It was nice that there was such a drive in recent years to acknowledge the beauty of thicker women, body positivity and all that, but it had come too late to override the negative societal programming she'd grown up with. In the back of her head there was always a wispy slip of a supermodel telling her that she was too fat. As if she didn't have enough to be anxious about already!

He smiled at Athena and Miranda, mumbling a hello as he moved off into the kitchen, dropping the paper bag he'd been carrying into the stainless steel trash can. He held onto the large cup of soda though, taking a loud slurp through the straw. Athena noted the McDonald's logo on the cup.

"Ah, so you've already eaten?" Athena asked.

"Damn! Nothing gets past you, does it?" Dennis quipped back sarcastically.

"Smartass!" Athena replied laughingly.

"Well, that last job took waaay longer than expected and I knew the meeting was supposed to be starting soon, so I grabbed a bite on the way home and wolfed it down while I was driving. I figured you'd already eaten. I didn't want to be hangry during the whole meeting," he explained unnecessarily.

"How could you possibly be hangry with this amazing cornucopia of snacks to choose from?" Athena asked, waving her hands over the contents of the table like one of the models on *The Price is Right!* when the grand prize was revealed.

"That's hardly a healthy meal!" he protested.

"And McDonald's is?" she teased back as she moved into the kitchen and began putting the leftovers she'd kept out on the oven for him in the fridge. "I suppose you can enjoy these delectable pork chops and mashed potatoes that I so lovingly labored over tomorrow - if I don't gobble 'em up first!" she said airily.

"Sorry. I guess I should've waited. I just didn't want to eat my dinner in front of everyone."

Athena smiled to herself. It amused her how formal and proper he could sometimes still be around people that were practically family by this point. She was sure that under the circumstances, none of the other members of the JSPS would have cared if he ate something a bit more substantial than what the table currently had to offer.

She pecked him on the cheek as she finished putting the last remnants of the meal in the fridge. "Your manners are as impeccable as ever."

Dennis blushed at this display of affection right in front of Miranda (who was studiously pretending not to notice). Athena knew that was how he'd react, which was exactly why she'd done it. She really enjoyed messing with him like that!

He reached into a pocket and pulled out his cellphone, checking the time. "Anyhow, I hope some of the others get here soon. I can't wait to see what you've been hiding from me. You'll tell me, won't you Mira?" He looked pleadingly towards his guest.

"Huh? What makes you think that I know anything about it?"

"Because she tells you *everything!*"

"True, but I also know better than to risk her wrath by spilling the beans. I'm afraid you'll have to wait for the big reveal like the rest of the team."

"You see? All your puny efforts at gleaning the truth are wasted! I've trained her too well!" Athena said triumphantly in her best super villain voice. She almost added a hammy cackle, but thought better of it. She was afraid that her cackling skills weren't up to par.

"I know when I'm beaten," Dennis sighed and pulled out a chair to sit down at the table.

"Not that chair!" Athena cried out in a panic. He was about to sit in the chair where she'd hastily hidden the tell-tale stack of books!

"Why, hello! What do we have here? A pile of books all about the Jersey Devil?" he grinned as he lifted them up. "This doesn't mean — "

"I will say no more before the meeting officially starts!" Athena haughtily replied, holding up a hand as if trying to stop traffic.

"So I was right when I guessed that you wanted to go out on a Jersey Devil hunt? But you've always said that he's nothing but a piece of folklore! What changed your mind?"

"I will say no more before the meeting officially starts!" his wife repeated, albeit more quickly and testily this time.

"I wouldn't keep pressing her, you're playing with fire!" Miranda teased.

But Dennis was far too pleased to say anything back. He was completely lost in happy thoughts of traipsing through the pines, searching for his favorite cryptid with his woman by his side. He'd been on such investigations before, but with other local paranormal groups that they'd befriended. There'd even been a group especially dedicated to hunting the Jersey Devil a few years ago that he'd sometimes joined until they'd eventually folded.

Athena thought the Jersey Devil was a bunch of bullshit, and she wouldn't allow the JSPS to investigate it because she was *very* protective of their reputation. This irritated Dennis as much as it made him laugh. The JSPS had been his idea originally and he'd even had to twist her arm a little to get her to join. Now she acted as if she ran it! Not only that, but the Jersey Devil was, and always had been in the group's logo, so they were already hopelessly associated with it. Athena had told him that she didn't mind that because the Jersey Devil was also a symbol of regional pride, but she *did* mind the idea that people might think that their group took such a ridiculous creature seriously enough to really go out searching for it. She was sure it would destroy their credibility. Dennis wasn't quite sure who she was trying to impress. They did enjoy a decent reputation as one of the less flaky paranormal research groups, but at the end of the day most scientists would still think they were a bunch of fools for wasting their time on all of this stuff. The sad fact of the matter was that to those people, *anyone* involved in the paranormal was a gullible idiot at best, and an attention-seeking charlatan at worst.

He couldn't believe that he'd finally be able to take his own paranormal team out on a search for the Jersey Devil. He'd been obsessed with the Jersey Devil ever since he was a small child. One could even say that it was the gateway drug that spurred his interest in all things paranormal. He recalled way back in first grade, when he'd found a book in the school library with a bright red cover and an eye-catching illustration of a dragon-like creature curled around the words "The Jersey Devil." He had immediately checked out the book and kept on renewing it until he'd gotten in trouble for keeping it out too long and had had to return it nearly six months later. That book had really fired up his imagination. The idea that there could be a real life monster flying around somewhere in the very same woods that he could see through his bedroom window had fascinated him more than it frightened him. He'd been intrigued by the notion that the world was a far more interesting and exciting place than it often appeared to be. He'd dreamed of being the first person to capture the creature and prove its existence to a disbelieving world. To this end, he'd copied by hand (despite not being particularly artistically inclined) the many maps included in the book showing the locations of alleged sightings of the monster. He'd constantly searched the woods in his own backyard and beyond. Unfortunately, he'd only ever seemed to find squirrels and the occasional turtle or deer. The Jersey Devil was one elusive hombre. He'd read about other mysterious creatures that were said to inhabit the American wilderness, adding them to the list of targets on his amateur monster hunts, even when they weren't known to live anywhere near southern New Jersey.

Eventually, his interests had drifted to include ghosts, too, especially when he met a cute little dark haired classmate who'd confided in him that she sometimes saw the spirits of the dead. A little girl named Athena Anderson.The other kids had thought she was a little weird and spooky, not to mention a brace-faced freak who always had her face stuffed in a book and liked to show off by confusing them with all the big words she picked up from those books. But to Dennis she had been an angel - a real life superhero blessed with the ability to see what others couldn't. Dennis had realized that maybe he could never be Batman, but perhaps he could be Robin. That didn't seem like such an unattainable goal. And so he'd attached himself to Athena. And all these years later, they were still attached to one another, only now in the most intimate of ways.

As he'd gotten older and wiser and read more on the subject, even Dennis had to reluctantly admit that the Jersey Devil was one of the more unlikely cryptids to actually exist. The more well known creatures like Bigfoot or Nessie benefited from the fact that the fossil record showed that creatures resembling them had definitely roamed the earth at one time. This fact always made the idea that some of them had escaped extinction a tantalizing possibility. The Jersey Devil, on the other hand, had no such luck; he didn't resemble any kind of known animal. He was often described as an unholy cross between a bat, a horse, and a kangaroo. Sometimes even a dog and a camel were thrown into this improbably chimeric mix of body parts. The Jersey Devil didn't seem like anything that could've ever naturally evolved at all, which was a big reason why Athena refused to take him seriously. Dennis' own occasional efforts to find the beast as an adult had proven as fruitless as his childhood attempts, prompting many an infuriating "I told you so" from his wife. Still, Dennis couldn't quite let go of his first love. He so desperately *wanted* to believe that the Jersey Devil was real, even though he knew that such a bias was anathema to the objectivity he tried to maintain as an investigator.

Dennis was completely lost in such thoughts. So much so that he absently ran his hand over the fuzzy back of the cat that had just landed on the table.

"Hello! Earth to Dennis! Don't pet that little booger! Get her off the table before she gets into the snacks!" Athena admonished from the big living room window where she'd drifted.

"Huh? Oh yeah." He gently slapped the cat on its butt. The pet stubbornly ignored the gesture and he had to sweep her off the table with his arm, earning himself an indignant hiss from the displaced animal. They had five cats and two old dogs. The animals were the closest thing they had to children. At 46 years of age, there wasn't much of a possibility of them having any kids even if they wanted to, which they didn't. Long ago they'd agreed not to have children, contenting themselves with spoiling Dennis' sister's kids and Miranda's son instead. Not having the financial burden of raising kids had enabled them to travel the country, and even the world. For the most part, Dennis didn't regret the decision. Although occasionally he couldn't help but wonder what a mixture of Athena and himself would be like. Also, when he saw all the mean and dumb people around him who were constantly breeding he sometimes wished he'd produced an army of his own kids to offset them.

Dennis saw Athena clap her hands in excitement as a familiar dark blue vehicle parked on the street in front of their house. Miranda was closer to the front door and rose up from the sofa to unlock it and throw it open. The final two members of the team who they could expect to actually show up for tonight's meeting had just arrived. The meeting would be starting soon and with it, all of Dennis' questions would hopefully soon be answered.

It wasn't long before Mark and Tyler walked into the house. "What's up bitches?" Mark said as he entered the room, which was his standard greeting. Mark was Athena's younger half brother. They shared the same father, but had different mothers. Athena's parents had split when she was a teenager. Her father had remarried and Mark was born a few years later. Athena's mother Barbara had also briefly remarried, to some guy who lived down in Egg Harbor Township, but that marriage had imploded after roughly a year and she'd been single ever since.

Mark Anderson was a good looking, well muscled twenty something young man with cappuccino colored skin and striking green eyes. He was also, as he was fond of telling people, "outrageously gay." He often kept everyone entertained with his crazy sense of humor and sassy remarks. Yet everyone knew that his humor masked his lingering feelings of being an outsider. He'd had a tough time growing up gay and half African American in a part of the state that tended to skew towards the conservative end of the political spectrum. Even though they didn't grow up in the same household and there was a large gap in their ages, Athena had always done her best to play the role of the dutiful older sister. To a large extent, she'd been successful. Mark trusted her implicitly and she was the first person he'd come out to. He'd picked up on her interest in the paranormal and been joining them on their investigations ever since he was a kid, often helping

Dennis set up their equipment. Indeed, he was the only one who Dennis trusted to touch some of his more expensive devices. When Athena's dad and stepmother retired to Florida a few years ago, Mark had chosen to remain in Jersey, moving in with his boyfriend. This was at least as much to remain near his big sister as it was to keep his romantic relationship intact.

The other new arrival, Tyler Lambert, was very much the opposite of Mark both in temperament and physicality. He was short, wiry, and pale as a sheet, with thick glasses and long, black, slicked-back hair. His style of dress was definitely in the "metal dude" category. He was always wearing torn jeans and concert t-shirts, mostly from bands that Athena had never heard of. Whereas Mark was often a bit loud and outgoing, Tyler was more quiet and reserved. However, once you got him going on certain subjects, he never seemed to shut up. He loved to show off his encyclopedic knowledge of the paranormal. His enthusiasm for these topics was often mistaken as arrogance by the others. He was also the most skeptical member of the team, with a tendency to want to debunk everything. This also earned him the disdain of the other team members, although Athena enjoyed having him around to play devil's advocate and help keep some of their wilder flights of fancy in check. He also happened to be one of the most faithful and reliable members of the team. He was now in his early thirties and had been coming to meetings since he was in his mid twenties. He never missed a meeting or an investigation.

The same could not be said for many of the other members of the team. Outside of this core group meeting tonight, few of the JSPS members could be counted on to show up on a regular basis. There were actually many more JSPS members out there, including people who were part of some of the satellite branches in the neighboring counties. However, those other branches held their own meetings. It was a rare day when some of the other members of this original branch showed up in the flesh, although many of them were at least active on their website. Scheduling conflicts and the like were often cited as the excuse. It frequently upset Athena to see how difficult the simple act of hanging out became the older you got. Things had been so much simpler when they were in grade school and everyone you knew was on the same schedule. When you grew up, everyone had wildly different routines and it became harder and harder to keep in touch. It took effort and planning. No wonder people tended to drift apart so easily!

But not this team, she thought with a touch of pride as she watched them move towards the dining room and take their places around the table. *These are my stalwarts. My fantastic four.* It wasn't lost on her that at least half of them were related to her and one of the others was her best friend, but it hardly mattered. The JSPS had a solid reputation in the paranormal community and a strong online presence, and most importantly they helped people - that made it a success in her eyes.

After Dennis had been snapped out of his daydreams by the cat, he'd realized that he needed to set up his digital camera to record the meeting. He placed it on its tripod at one end of the dining room and inserted a fully charged battery. Later, he'd edit the footage and post it to their website. Having started the camera, he sat down and pulled the bowl of Herr's sour cream and onion chips to his side. He could control the camera remotely through an app on his phone, which he now swiped open.

Athena took her place at the head of the table, but didn't sit down. The pile of books on the Jersey Devil was now stacked in front of her.

She looked into the camera and smiled. "Thanks for coming, everyone, and thanks to everyone watching online. I now call this meeting of the Jersey Shore Paranormal Society to order!"

Chapter Two: Athena Holds Court

There was a time when the idea of giving a speech like this would've absolutely mortified Athen Arden. But she was more comfortable in front of these people than anyone else on the planet, plus she'd been doing this for years now. Talking in front of an invisible audience on the internet was quite different from talking to an auditorium packed with strangers. That's why when her group was invited to participate in some of the local paranormal conventions, she let Dennis do most of the talking.

"Tonight, we're going to discuss our official state demon, the Jersey Devil. So, what do you guys know about the Jersey Devil?"

Dennis began to open his mouth, but Tyler, as usual, was quicker on the draw.

"What *don't* I know about the Jersey Devil?!" he interjected.

"Oh, so we have an expert, do we? Please, Mr. Lambert. Enlighten our audience." Athena knew that he'd probably keep on talking, whether or not she granted him her official blessing, but she had to at least pretend that there was some degree of order to this meeting.

"It's pronounced 'lam-bear,' actually," he corrected her. Everyone around the table grinned a little. They all knew perfectly well how to pronounce his last name by now, but they kept on saying it wrong just to needle him. It never failed to produce the desired effect.

"According to legend, the Jersey Devil was born a little south of here, down in Leed's Point way back in 1735. His mother, who is only known to history as 'Mother Leeds,' was rumored to be a witch. She already had twelve children and when she discovered that she was pregnant for a thirteenth time, she reportedly shouted out 'let it be a devil!'"

"Twelve kids? Shit! I can't say I blame her!" Mark laughed. "That vajayjay would be *all* stretched out!"

Tyler glared at Mark for interrupting his diatribe. Athena glowered at him for completely different reasons.

"Mark, please try to keep your comments family friendly," she reminded him, although she knew that such things could be "fixed in post" when Dennis got around to editing the video.

Tyler continued his retelling of the legend "Another version of the story has Mother Leeds' unborn child being cursed by a preacher because she was rude to him when he tried to convert her."

"Damn! Those 18th Century Jehova's Witnesses sure didn't play around, did they?" Mark interrupted again, earning himself another stern look from Athena, although he could tell from the smile playing around the corners of her mouth that she was secretly amused by his running commentary.

"*Anyway*," Tyler said more loudly, "when the child was born it was a hideous monster. Some stories say that it killed the whole family and flew up the chimney. Others say that it just killed the midwife and escaped, once again up the chimney. Some versions assert that it was confined to the attic or the basement for years before eventually escaping into the Pine Barrens."

"Wow! So that's the legend? All I know about it is what my father used to tell me," Miranda commented.

"What did he tell you about it?" Dennis asked gently. It was rare that Miranda even acknowledged that she'd ever had a father.

"Well, you know that house on route 9 with the chair on the roof?" They all nodded. The house was a well known local landmark.

"Dad used to tell me that the Jersey Devil would sit up there, looking for victims. He said that whenever it rained he'd swoop down and rip people right up off of the sidewalk. I really used to believe it because I was just a little kid. It scared the bejesus out of me!"

Athena pursed her lips. If she didn't already have enough reasons to hate Miranda's late father, Dean Drake, she did now. He was a certified madman who'd killed his wife and then himself, right in front of his daughter. Then, years later as a ghost, he'd tried to kill Miranda and the rest of the JSPS. What kind of a sick, twisted person tells that kind of a thing to a little kid?

Athena turned from these dark musings to the comfort of her researched tale. "The Leeds family didn't enjoy a great reputation amongst their neighbors. Back then the Quakers dominated the religious and political life of this part of the state. The patriarch of the Leeds family, Daniel Leeds, had gotten himself into trouble by publishing an almanac which contained astrological information. To his fellow Quakers this was tantamount to practicing witchcraft. When he wouldn't stop publishing his almanac, a long and bitter feud started between himself and the Quaker establishment."

"I guess some people really don't like reading their horoscopes! What'd they do to him? Make him eat nothing but Quaker Oats for the rest of his life?" Mark quipped as he dipped a chip.

"Nah, they wrote nasty things about him. He answered in kind. It went on and on for years, and got to be pretty tedious after a while. Anyhow, my point in mentioning all of this is that the Leeds family came to be associated with Satanic, evil things. Daniel's critics called him a devil. The Jersey Devil was originally called 'The Leeds Devil.' I believe that the entire legend began with this slandering of the Leeds family. I got this idea from this book, written by an actual descendant of Daniel Leeds." She lifted up a book with the curious title of *The Domestic Life of The Jersey Devil: or Bebop's Miscellany.* "It's quite good. In fact it's the best one on the subject. If anyone wants to borrow this or any of the others I brought out for the meeting tonight, all you have to do is ask."

"Hey! All of those books actually belong to me!" Dennis reminded her.

She winked at him. "I know, but I didn't think you'd mind sharing your knowledge of your favorite cryptid with your friends."

"Well, sure. Yeah when you put it that way, I guess it's alright. Just take good care of 'em if you end up borrowing one. Use bookmarks, don't fold the pages! Some of those books are probably collector's items by now, ya know?" he cautioned the table.

"I think we can all agree that the legend is just that - a legend," Athena cut in. "It doesn't really hold water as a factual account of real historical events. Even if we're prepared to believe that a child was somehow cursed into being born a demon, how could such a creature possibly still be alive today? Then there's the physical descriptions of it." She pulled a few pieces of paper out of one of the books she had next to her and held one up. Dennis zoomed the camera in on it.

On the paper was an old illustration of the Jersey Devil that had originally appeared in a Philadelphia newspaper in 1909. It was a well known image - one of the first results that popped up when one Googled "Jersey Devil." It depicted a decidedly non-threatening creature with a horse-like head, large ears, bat wings, and an elongated body with a pair of almost comically thin legs that looked like they could barely support its weight. The legs terminated in a pair of cloven hooves that were somehow absurdly wearing horseshoes. The beast had a long, skinny tail that split into three prongs at the end. A pair of tiny, T-Rex-like foreclaws (or are they hooves?), and a bemused facial expression rounded out the surreal picture.

Athena held the paper up for a moment longer before setting it down and continuing. "This is the popular image of what it looks like, although sometimes it's described as also having horns or antlers. As you can see, it's a strange mishmash of various types of animals. The chances that something like this could naturally evolve and represent a member of some unknown class of animal isn't terribly likely."

"I dunno. A platypus doesn't seem very likely, yet it exists," Dennis argued. Athena smiled thinly. This was something he often said when she brought up her belief that the Jersey Devil couldn't possibly have evolved. It was true, the world was full of some very strange and wondrous animals.

"God was doing *all* the drugs when he created the platypus!" Mark added. Even the normally dour Tyler chuckled a little at that one.

Athena pressed on with her presentation, unfazed. "Worst of all, most of the features you saw in that picture stem from a rash of so-called sightings that occurred over the course of a week in January, 1909 - most of which were undoubtedly part of an elaborate hoax. There was a Dime Museum in Philly back in those days which was really more of a freak show than a real museum. The publicist for the museum later admitted that he planted many of the stories of Jersey Devil sightings in the papers to drum up business." Athena next produced a photocopy of a map and held it up.

Dennis immediately recognized it from *The Jersey Devil* by James F. McCloy and Ray Miller Jr., the very same book which had ignited his interest in all things uncanny as a child. Indeed, the map was one he had made crude attempts to draw when he was in first grade. It showed the lower half of the state of New Jersey, various spots marked with dots, their place names written out in cursive. She had made copies of several different maps which appeared in the book, and now held each one up for a few seconds.

"These maps show all the sightings recorded during that notorious 1909 wave. As you can see, they're mostly clustered around the south western part of New Jersey, with a few sightings crossing over into Pennsylvania and even Delaware. All conveniently close to the Dime Museum rather than the cryptid's traditional stomping grounds to the east, in the Pine Barrens along the shore, near the Devil's alleged birthplace in Leeds Point. The publicist for the Dime

Museum borrowed a kangaroo, painted it green, and attached wings to it. He made sure that the descriptions of the monster in the stories he gave to the press matched that of the beast he'd created with the unfortunate kangaroo. He then staged the capture of this creature and advertised that it could be seen at the museum. The spectators were led into a darkened room where the caged 'Devil' was kept behind a curtain. The curtains were parted and a boy with a board that had some nails in it would smack the poor kangaroo on the back, and it would bound forwards into the light. The curtains would quickly close and the suckers who paid to see this spectacle would be led onto the next exhibit."

"That poor animal!" Miranda exclaimed, outraged by its inhumane treatment.

Athena nodded her head enthusiastically, "You don't know the half of it! They almost killed him the first time they painted him green. He licked off the paint and poisoned himself! Fortunately, they eventually found a less toxic paint. This whole wave of sightings is often held up as though it's evidence of the creature's existence by unscrupulous researchers, despite the fact that the publicist admitted that most of the newspaper accounts at the time were complete fabrications."

"The key word here being *most*," Dennis interjected pointedly. Athena sighed. This was another frequent bone of contention between them whenever they discussed this topic.

"Yes, we can't prove conclusively that *all* the stories were planted by him. The initial story that kicked everything off, which was the discovery of some mysterious tracks in the snow, was what supposedly inspired him to create the hoax. However, in the 1960's someone fessed up to hoaxing some of the tracks. It's *possible* that a few of the sightings were sincere reports of misidentified animals made by people who'd been whipped into a panic by all the press about a monster on the loose." She brought out yet another piece of paper and held it up for everyone to see. This one showed a large bird.

"This is a SandHill Crane. They used to be native to New Jersey. They're still found here occasionally, but mostly they've moved south. They can grow to be up to four feet tall with a five foot wingspan. A popular theory is that these were mistaken as the Jersey Devil."

Dennis sputtered out a derisive laugh. "Those things don't look anything like the Jersey Devil! The head is way too small. There's no long tail. It's covered in feathers and obviously a bird. You'd have to be an idiot to think that thing is a monster."

Again, Athena was familiar with this criticism. She wasn't trying to reenact their past disagreements about this cryptid in front of the whole internet, but it seemed unavoidable. "Really? Can you be so sure that if you saw one a few hundred feet away through the woods at night that you wouldn't mistake it for a monster? Especially if you're already expecting to run into something strange out there? I hear that they make a terrible screeching sound too, it can be pretty terrifying if you don't know what it is."

"It sounds reasonable to me!" Tyler agreed a little too strongly. Sometimes Athena wondered if he had some kind of a crush on her, his skepticism a misguided attempt to impress her.

Athena looked Dennis right in the eye. She'd spent most of her presentation so far winding him up, now it was time to give him a little joy. "For all the reasons I've just given, in the past, I've refused to take the Jersey Devil seriously. I've considered it a charming piece of regional folklore rather than anything real that's worth searching for. But lately, I've developed a different theory. Some of the reports don't fit so neatly into the standard description of the monster. Anytime that someone runs into something anomalous in these woods, people call it the Jersey Devil. There's a common thread that runs through some of these sightings - a description of a horribly disfigured wild man is sometimes reported. Lately that particular kind of sighting has been on the rise. The esteemed members of our Atlantic County branch have been discreetly documenting quite a few of them recently. I say discreetly because it's well known that I've never considered the Jersey Devil to be an appropriate subject for our investigations. They were brave enough to email the reports they've been collecting to me anyway."

"Those guys must be pretty brave - she's been known to bite!" Mark interrupted.

Dennis held up a finger. "Only in the bedroom!"

Athena blushed and tried to carry on. "Those reports were pretty compelling. I've become convinced that people are seeing *something* out in those woods. It's made me reassess my assumptions on this topic."

She placed both hands on the table and leaned forward. "What if everyone's gotten it all wrong this whole time? What if instead of looking for some kind of unknown animal we should be looking for a ghost? The ghost of a person who was born with birth defects that would've been frightening to the people of his time?

That would've been seen as some kind of divine punishment for the imagined sins of his family? What if this person was hidden away and mistreated by his own flesh and blood who were embarrassed and ashamed of him? Then, one day he escaped into the forest, forced to live off the land like some kind of a wild animal? Sometimes this 'Leeds Devil' is seen by other people, raiding their crops and stealing their livestock to survive. What if he managed to live like that for who knows how long before finally passing away - only for his restless spirit to continue haunting the woods near where he was born to this very day?"

Everyone at the table was speechless for some time. Athena smiled in satisfaction at the effects of her new hypothesis on them. Of course it was Tyler who broke the silence.

"It's definitely an interesting idea, but it sounds like you're trying to explain one impossible thing by invoking another."

She looked at him pityingly. "Oh Tyler, after all we've been through together you still want to pretend that spirits aren't real? I know for a fact that sometimes they are. I can see them, remember? As clearly as I can see you right now."

He shifted uncomfortably in his chair and took a swig of his Pepsi. "I'll admit that in my years with the JSPS I've sometimes witnessed things that are *difficult* to explain away. It's part of what keeps bringing me back."

"That, and the snacks!" Mark joked. Tyler ignored him.

"But my criticism still stands."

"And it is duly noted." Athena assured him.

"So to be clear, you're suggesting that all the reports that don't match this wild man version of the Jersey Devil are nothing but hoaxes?" Dennis asked.

"I'm saying that a specific image of the Jersey Devil was created solely to sell tickets to a freak show attraction. All the alleged sightings of such a creature are deliberate hoaxes or misidentifications of real animals which are known to science," she clarified.

"Is there any evidence that this 'Mother Leeds' ever existed and had thirteen kids? Couldn't that whole thing be a myth?" Miranda wanted to know. "I mean, they had birth records back then, it shouldn't be impossible to prove."

Athena once again held up *The Domestic Life of the Jersey Devil.* "According to this book, Daniel Leeds' son Japhet married a woman named Deborah and together they had twelve children. No thirteenth child is officially recorded, but if the child was an embarrassment perhaps they would've tried to hide his existence from the world? The likelihood of having a child who was born with serious deformities would've increased significantly if she was in her late thirties or in her forties by the time baby number thirteen was born. That's still true today, it was probably doubly true back then."

"I think it's an amazing theory!" Dennis gushed. "So you want to apply ghost hunting techniques to the search for the Jersey Devil, is that the idea?"

"Yes, in a nutshell."

"What do you think triggered this new wave of sightings?" Miranda inquired.

"Hard to say. Ghosts are usually stirred up by new construction and there has been a little bit of development out that way recently. They're not allowed to infringe on the Pine Barrens all that much, it's mostly protected land, but they build it up wherever they can. Maybe they've started building too close to the real Jersey Devil's final resting place?"

"Where do you plan to start the search?" Tyler asked her eagerly.

"I was thinking of checking out a spot that's supposed to be the remains of the old Leeds house, although nobody's sure if it's the right location. I figured I could see what kind of vibes I pick up around it. If it turns out to be a dud, we can hit the area where the most recent sightings have taken place. There's a lake down there, deep in the woods - well more of a pond, really. It doesn't even appear on many maps. That's where it's been reported lately."

"Hold on, that sounds like the area where all those murders happened a few months ago! I'm not going out there!" Mark exclaimed.

Almost two months earlier, in June, an archeologist and his students had gone on a dig in those woods, looking for native artifacts. Their mangled and mutilated bodies were discovered shortly afterwards. As sensational as the story was, it was barely mentioned by the press anymore; but people in the region still talked about it nonetheless.

Athena was having none of it. "C'mon, Mark! They caught the psycho who killed all those people, remember? She's currently cooling her heels in jail, awaiting trial."

"Didn't she say that she didn't do it? That it was the work of a monster?" Tyler said.

"A classic case of disassociation. She can't face the terrible things that she did, so she blames it on a monster, when the only real monster is herself. She's a total loony. Or maybe she's just angling for an insanity plea? Either way, we can't take anything she has to say seriously. They say they caught her red-handed - literally!"

Mark shook his head animatedly. "I'm not sure it *is* safe. I had a cousin who used to live in some apartments near that lake. He said that kids sometimes went missing around there. Wandered off into the woods and never came back. I used to get the willies whenever we went out there to visit him."

This was news to Athena. She didn't have any cousins that she knew of who'd ever lived down that way. She decided that they must belong to Mark's mother's side of the family. It was an uncomfortable reminder that even though he was her brother, there were whole sides of his life that she knew next to nothing about. "Maybe they just got hopelessly lost in the woods or fell in the lake?"

"Or a monster got them. Or, if you prefer, the ghost of one," Mark told her flatly.

"You know that ghosts aren't powerful enough to do that!" she argued. This earned her a withering look from Miranda.

"And you know damn well that sometimes they are!" She said it more fiercely than she'd intended. Of course Miranda could never forget how her own father's ghost had nearly killed them all on their very first case.

"Yes, but that's pretty rare. Like one in a thousand rare," Athena admitted grudgingly. In all her years of ghost hunting, Athena had yet to encounter any spirit quite as strong as that of Dean Drake.

"Well, you can count me in! This is an exciting new spin on the Jersey Devil and I can't wait to get started!" Dennis was, unsurprisingly, not so easily dissuaded.

"It could be just some sad homeless dude who's gone feral," Tyler countered.

"Possibly, but some of these reports go back decades," Athena told him. "It's difficult for me to believe that a homeless person could survive that long out there on their own."

"It'll be interesting to see what, if anything, we happen to uncover. When do you plan on going down there?" Tyler asked, which was as close to an endorsement of the expedition as she could hope for from him.

"I was hoping for this weekend. We'll meet at the WaWa on West Bay Ave on Saturday morning at 11 AM and head out." She looked into the camera and put on her best smile. "Of course, as always, contributing members of any branch of the Jersey Shore Paranormal Society are welcome to join us. If you do decide to come along, be prepared to spend the night in the woods. If the weather permits, we'll be camping. I'll be posting updates to this page all week just in case there's any last minute change of plans. Thanks for joining us, and remember to always keep an open mind - it's a weird world out there!" That last phrase was how she typically signed off, and Dennis knew that he could stop the recording as soon as she finished uttering it. Athena visibly relaxed as soon as she saw the light on the camera fade out, as if she were a balloon that had just deflated. She hadn't realized how tense she'd become until then.

"So, how was that?" she asked the room.

"Great as ever Triple A!" came Dennis' response as he shoved a few sour cream and onion chips into his mouth. He'd tried not to eat too many snacks while the camera was rolling out of a combination of concern that his loud crunching would be picked up by the mic and self-consciousness about being filmed while eating. Now that the cameras were off, he could go wild on the bowl in front of him. Many of the other team members who'd been similarly restraining themselves also cut loose on the snacks arrayed before them. "Triple A" was one of Athena's nicknames, which stemmed from her full name: Athena Anderson Arden.

"It's a good theory, but I don't think I can join you on this one, Sis. Too many people have wound up dead down there lately and I'm far too young and handsome to join them," Mark told her.

Athena couldn't conceal the disappointment on her face. She loved having Mark along on these investigations. It was some of the only quality time they got to share together anymore. He wasn't usually so easily spooked, either; they hung out in real haunted houses routinely. The combination of the recent murders and his memories of the bad feelings he got from visiting those apartments in his childhood must've coalesced into the perfect storm of misgivings in his mind. Still, she didn't want him to feel pressured into joining them, so she said nothing.

"Are you sure, man? I could really use your help with all the tech stuff," Dennis urged.

"I'll think about it. But I have to say that unless someone can convince me it's safe I'm leaning towards a no."

"What about you, Mira?" Athena asked her friend.

"I have to say that the idea of the Jersey Devil still scares the shit out of me on some level, but I'll be there." Athena grinned approvingly, she knew she could count on Miranda.

Athena sighed. Most of the core team would be able to make it, and it was always possible that some of the irregulars might show up too. She knew that at least some of the members of the Atlantic County branch, the ones who'd been emailing her the stories they'd gathered, would want in as well. If only she could get Mark to commit to it! It wouldn't be the same without him.

Suddenly, the vague outlines of a plan to bring him around to her point of view began to form in her head. It was a long shot, but it might just work.

Athena smiled to herself.

Chapter Three: Off the Beaten Path

The white sandy path stretched out before Dustin McCloskey, the tops of the pines swaying in the gentle summer breeze along either side of the trail. He threw open the door and slid out of his yellow VW bug (a real vintage one from the twentieth century, not one of those newfangled numbers) and stretched. The trail was getting too narrow at this point to drive much further and part of the point of this whole trip was to get in a little exercise anyway. He leaned back into the car and liberated his backpack from the passenger seat. He'd packed lightly, the bag only held a few bottles of water, a bag of beef jerky, and a can of Deep Woods Off (which he'd already liberally applied to his body). He shouldered the pack and set off, a lively spring in his step.

It was good to be outdoors again. He'd spent far too much of his time cooped up inside at work lately. His plan was to locate the small lake hidden away in these woods. He hadn't even been aware that it existed until he'd heard about all those people who'd been murdered close to its shores recently. When was it that happened? Was it two months ago already? He wasn't sure. Long enough for the news to have gotten bored with trying to report on it anymore. The news cycle had moved on quite some time ago, looking for fresh atrocities for the endless grist mill. He hadn't been brought here by any sort of morbid curiosity about the tragedy, he was simply drawn by the attraction of a new fishing hole that was so remote that even most of the locals seemed to have forgotten it existed. He hadn't been fishing all summer, which was practically a crime. He hadn't brought any of his fishing gear with him though, today was purely a scouting expedition.

Hell, if this spot was nice enough, maybe he'd dare to ask Stacy out and bring her here. He didn't know if she was really into fishing, but maybe he could entice her with the promise of a remote place for a nice swim and a picnic. That sounded romantic, right? Girls liked that sort of thing, didn't they? He tried to picture her in a bikini and smiled at the mental picture. He was pretty sure that she liked him. Or was he misinterpreting her playful friendliness for something more than what it actually was? People always said you shouldn't date your coworkers, but honestly now that he'd dropped out of Stockton State College, how else was he supposed to meet new people? He'd tried out the bar scene in Atlantic City and on Long Beach Island but he always found himself just standing around, too shy to dance or talk to anyone else. There was always online dating, but he felt like that was for losers.

He decided to check Google Maps. He already knew that this path would eventually take him to the lake, but he was curious to see how much farther away it was. He couldn't see even a hint of it through the dense greenery surrounding him. Tapping his phone to life, he was surprised to see that he had no signal. Even though it looked like he was in the middle of nowhere, he was only a few miles away from Route 9 and this area was normally very well covered by cell phone towers. He thought he'd seen one on his way into the woods, right before he came across that weird stone archway he'd passed under that looked like it was a part of Stonehenge. He'd been grateful that his car had been able to squeeze under it. He wondered what it was doing out here? He'd heard that there had once been a campground on the other side of the lake, maybe it had once been part of that camp? He'd felt an odd, nameless feeling of disquiet as he passed through the arch. It was like a sudden punch to the gut. This feeling of unease still lingered, but he'd resolved to ignore it and try to enjoy himself.

Without any signal his phone was frozen on the map from the last time he'd pulled it up. It wasn't giving him any idea of his present location in relation to the lake. He could still see the lake on the zoomed-in satellite image and the bright outline of the trail he'd driven in on. The path meandered a little to the south before curving off to follow the shoreline. He sighed and slipped the phone back into his pocket. He didn't need the map, he was already obviously on the right trail. It would only be a matter of time before he was sure to see the sunshine reflecting off the sparkling waters of the lake. What was the lake actually called? Deer Crest Lake? That sounded right. He wondered what a "deer crest" actually was. He swore that half of the place names around here just sounded woodsy and didn't make any actual sense.

For some reason he suddenly recalled the shocked looks on the faces of his coworkers at the WaWa when he'd told them what he planned to do on his day off. They'd thought he was nuts to come out here all by himself. Even though the killer had been captured, they still thought it was a bad idea for some reason. What, did they think that the ghosts of all those dead students were gonna come after him? Or the Jersey Devil? He didn't believe in any of that silly supernatural crap! Nor did he have much patience for those who did. He was happy to note that Stacy had thought it was pretty ballsy. If anything, she admired him for daring to come out here like this. Yeah, she liked him. She was his for the taking, if he could just work up the courage to bust a move. If only he could find the right moment alone with her to tell her how he felt.

No sir, there was nothing out here that was threatening, nothing but sunshine and pine trees. The unexpected lack of cell service actually did bother him - just a little bit. He didn't expect an emergency, but who ever did? He didn't like the idea of not being able to call for help if he *did* need it. The only thing that he was slightly concerned about was the fact that due to the success of conservation laws, the bear population was on the rise. They were even showing up in people's backyards in some of the bigger housing developments lately. He knew what to do if he ran into one: don't run away, make yourself big and make lots of noise to scare it away. Nevertheless, he didn't particularly relish the idea of putting these ideas to the test. He'd grown up in the woods, and had never seen a bear outside of a zoo or a nature special on TV, so it wasn't much of a concern. Not really.

He tried to distract himself from the inability to call for help by enjoying simply being out in nature. Wasn't that part of the whole point of this? To escape the merciless artificial glow of fluorescent lights and air conditioning in favor of real sunshine and fresh air? He passed another NO TRESPASSING sign. They were a dime a dozen out here. He paid them no mind. They were a common sight in many parts of the Pine Barrens and you'd never get anywhere in these woods if you actually tried to obey them.

Suddenly his attention was drawn by the reflection of light shining off of something. Was that a camera mounted high up near the top of that tree? Fortunately, it seemed to be pointed in the other direction, although with no cell service around here he wondered how it would get a signal out. He didn't see a cable running down from it, so it had to be some sort of wireless signal, right? Satellite maybe? He didn't know, tech stuff wasn't really his forte. Perhaps it didn't work at all and was just for show? Meant to scare people away?

Off to his left, he saw something else reflecting the afternoon sunshine. There was no mistaking it, through the tangle of branches he could see the shimmering waters of the lake. He decided to break off of the trail and go straight through the low underbrush towards the lake. If there were more cameras, they were likely to be mounted along the main trail. He didn't want to chance getting busted by anyone, just in case those cameras really did work.

He crashed through the woods, blazing his own path until he reached the edge of the lake. It wasn't particularly large, but big enough to be harboring some decent-sized fish. He walked along the uneven ground of its shores, his shoes squelching in the soggy soil. Across the way, he thought he could spy the occasional tumbled down ruin of one of the wooden cabins from the abandoned camp. When he reached a moss covered tree stump, he decided to take a rest. He dug the bag of beef jerky out of his backpack and chewed on it absently, occasionally taking a swig of water to wash it down. He stared out across the still waters of the lake, letting his mind wander.

It sure would be strange fishing without his dad. Fishing has always been their thing - his dad's way of avoiding a confrontation with his mother. But such deep-seated marital problems could only be avoided for so long. Divorce was inevitable, and once it happened, his mother had gotten primary custody. He'd only seen his father every other weekend after that, weekends that were usually still filled with fishing.

It had been almost a year now since his dad had been killed by a drunk driver. It had soured Dustin's own appetite for alcohol and was another one of the reasons why he'd been so uncomfortable exploring the local bar scene. Dad had never remarried, and Dustin was an only child so there wasn't anyone else to leave his stuff to. Dustin had inherited his old VW bug and the house. He'd also inherited Dad's small fishing boat, but even if he could get his car all the way back here, he didn't see anywhere to launch it. He was still pretty shook up by the sudden loss of his father, who had only been in his forties. So shook up that he'd dropped out of college. School had just seemed so pointless after Dad's death. Everything did. He'd let his life become an endless, boring cycle of waking up to go to work and coming home to sleep with barely anything else in between worth mentioning. Rinse and repeat. The unremarkable days and weeks bled into one another until before he knew it nearly an entire year had slipped past him. A whole year of his early twenties gone and nothing to show for it.

Something had to change. He couldn't keep going on like this forever, existing but never really living. It was time to take control and get back to doing the sorts of things that he loved and figure out what he was going to do with the rest of his life. He'd be damned if he was going to let that drunk asshole's car claim two lives.

Here, on the shores of this forgotten lake, he felt like maybe he was beginning to do that. Despite the all-pervasive aura of dread which hung around these woods, he'd managed to dial it down enough to find a certain degree of inner peace here. He let his eyes wander over the clear blue waters that mirrored the cloudless skies above. It was remarkably quiet here. He saw no birds and didn't even hear any squirrels rustling in the underbrush. Hopefully the lack of wildlife didn't indicate that the lake was devoid of fish. There was only one way to find out. He daydreamed about returning here with Stacy by his side to plumb the depths of the lake with his fishing line. He really didn't know all that much about her, but something about her intrigued him.

He lost all track of time sitting there, its nebulous passage marked only by the fact that he'd somehow drained his first water bottle and emptied his bag of jerky. Eventually, the march of time began to make its mark known in more unmistakable ways. The sun began to slip down towards the horizon, casting its dying rays over the water and painting the sky around it in hues of pink and orange. It was a beautiful spectacle.

Suddenly, the thought of being caught out here after dark started to fill him with an uncharacteristic unease. His mind wandered back to his coworker's silly worries. The place where those archeology students had been murdered might not be far from where he was sitting. He knew that the site where they'd made their camp had been somewhere on the same side of the lake he was on, across from the old campground. He didn't believe in ghosts, but as the light grew dimmer all around him, ghosts suddenly *felt* far more possible than he'd ever imagined. If any stretch of forest was haunted, it would probably be this one.

The unfortunate murder victims had been out here digging for Native American artifacts, only to wind up getting hacked to pieces by a deranged couple. The woman had apparently become so blood crazed that she'd turned on her partner in crime and fiancé, killing him too. She'd been discovered when a concerned colleague came to check on the students after their professor hadn't answered her calls. Fortunately, she'd persuaded the local cops to come out there with her. They said the woman was found sitting in a pool of blood, surrounded by the bodies of her victims and laughing maniacally. To Dustin, the whole story sounded pretty fishy. The couple that had supposedly done the killing hadn't had any previous history of violence or criminal behavior. Also, he'd failed to hear a decent explanation of how they knew that the students would be out here to stalk and kill. Still, the fact that something so terrible might have happened only mere steps away from his present location sent a shiver down his spine. The feeling of dark foreboding he'd done such a great job of shutting out now came flooding back in, more powerful than ever before. He began to strongly regret the fact that he'd put himself in a position where it was impossible to call for help.

A thought suddenly struck Dustin. Of course that professor couldn't answer his cell phone! It wasn't necessarily because he was already dead at the time, it was because there wasn't any signal out here! Unless there was a better signal closer to the lake? He hadn't bothered to check his phone in hours. He pulled it back out now to see if he had any bars. He grunted in disappointment. It was just as bad as before. Even worse, he now saw what the actual time was and realized it was even later than the setting sun had indicated. It was definitely time to go. Well past time.

He finally rose up off of the stump that had been his seat for the past few hours, vigorously massaging his suddenly-sore ass with the kind of unconcerned abandon that one can only get away with when completely alone. Since he hadn't come to the lakeside via the main path, and it was already starting to get quite dark, he was beginning to worry that he'd get lost. He hoped he could find the spot where he'd first veered off the trail before he lost all light. Had those murdered people walked along this very shore as they fled from their attackers? Was he now moving through the spot where their pursuers had caught up with them? Cornered them and chopped them to pieces? He felt himself beginning to panic, but then recalled that his phone had a built-in flashlight. The surprisingly brilliant beam illuminated the ground before him, and in time he found himself back in familiar surroundings as he identified the area where he'd emerged from the woods. He stumbled his way through the brush and back onto the sandy path, which now gleamed in the fresh moonlight.

He began trudging back towards his car, unconcerned by the camera he'd seen earlier. He'd been here for the better part of the day and nobody had come out to hassle him. Either the camera really was just a decoy meant to deter trespassers, or nobody was bothering to monitor it. His yellow car, which his father had named Bumblebee (like the character from *The Transformers*), was a bright beacon of hope in the now pitch-black night. He'd had a pretty nice day out here, and he planned to return soon, but the thought of leaving filled him with relief. Suddenly, his dull old life was starting to look pretty good to him and he couldn't wait to get back to it.

He shrugged off his backpack and climbed behind the steering wheel. With a turn of the key, Bumblebee shuddered to life and he switched on his headlights, twin cylinders of light piercing the blackness enveloping him. He'd forgotten how uncannily dark it could get in the forest at night. Dustin threw the car into reverse, planning to back into a part of the trail which was wide enough for him to execute a sharp k-turn so he could get out of here. After backing up a few feet, to his horror the wheels began spinning uselessly. He tried driving forwards, but the car stubbornly remained right where it was.

Stuck. He was stuck! The soil of the Pine Barrens, which wasn't terribly different from the sands of a beach in places, had proven too much for his tiny car. He shifted into neutral and clambered out of the vehicle. He tried to push on the car with all of his might, first in one direction, then the other, but he couldn't budge the small vehicle out of the ditches his spinning back wheels had created around themselves. He swore and pounded his fist on the roof of the car so hard that he nearly dented it. It wasn't as if he could call a tow truck to pull him out. In desperation he checked his phone one more time, but nothing had changed since the last time he'd examined it except that the battery was now significantly lower from using the flashlight.

He could try to walk to the end of the trail and flag someone down on the road, or maybe get far enough to pick up a signal and make a call? Though it might take him quite a while to get that far on foot. In this darkness, if there were any predators out there he wouldn't see them before it was too late and he didn't want to use his phone's flashlight again since it drained so much power. New Jersey not only had black bears, but also packs of coyotes and even bobcats in some places. The woods that encircled him remained as eerily silent as ever, but that didn't mean that there wasn't something deadly out there. Something that could be watching him right now. No, he decided that as much as it sucked (and it sucked quite a lot!) he'd have to spend the night in his car and try to go for help in the morning.

He relieved his bladder (which felt like it was about to burst) in some bushes, then climbed back into Bumblebee. Once inside, he killed the engine and the headlights. The darkness around him was all-encompassing now, and weighed heavily upon him. He was a rather tall fellow, and as such, he knew he couldn't fit lying down in the back seat unless he planned to spend the entire night curled up into a fetal position. He did *not* have such a plan in mind. So instead, he lowered the driver's seat back until he was facing the ceiling of the car.

Even though it had been a fairly hot summer day, much of the heat trapped inside Bumblebee had already dissipated. There was a strange chill in the night air which made it hard for him to fall asleep. He wished he'd had the foresight to carry a blanket in the car. His stomach rumbled and he found himself also wishing he'd brought more food with him than just that bag of jerky. It wasn't just the cold air and hunger keeping him from resting. He was worried about how much he'd have to pay for a tow truck to get him out of here. He didn't make much working at the WaWa. If Dad hadn't already had the house paid off he would've had to sell it. He sighed. He supposed he'd have to add it to his already burgeoning credit card debt. He'd also be late for work in the morning - he'd have to pick up some overtime to make up for it.

Oh well, it's not like I've got anything better to do than work anyways, he thought gloomily.

He tried to look on the bright side: at least he wouldn't have to pay for the car to be towed to a garage and deal with repairs on a vintage vehicle for which replacement parts were becoming increasingly hard to find, not to mention expensive. Once Bumblebee was liberated from the sand, Dustin would be back on his way home. Dustin didn't dare get rid of Bumblebee, even though it was hardly the most practical of vehicles. It had been his dad's pride and joy. He'd somehow kept it running for Dustin's entire life. Dustin had virtually grown up in this car, there were a thousand precious memories associated with it. No, he intended to hold onto it for as long as he could. Sometimes he could swear that he could feel his father in the car with him, every bolt and rivet of it was so thick with his presence. Yet the normally reassuring confines of the car brought him no peace on this night.

Even worse than all the other things keeping him awake was the idea of the restless spirits of the people who'd been murdered here coming to knock on his windows, begging for him to take them away before their murderer could catch up with them. He shook his head. He didn't know why that particular image had just popped into his mind. He didn't believe in such things! Despite that, he could almost see them, dripping blood, crimson gashes riddling their bodies, surrounding his tiny car, rapping their fists on it relentlessly. Rocking the small vehicle back and forth like a pack of hungry zombies....

He tried to force the grisly pictures out of his head. For a moment he succeeded, but what replaced it wasn't much better. He recalled his father's tales of the Jersey Devil, and a mental picture of that mysterious beast began to form in his mind's eye. Red eyes set in a horse-like head glared balefully at him out of the ebon night, and wide, leathery wings flapped as it took to the sky and lashed at his car with a long, forked tail. The vision seemed so real that Dustin gasped. His father's insistence that the Jersey Devil would get him if he didn't get home before dark had always had the desired effect when he was a little kid. He'd always faithfully returned home from his friend's house down the street before the sun went down and the suburban street lights flickered to life. It had been years since he'd taken the idea of the monster seriously and he wasn't about to do it now. He didn't really believe that there were any large animals still lurking in the wild that science hadn't found yet. *Especially* one as weird as the Jersey Devil. Yet out here in the middle of nowhere, it was almost impossible to hold onto his certainty.

Hours passed like this, Dustin caught in a kind of fever dream - or more accurately, a nightmare, as his wandering mind continued to manufacture more disturbing imagery to torment him. Eventually, his weariness won out and he sank into a deep, dreamless sleep.

He was suddenly startled out of this stupor by a strange, deep, buzzing sound coming from somewhere behind him. His eyes flew open and he cried out in alarm. He saw blindingly bright lights reflecting in his rear view mirror, a pair of them which were growing ever closer as the strange sound droned ever louder.

Motorcycles! It now dawned on him what the sound was. *Those are dirt bikes!*

He couldn't imagine what anyone was doing riding through the pines this late at night, but he realized that the presence of someone out there might help him get home sooner. He threw the car door open and stumbled out, almost getting hit by one of the bikes as it screamed past him. On the opposite side of Bumblebee, another dirt bike went whooshing past him.

"Hey! Come back here!" he shouted at the top of his lungs. "Please! I need help!" He lost hope as he watched the crimson dots of their tail lights disappear into the inky depths ahead of him.

Where the fuck are they headed in such a hurry? he wondered.

Then suddenly, he heard another odd sound from somewhere behind him. A sound of wheezing, labored breaths accompanied by heavy, clumsy footfalls. An unbelievable stench blasted Dustin's nostrils, nearly causing him to double over. A blood curdling, inhuman screech pierced the night and he whirled around to search for its source. Even in the faint moonlight he could see it rushing towards him from the gloom.

It was coming straight for him - something vaguely shaped like a person, yet not a person - or at least nothing like any person he'd ever seen before. It was *horrible.* Something impossible, something which simply should not be! It was dressed in tattered, flapping rags. It was a heaving, pulsating pile of crawling flesh - some of it blackened and rotten looking while other parts seemed raw, pink and new. Long strings of dark matted hair burst irregularly from what he supposed must be its scalp, and flew wildly behind it. One unblinking eye fixed upon him with a crazed, glassy gaze and filthy, yellowed teeth chattered away manically. It moved with a completely graceless, jerky, twitchy, painful-looking gait, yet some relentless determination drove this vaguely humanoid mass of twisted body parts forward with an astonishing speed.

He screamed and tried to jump back into the car, but it was too late.

The terrible thing was upon him in an instant; gnarled, broken-looking fingers digging long nails into his skin with lunatic strength, driving him down into the white, sandy earth. He fell to his knees and whimpered as its teeth ripped into him, sending gobs of flesh flying up into the air as it greedily fed on him. He cried out in pain with each new savage bite. He tried to bat at the thing, pummeling it with his fists, but it was useless. Nothing could stop its frenzied, single-minded need to feed. The horrible stink of it, its hot, fetid breath, the slick, wet, slobbering sounds it made as it feasted upon his flesh completely filled his awareness. His strength faded fast, his attempts to fight back becoming ever more feeble, until he stopped moving of his own volition completely. His listless limbs leapt and jerked now only in response to the excited movements of the thing straddling him as it continued to wildly rend at the meat of his body.

I'm coming home, Dad. See you soon, he thought dazedly as this world of pain finally, mercifully faded to black.

Chapter Four: Enter Lars

It was another uneventful day at the library, where Athena reigned as queen over both pulpy potboilers and highbrow classics. That was okay, she preferred it like that. The predictable rhythms of her workday brought her comfort. This was her own little world and she was in control here, or at least as in control as anyone can ever fool themselves into believing they are when someplace is open to the public. She was alone in her office, a chaos of tall stacks of paper and even taller stacks of books, devising a cunning plan to convince Mark to join the JSPS expedition this weekend.

To this end, she decided to call up her old friend Lars Ericson. She'd known Lars since middle school. Lars had been the type of kid that had always been a grownup. He used to wear button down dress shirts and even business suits to school. This had made him either deeply cool or deeply uncool depending on who you asked. In retrospect, Athena realized that what he was actually doing was following the age old advice of dressing for the job you want. Lars had wanted to be a TV news anchor, and as such he was active on their high school's TV channel, reading stories about PTA fundraisers and lacrosse games with all the gravitas of Dan Rather. He also practically ran the school newspaper which was how he and Athena had first gotten to know each other. Unfortunately, he had proved to be far too ginger for prime time, but Lars eventually landed a job at one of the larger papers in

New Jersey, the Asbury Park Press. He still lived locally and was a frequent patron of the library. Athena often helped him find research materials for his stories, and the two would catch up with each other or reminisce about old times.

Most importantly, Lars was also interested in the paranormal - possibly to the detriment of his career - and was known for covering the weirder local stories. He'd already been out with the JSPS on several investigations in the past and was a reliable source of good press for them.

So it was that Athena dialed his number and was pleased when he actually answered.

"Well, what have I done to warrant a call from the Goddess of Wisdom herself?" Lars quipped. Athena smiled. She always liked it when people equated her with her mythological namesake, although she often felt more like a wiseass than a font of wisdom, and she most decidedly *didn't* feel like a Goddess!

She decided that the direct approach was the best one. "I need a favor from the only ace reporter I'm friends with."

"Hmm, now I'm worried! What mischief are you cooking up?" he replied playfully. She was lucky to catch the usually serious Lars in such a buoyant mood.

"I was wondering if you could wave that big press pass of yours around and get me in to see that lady who murdered all those people in the woods last month."

"What? You want to talk to Rebecca Greene?" He was incredulous. "Isn't that sort of outside of your usual wheelhouse?"

She leaned back in her chair which squeaked in protest, and nervously twirled around a pen she'd snatched off her desk.

"I'll level with you, it's not for me, it's for my brother. You see, we're set to do an investigation of the Jersey Devil down near Leeds Point this weekend, but Mark won't go. He doesn't buy the idea that she did all those murders. He believes her cockamamie story that someone or something else was to bIame. I thought if he could just see her for himself, see what a loony toon she is, that he'd believe she's guilty and therefore it's safe to go on this investigation."

She heard Lars laughing on the other end of the line, frowned, and lost control of her pen, inadvertently sending it sailing across the room to disappear into an abyss of yawning cardboard boxes.

"I've gotta hand it to you, Athena! That's gotta be the weirdest reason I've ever heard to want to meet a mass murderer!"

"Do you think you could get us in?" Athena inquired as she slipped out of her chair with a distinct lack of grace, crawled on her hands and knees over to the boxes and began searching through them for her lost pen.

"Perhaps. As it happens, your interests do align with my own. I've been bugging my editor to let me cover that story. I think there could be a book in it somewhere down the line. I was planning on trying to snag an interview with her anyway."

"Well, I *am* psychic, remember? Is it really so surprising that my hunch that you could help me turned out to be correct?" *Where was that fucking pen?* Her entire upper body disappeared into the largest of the boxes. Why couldn't her vaunted clairvoyance help her locate the lost writing implement?

Lars chuckled. "No, I suppose it isn't. I guess I can see if you and Mark can tag along. I can say that you're interns helping me with the story. Of course I'll have to get her to agree to an interview to begin with. Her lawyers probably won't want her talking to the press," he mused out loud.

Athena pulled her head out of the box, her hair now looking quite disheveled, and immediately began diving into the next one. "Aren't I a little old to be your intern?"

"Athena," he said with all his patented anchorman gravity, "you're never too old to learn."

Athena chuckled at his use of his Six O'Clock News voice.

"Besides, I can make it official. I can temporarily deputize you into the esteemed legions of summer interns."

"What? Really?" She was flabbergasted. She didn't think her friend had that sort of pull at his job, but then again, he had been there for decades. Having finally succeeded in fishing her pen out, she triumphantly cried, "Aha! Now I've got you, you fucker!"

"Excuse me?"

"Oh! Uh, sorry, that wasn't directed at you! I just found my favorite pen that I accidentally threw across the room and then it turned into a whole thing..." Her voice trailed off as she came to understand how ludicrous the whole thing sounded.

"It's okay," he said and she could hear the bemusement in his voice. "You know, if this is going to work I'll need a little info on you and your brother. The county jail will likely do a background check on anyone wanting to visit Becca Greene before granting permission. I'll email the internship forms for you guys to fill out so I can pass that info along to them."

"Yeah, that makes sense." She stood up, smoothed out her skirt and plopped back down into her chair with a sigh of satisfaction. "They need to make sure we're not smuggling in any files hidden in birthday cakes and all that." She began twirling her pen around again.

"Exactamundo! So it's settled then. I'll work on getting us an interview, and if I'm successful you'll owe *me* something."

Athena dropped her pen again. "Sonuvabitch!" she exclaimed reflexively. At least this time she'd felt it bounce off her foot, which meant it was probably somewhere under her desk. She leaned forward to look for it. "Sorry! Once again, not directed at you. What do you mean I'll owe you something? Is that what we're doing now? Tit for tat? Quid pro quo? Is that any way to treat an old friend?"

"Relax! I saw that last meeting you posted on the web," he started. Athena wasn't terribly surprised to learn this, Lars was fairly active in commenting on her posts. She honestly didn't know why he didn't just officially join the group, he was clearly interested in all of this stuff. She figured that it probably had something to do with not showing a journalistic bias.

"And?" she asked as she felt around on the carpet beneath her desk.

"And I found your theories about the Jersey Devil being a ghost very interesting. I want in on the investigation this weekend. I want to cover it for the Press."

"Oh is that all? Lars, you know you're always welcome to join us anytime you want to! Just show up! And who am I to turn down free publicity?" She was all the way out of her chair by this point and fully beneath the desk.

"Glad to hear it! Although if I can't get an interview with Becca Greene this week you might have to push it back to next weekend."

"That's not a problem. It was starting to look like I might have to reschedule if the forecast keeps calling for rain anyways. In all seriousness though, is it really smart for you to keep covering us like this? It's probably on account of your writing so many stories about ghost hunts and UFOs and the Jersey Devil that your boss gives you such a hard time when you want to cover an actual real life criminal like Becca Greene."

"Yeah, It probably isn't very smart, but it's what I like to write about. And my stories on those kinds of things get more clicks, which is ultimately all that really matters to the paper anymore."

"Yes!" Athena said a little too enthusiastically because her fingers had just brushed against the elusive pen. She grabbed it and went to stand up before her head had cleared the desk. "Ouch! Goddamn!"

"Are you okay?" Lars' voice was flush with concern.

Athena rocked back and forth on the floor, massaging the back of her head. "Yeah, don't mind me, I'm just one big hot mess today."

"Okay, then I'll work on getting an interview and getting us into that jail. Look out for my email and I'll be in touch if I'm successful."

"Sounds like a plan! I'll see ya around, Ericson," she said, hoisting herself back up into her chair.

"Goodbye, Athena."

Great! Now all I have to do is convince Mark to come to the jail with me and meet a mass murderer!

She found herself wondering why she was so hell bent on convincing him to join them on this particular investigation. Sure, the JSPS was the major thing that brought them together these days, but it wasn't like he hadn't sat out on an investigation before. Of course on those occasions he usually had a more valid excuse, like prior plans or feeling sick. This was the first time he'd straight up chickened out. That area where his cousin used to live must've really spooked him, or maybe he was picking up on something she couldn't sense. Since her mother was almost as psychically gifted as she was, Athena normally attributed her abilities to that side of the family, but sometimes she wondered if Mark had some abilities too. Perhaps Athena had inherited her powers from both her mother and her father? She didn't know.

At any rate, what her psychic instincts were telling her now was that she was following the correct course of action. For whatever reason, the universe was nudging her to talk to Rebecca Greene, alleged slayer of grad students. If nothing else, it would certainly be interesting. She hadn't talked to a bona fide psycho killer before - or at least none that were still living, if you counted Miranda's dad. She wondered what made someone who seemed perfectly normal on the outside suddenly snap like that? She sighed, supposing if she knew the answer to that question she'd be a killer herself.

Instead of continuing to ponder such impenetrable mysteries, she texted Mark.

Hey, wanna meet a mass murderer?

That oughta get his attention!
She was right, he wasted no time in texting back.

I've already met Tyler. He even showed me where he keeps the bodies once.

She giggled at that one. He loved to rip on his fellow JSPS team members, and Tyler often made the most tempting target.

No, you silly! I mean the lady who killed those people in the woods! My reporter friend Lars wants to interview her and if he gets permission we can tag along.

Why do u wanna talk to her? Why drag me along for the ride? You're hoping it'll convince me that it's safe to go on that JD hunt this weekend aren't u?

Athena groaned. She wasn't sure if it was because her brother could so easily see right through her, or if his use of "u" instead of "you" when texting rankled her. She just couldn't bring herself to use such linguistic shortcuts, she was too old school. She decided that honesty was *not* the best policy and doubled down.

I don't know what you're talking about! I know how you love all that true crime stuff and thought you might be interested, that's all.

ur a terrible liar, even when texting. But yeah, I'm interested.

Athena smiled as she watched that last response appear on her screen.

I knew you would be.

Don't flatter yourself. I just wanna see your face when you realize she's innocent!

C'mon, you don't really believe that do you?

If there's one thing all these true crime shows have taught me it's how fucked up the system is. How much they like to frame innocent people, especially when they look like me.

For a moment Athena was tempted to remind him that Becca Greene wasn't black, but she thought better of it. The kid had a point, the system was corrupt as all get out, but she still felt like this case was pretty open and shut.

If she didn't do it then who did? The Jersey Devil? There's no credible cases of the JD ever killing anyone. Besides, he's just a ghost!

Says you! Anyhow you'll see that I'm right.

Oh yeah, wanna put some money on it?

My broke ass can't afford to put any money on anything!

He sent that last one with a laughing face emoji.
That was true enough. Her brother always seemed to be hurting for cash. Ah, to be young and broke!

Join the club!

Although, truth to tell, she and Dennis were actually doing pretty well so it wasn't really a fair comparison, but Athena never truly *felt* that they were as financially secure as they were. Money was just one more thing she was constantly anxious over.
There was a long pause and Athena thought he might've set his phone down to do something else. For the most part Athena preferred texting to talking, generally finding it less awkward, but this was something she hated about it - not knowing what someone else was doing or when the conversation was over. Her need to fill this interminable void won out and her thumbs were soon flying over her screen again.

It's all hypothetical right now anyway. My friend doesn't even know if he can get in to see her.

Happily, shortly after sending that last message she saw the trio of dots which heralded the arrival of an incoming text.

Cool, just let me know when u know something definite.

Sure thing. Love you little bro.

She punctuated it with a trilogy of hearts.

Ditto, big sis.

He returned the hearts and added a smiley face.

Athena stared at the screen for a moment, soaking in the virtual love and allowed the screen to go dark, satisfied that for once, the conversation had actually come to an easily identifiable conclusion.

Chapter Five:
The Consequences of Negligence

That very same day, and a bit further to the south, Agent Method was shaking her head in disgust at the mess on the ground in front of her. The object of her disdain was a set of human remains which had been picked so clean it was nearly skeletal. Here and there, raw chunks of flesh still clung stubbornly to the corpse along with several torn and bloodied strips of cloth which she supposed must've been clothing at one time. More such bits of clothing were strewn around the body, in white sands stained red by the victim's vital fluids. The scalp remained; hair was apparently as indigestible as clothing for the thing which had done this.

The stench was stomach churning. It took all of her willpower not to throw up.

Method's gun was drawn this time. The creature was nowhere to be seen at the moment. Method was grateful she didn't have to look at its awful face, but also didn't like the idea that it could burst out of the bushes at any moment to attack.

Someone had recently spotted the body on one of the cameras mounted high up in the treetops. Method and her team had been ordered to secure the body and assess the situation, and were promptly teleported to the location thanks to one of Agent Ember's spells.

"This one looks even worse than those students did. He must've been really hungry!" Agent Fresh remarked, displaying his penchant for stating the obvious. She decided to cut the guy a little slack, though - she knew he was just talking because he was nervous, and this time she couldn't blame him. She was nervous too, knowing that thing was lurking around.

"It probably doesn't get to feed very often. Even most of the animals are spooked by the mystical energies thrown out by the standing stones that keep it contained," Agent Ember replied dispassionately in her usual smooth, whispery soft voice.

Method frowned. "Hasn't anyone ever thought about airdropping some meat in here for it?"

Ember laughed at the idea. "That thing is an *abomination.* Its very existence is an embarrassment to my people. The last thing anyone wants to do is take care of it. As far as the Director is concerned, we're already spending far too much money keeping it contained."

"It's still a living thing!" Agent Method argued, kicking at the dirt with her toe in frustration at the obstinate attitude of her superiors. The thing deeply horrified her, but so did their own negligence towards it.

"A living thing? Barely!" Agent Ember said without looking up as she typed the number on the old Volkswagen's license plate into her wrist computer. Within seconds a display projected onto her sunglasses showed her the name of the person the vehicle was registered to.

"Dustin McCloskey," she muttered sadly.

"Huh?" Fresh asked.

"Dustin McCloskey. It might be the name of our John Doe over there. See if you can find a wallet in some of those torn clothes to confirm it," she commanded.

Agent Fresh made a face as he pulled a pair of medical gloves from his ebon sports jacket and put them on. "Why do I get all the nasty jobs?" he wondered aloud as he leaned down to sift through the shredded strips of fabric strewn around the body.

"It's the price you gotta pay for being a newbie," Method replied unsympathetically, her eyes never leaving the woods that enclosed them like an arboreal tomb.

"When exactly do I stop being a newbie? I've been an agent for over a year now!" he groaned as he shook some gore from his fingers.

"Maybe when you can do your job without complaining so much?" Method offered with a sarcastic smirk. He rolled his eyes at her, but she couldn't see it behind his sunglasses.

Throughout this entire exchange, Agent Ember had been frantically typing into her wrist computer. She finally let her hand fall to her waist and turned to smile at her two subordinates. "The cleanup crew is en route and should be here in about twenty minutes. We won't have to hang around here much longer."

Technically, a cleanup crew wasn't necessary. Ember could cast a spell that would disintegrate all traces that Dustin McCloskey had ever set foot in these woods - the body, the car, it would all be reduced to dust. However, their science division was intrigued by the monster and believed that they could learn more about it by studying the remains of its victims. And cars recovered from cases were an important source of income for her organization. After all identifying serial numbers were removed, it would be offered at a discount to other agents. If nobody bit, then it would be auctioned off on the black market. Method had obtained her own personal vehicle this way. Her husband Tristan, who, bless his heart, was completely ignorant of what she really did for a living, had been amazed that she'd gotten such a great deal on such a nice car. She often thought he might feel differently if he knew what had happened to the last people who'd owned it. It was something she tried not to think about.

"I hope you remembered to tell them to bring a tow truck. The victim's car obviously got stuck," Fresh mentioned as he pointed one dripping, red finger towards the small ditch behind the rear tires. "We won't be able to just drive it back to base."

"A tow truck? Did you forget that I'm a witch?" Ember said with an air of self satisfaction. She began chanting a spell and within moments the car was lifted up into the air. With a wave of her hand she spun it around so it faced the opposite direction, and with another gesture she gently set it back down on the trail.

"I believe the keys are still in the ignition. Now please tell me that one of you knows how to drive a stick shift?" the raven-haired senior witch inquired.

"I'll drive it, my dad taught me how to," Method told her. Something was still bothering her. "I don't understand how this happened! Why install all those cameras and motion sensors around here if we're not going to do anything when somebody trips them? This poor bastard couldn't have gotten this far back here without being detected."

Was this going to be her life now? Cleaning up after this thing? She was beginning to regret transferring to the South Jersey base. When Ember had been promoted to field leader she had wanted Method on her team. Since the two had worked so well together in the past, Method had readily agreed.

"That's precisely what I've just been talking to HQ about. A full investigation is being launched, but I have a feeling it'll be a short one. Apparently Agent Titan was on monitor duty when this occurred. It's pretty obvious what probably happened."

"Agent Wanker! That's great! That's just great!" Method was outraged, "Why was he allowed to be on monitor duty?"

"Apparently Agent Starbird's daughter had her Bat Mitzvah, so he switched shifts with Titan."

Method couldn't believe that someone had approved such a shift swap. Everyone knew that Agent Titan had an addiction to internet porn. He'd been caught several times in the men's room indulging himself, hence his unfortunate nickname. The only reason why he hadn't been fired was because he was related to an influential leader in one of the numerous secret societies whose activities her organization covered up. Getting rid of him would've created a political brouhaha, so instead he'd simply been relegated to the most menial duties. While this did include monitoring the numerous cameras they'd planted in various places of interest to her group throughout South Jersey, she assumed that someone would've been smart enough to know that he couldn't be entrusted with keeping an eye on an area this lethal. Worst of all, she was certain that due to his family connections, he'd get off with only a reprimand.

"Hey! I found it!" Agent Fresh exclaimed as if he'd just won the lottery. He pulled a dark brown wallet out of a pocket in a blood-drenched chunk of fabric that had once been part of a pant leg.

"Keep it down!" she hissed, "That thing is still out here, remember?"

"Chill out! If it gets too close, I'm sure someone monitoring things from HQ will alert us," he assured her as he stood up, opened the wallet and read the name on the driver's license. "Yeah, it's Dustin alright."

Agent Method ignored his confirmation of the corpse's identity. "You still trust this process to keep us safe after seeing that?" She waved her gun in the direction of the body.

"Sure. I assume that somebody more competent than Agent Wanker is looking over things now. This system wouldn't have saved poor old Dustin anyway. Even if somebody had spotted him on a cam, there were no magic users on duty last night who could've teleported in a rapid response team quickly enough. It takes about 45 minutes to get here from our base in Ong's Hat by car; he probably would've been toast by then." He snapped off his gloves, dropped them in the pile of bloody clothes, and placed the wallet in an evidence bag he produced from an inner jacket pocket.

He was probably right. Method hated to admit it, so she didn't out loud. Their science division was working on a technological method of teleportation based on some alien tech they'd recovered back in 2013, but so far they'd met with no success. Fresh's words only served to further convince her how idiotic it was to not put up a high wall around this entire area. She understood that the creature couldn't be removed from the land, but did they have to make it so easy for people to wander in? Especially if they couldn't always get here in time to save them?

Just then she heard a twig snap off in the distance and swung her gun to cover the dark stretch of trees in the direction where the sound seemed to have originated. She sighed when she saw a squirrel come shooting out of the bushes and up the side of a cedar tree.

Ember punched a few keys on her wrist computer. "Looks like Dustin didn't have much family. He shouldn't be too hard to disappear." She sounded entirely too pleased as she said it, in Method's opinion. She thought it was incredibly sad that this guy's family and friends would never know what happened to him. Ember was a good woman, but Method had borne witness as she'd grown ever more detached and callous as the years wore on. She hoped she never ended up like her. Not for the first time she wondered how much longer she could stay in this job - the excitement of it was starting to wear off. She'd leapt at the opportunity to join this organization because she'd been such a big *X-Files* fan, even patterning her appearance after Agent Scully. However, the reality of such a job was often far less satisfying than watching a show about this kind of stuff from the safety of your home.

Fresh took out his trademark breath spray and squirted it into his mouth, then froze as he noticed something on the ground a few feet away. "Aren't those motorcycle tracks? Was someone else out here before us? For that matter, how do we know that our buddy Dustin came out here alone? There could be other victims in this forest."

Ember shook her head, her long dark tresses swinging as she did so. "They've been reviewing the footage from last night back at HQ. He *was* by himself. There had been a pair of men on dirt bikes riding through here shortly before the creature got Dustin, but they got away."

"Oh boy, witnesses! Shouldn't we be going after them next so we can wipe their memories?" Fresh asked.

"We can't get a positive ID on them. Dirt bikes don't need license plates in this state and they never took off their helmets while they were within range of our cameras, so trying to identify them with facial recognition software is off the table. It's not a big deal. If they talk, nobody is likely to believe them anyway."

Method wasn't so sure about that. People seemed to believe all sorts of strange things these days, like the idea that a reality TV star might make a good President. Before she could say anything, her attention was drawn to an alert that flashed on the screen inside her sunglasses. They all saw it. It was a warning that the creature had just been picked up by both cameras and motion detectors. It appeared to be moving towards their position. She tensed and swept the treeline with her gleaming silver pistol.

Agent Fresh fixed her with a smug smile. "See? I told you that the system wor–"

His voice trailed off as the thing burst from the greenery, tackling him to the ground. So powerful was the impact that his gun went flying out of his hand before he could get off a shot.

The helpless agent squirmed and kicked at the thing. "OMIGOD! GET IT OFF OF ME! GET IT OFF! GET IT OFF!" he screamed, until his cries degenerated into incoherent declarations of agony. Torrents of crimson jetted into the air.

Agent Method pointed her weapon at the beast, but faster than she could register, Ember was upon her, batting the gun out of the way.

"Are you nuts?" Method howled at her superior.

"You'll hit Fresh! Let me handle this!"

Agent Ember cast her levitation spell once more, this time lifting the creature off of Fresh. It hung there in mid air for a moment, its one drooping, deformed eye blinking in confusion and rage before she hurled it into the trunk of a distant tree with such force that the trunk snapped in half and crashed down into the underbrush. Such a counterattack surely would've shattered its spine, yet Method knew that within moments it would be recovered enough to come at them again.

Ember's voice invoked another spell, and a shimmering green wall of energy encircled the three of them and the car. As soon as it had been erected, she wasted no time in dashing to Fresh's side. Method followed.

Things didn't look good for Agent Fresh. There was blood everywhere. So much blood! Method could see that the entire left side of his face, including his ear, had been torn off. A pity, he'd once been a handsome man. Annoying, but handsome.

Now we'll have to start calling him Agent Van Gogh, she caught herself absurdly thinking. Her face flushed with shame at her own insensitivity. For all his faults, overall he was a good guy, and he might even have had the makings of a decent agent. At any rate, *nobody* deserved this.

He's not gone yet. Don't think of him in the past tense! Not yet!

She could see the exposed tendons and ligaments of his jaw like something out of an anatomy textbook. She could hear Ember reciting another spell. She recognized the healing enchantment. She'd seen Ember use it before. As her superior laid one glowing, golden hand on Fresh's ruined face, he stopped screaming so abruptly that Method was shocked by just how much she'd already gotten used to hearing his pained cries.

A forlorn Ember looked up at Method. "I've stopped the bleeding, but I need to teleport him to the infirmary ASAP! Take the car and get out of here before this shield spell expires. I'll make an opening for you, now *go!*" She practically shouted the last part, which showed how desperate things were for Agent Fresh, as Ember's voice was rarely ever raised above a raspy whisper. As if to punctuate her point, the thing hurled itself uselessly into the energy barrier just inches from them and snarled. Agent Fresh's torn flesh still dangled from its jagged, ruined teeth. Fresh screamed again.

Method wordlessly nodded her understanding and whirled around to dash towards the waiting VW Bug. She nearly tripped over what was left of the car's previous owner as she did so. Flinging herself into the driver's seat, she felt for the keys, and with a groan of protest the engine shuddered into renewed internal combustion activity. She drove towards the energy barrier without hesitation, her eyes fixed on Ember in the rearview mirror. The senior agent was back on her feet, supporting Agent Fresh with an arm wrapped around his waist. She gestured with her free hand and a large hole opened in the barrier just big enough to accommodate the Bug. As soon as Method was through, it closed behind her. She could still see her two companions through the wall of green energy, but only for a moment. Soon there was a blinding flash of light and the two of them were gone, teleported to safety by Ember's magic.

I'm not out of the woods yet, she reminded herself. Not until she got past the stone arch further down the trail. She shifted gears and put her pedal to the metal. Sure enough, she soon saw the thing jump out of the bushes and felt it slam into the side of the vehicle before giving chase with its weird loping run. It was uncannily fast, but it was no match for a car, even one this old.

At long last, she saw the stones as she rounded the bend. It was difficult to resist the urge to floor the gas as soon as she sighted the arch. She was careful not to go too fast though, otherwise she'd get stuck just like poor Dustin had. It was difficult to maintain this discipline with that horrible, ugly thing still breathing down her neck. The car passed under the arch and it was with some satisfaction that she watched the creature run headlong into the invisible field. It looked like it had shattered what passed for its face in the process. As her eyes scanned the trail ahead for the turn off to the main road, they fixated on a rabbit's foot pendulously swinging from the rear view mirror. It certainly hadn't brought Dustin any luck. It was a sobering reminder to her that not all the magic people put their faith in was as potent as Ember's.

Chapter Six: A Trip to the County Jail

thena heard from Lars the very next day. Happily, he had good news for her. Rebecca Greene had agreed to an interview, apparently over the vociferous objections of her public defender. As it turned out, she was eager to have her side of the story made public - even at the risk of potentially damaging her case. Athena interpreted this as a sign of either extreme desperation or sincere belief in her own innocence. Athena also knew that just because Becca believed herself to be innocent didn't mean that she actually *was* innocent. People had an almost infinite capacity for self delusion, especially when confronting truths about themselves as ugly as the fact that they're a mass murderer. It could simply be even further proof that Becca was as cuckoo as Athena assumed she was, and she told Mark as much when she texted him the news. He naturally pleaded with her to try and remain objective and just listen to the woman's story. Athena promised, grateful that he couldn't see her crossing her fingers as she typed her disingenuous response.

Lars had reported that they possibly had another day or so to wait for their background checks to go through before they'd be allowed to visit the jail where Becca Greene was being held while she awaited her trial. "Assuming that none of you have secret axe murdering pasts," he'd joked.

"Damn, I always knew that would come back to haunt me one day," Athena had quipped back.

Visiting hours were on the weekends only, but that was alright since the weather forecast had remained lousy and they'd had to reschedule the investigation on account of rain anyway.

As it turned out, neither Athena nor Mark had secret axe murdering pasts or anything more serious than a few traffic tickets, and that Saturday afternoon the newly minted newspaper interns found themselves sitting in Lar's SUV on their way to the Atlantic County Gerald R.Gormley Justice Facility, as the place was formally known.

After undergoing a body search where Athena had to stop herself from slapping the corrections officer when she thought he was getting a little too handsy, they were ushered into a small, plain room with a table and four chairs. Three of the chairs were on one side of the table and the last one was looking rather loney by itself on the opposite side. Athena, Mark and Lars all took their seats and waited. And they waited, and waited some more. Athena fidgeted endlessly with the shiny new lanyard that declared she was an intern at the Asbury Park Press. Mark was on his phone, occasionally tittering at whatever funny video he was watching. Lars just looked around the room nervously, fiddling with the voice activated microcassette recorder he'd brought with him.

Finally, Becca Greene was ushered into the room by a guard. She was dressed in the kind of bright orange jumpsuits only worn by astronauts or inmates. She shuffled into the room noisily, as both her legs and wrists were chained together. The sound of rattling chains absurdly reminded Athena of the ghost of Jacob Marley from *A Christmas Carol.* All three of the visitors were shocked by the transformation in the woman's appearance. They'd all seen photos of a vibrant, pretty, athletic brunette in her mid to late thirties. The woman before them now was barely recognizable as the same person. Her hair was a frizzy, bedraggled mess. Gone was her well tanned skin, replaced by a sickly, jaundiced pallor. Dark circles underscored hopeless eyes in which only the barest glint of life still flared. She had been a thin, muscular woman in her photos, but now she was downright skeletal. This pathetic creature was guided to the chair by the corrections officer, her ass landing in the spartan plastic chair with a thump. The officer backed himself up against the wall behind her, but remained in the room.

Lars instinctively extended his hand to shake hers, but a warning glance from the guard reminded him that such physical contact was verboten. He awkwardly lowered his hand, letting it rest on the table. "Thank you so much for agreeing to speak with us today, Rebecca," he said in his best TV newsman voice. "I'm Lars and these are my, erm, assistants, Athena and Mark."

The other two muttered their muted greetings.

The woman shrugged. "I just wanna be able to tell my story, to get the truth out about what really happened." She looked down sadly. "I've had other offers to talk to the press, but I wasn't ready to talk about it then. Now I feel like I've got to set the record straight. They've got so much of it all wrong! Especially when it comes to the crazy things they're saying about Dylan! Oh, my poor Dylan.

Dylan was the name of her fiance, who had been posthumously accused of being her partner in crime before she had turned on him and killed him too, or so the official story went.

"I never hurt my Dylan. And he'd never hurt anyone else either! My lawyer showed me all these pictures that are going around on the internet of him dressed up like Michael Myers from those *Halloween* movies and they're trying to point at that as proof of him being some kind of a psycho who was obsessed with violence. Sure, he had a small collection of horror movies, but it was mostly that cheesy old stuff. *Dracula*, *The Wolfman*, all that *Universal Monsters* stuff. He didn't like things that were really gory. He just loved movies in general, all kinds of movies! When we were together, we mostly watched romantic comedies and Disney movies. *Disney movies!* Those were his favorites! Does that sound like a psycho to you? We were gonna have our honeymoon at Disneyworld." The thought of the honeymoon that would now never occur seemed to make her choke up. Her voice broke and she abruptly grew silent as she fought back the tears.

Lars leaned forward. "Why don't you just start by telling us what you two were doing out there on that day," he suggested in a calm, reasonable tone.

Becca seemed to regain her composure. She nodded and looked up at them. "Sure, we were out there to work on his fears. He was no psycho, but he *did* have a few minor mental issues, don't we all? It was nothing serious, he was just afraid of going into the woods. I like to go hiking and he was upset that it was something he couldn't share with me. He wanted to conquer his fear because of me, so we could spend more time together - *that's* the kind of man that he was. He was scared of the woods because of something that happened when he was a kid, when he lived in some apartments that are near the woods. So we returned to the scene of his trauma.”

Mark’s ears pricked up at the mention of apartments.

“Those wouldn’t happen to be the Deercrest Apartments, would they?” he asked.

Becca scrunched up her face in concentration. “Yeah, I think that’s what they were called. They’re all boarded up now. That’s where we parked his car.”

Mark glanced at his sister with a somewhat smug expression that definitely said *See, I told you there was something fishy about those apartments!* Athena just rolled her eyes at him.

Up until that point Athena had been too anxious to say anything, but Mark’s boldness in speaking up gave her the courage she needed to talk to the alleged murderer.

“What happened in those woods when he was a kid?”

“He and some friends were riding their bikes on the trails back there. There were stories of a man living in an old farmhouse in the woods who kidnapped the kids from the apartments. They didn’t believe it, so they rode out to check it out, but as they got close to the place they were chased away from there by *something*.”

“What kind of something?” Lars asked softly.

“He never got a look at it. The kid riding in front saw it and turned around to get away, and they all just followed his lead. But the feeling of being chased by something was very real to Dylan, and it terrified him. It stayed with him for his whole life - the feeling that he’d narrowly escaped death, and a fear of the forest. I *can* tell you what we both saw when we found that old farmhouse. Most of the building had collapsed, but there was a chicken coop next to it that was intact and there was something sleeping inside of it, something horrible...." Her voice broke off and she took a deep breath before continuing.

"It's hard to describe, but I'll try. It was kinda small, like a young boy, but it looked rotted in some places and in other places it looked like the skin was regrowing, like growing super fast right before our eyes! It was all lumpy and misshapen and dressed in dirty, torn clothes. It limped and was hunched over when it woke up and ran after us. It was fast despite all those deformities, impossibly fast! We ran away and hid. We thought we'd given it the slip, but somehow it snuck up on us and...it got Dylan. It was horrible! It started eating him alive right in front of me! I wanted to do something, to save him, but he told me to get away. He sacrificed himself so that I could live! He's a *hero*, not the monster they're saying he is! But there really was a monster living in those woods, that's what really killed those students!"

"Great! And that's where you want to take us next weekend?" Mark said, looking pointedly at Athena.

Becca's eyes went wide at his words. "You're planning on going out there? You can't! You might wind up like all the others! I don't know what they did with it, I didn't see! It could still be out there right now! You can't go! You can't!" She was getting increasingly agitated by the minute and started to stand up. The guard took a few steps toward her.

"Calm down and stay in your seat or I'll end this interview right now!" he commanded.

Becca's nostrils flared and her face turned bright red as she gestured wordlessly towards her visitors, her chains rattling with each movement. In the end, she frowned and sank back down into her seat, looking crumpled and defeated. The guard moved back to his spot up against the peeling, puke-green paint of the cinder block wall.

"So if I'm understanding you correctly, you're claiming that some sort of creature was responsible for the deaths of Dylan and the other people who were out in the woods that weekend?" Lars stated, somehow managing to keep the incredulity he was probably feeling out of his voice.

"Right! Exactly! My lawyer doesn't want me talking about it, he says it makes me sound crazy, but everyone already thinks I'm crazy, so what do I have to lose? I know how strange it sounds, but it's what happened! You have to believe me! What's really crazy is the idea that two people who have no previous history of violence or criminal activity would suddenly snap and decide to slaughter a bunch of people one day. We didn't even know those others were out there! I never even saw them until they were zipping them up into body bags when they brought me to their camp after they got me away from that monster."

"Others? Who are you talking about?" Athena was confused. Who was she trying to implicate in her crimes now?

Becca looked Athena straight in the eye. "The Men in Black. They're real, only some of them are women! Hell, some of them barely even seem human. I guess they've got their own monsters too."

Great, more riddles! Athena thought in dismay. What monsters was she talking about now? And now she was bringing the MIB into this? The MIB was something else that Athena was highly skeptical about. As far as she could tell, the only "evidence" of their existence was purely anecdotal. There was also the problem that representatives of any number of real government agencies could easily be mistaken for the MIB. Still, Athena wanted to know more, propelled at this point more by a morbid curiosity about how much more outrageous Becca's story could become.

"What do the Men in Black have to do with any of this? And what do you mean they've got their own monsters?"

"I wish I knew, but I don't understand any of it myself. I was running from that thing, trying to reach civilization and that's when I bumped right into the Men in Black. The thing chasing me caught up with us, but the Men in Black had something with them, they called it 'the test subject.' It looked like a bald guy with dark blue skin wearing a kind of tight fitting armored bodysuit. He was up in the trees, and he jumped down and fought the thing. He had these long blades that popped out of his forearms and he cut the thing's hands off! The hands grew right back! He kept on fighting the thing while the Men in Black took me to the camp. The place was crawling with the Men in Black, and a few cops too. They were cleaning up the crime scene, taking the bodies away. They drove me away, to some kind of underground base miles away. They kept me there for hours before turning me over to the police. They framed me for the whole thing! I don't know why, but they're out to get me! They're all in on it! Trying to hide the truth!" Becca's eyes blazed with an unbelievable intensity that bored into all of them.

Athena sighed. *They're out to get me?* Did this lady know how crazy she sounded? Athena had read up on human psychology quite a bit over the years, educating herself as a way to figure out how best to cope with her own sometimes nearly crippling anxieties over just about everything. This was textbook paranoia! No wonder her lawyer didn't want her talking, unless he was using reverse psychology on his client. Maybe he really *did* want her to talk as a way to plant the seeds for an eventual insanity plea.

As distasteful as it might be to visit the mind of a killer, Athena reluctantly stretched out her awareness to brush up against the edges of Rebecca Greene's consciousness. She sensed no duplicity within her. Becca truly believed everything she'd just told them, however that proved nothing. Over the years, Athena had come to learn that people had an infinite capacity for self delusion. People made up all kinds of justifications to cover their real motivations, justifications that they were far more comfortable with than the truth. Seeing what might lie under the surface of her beliefs would take far more finesse than Athena possessed with her psychic abilities. Besides, she didn't *want* to see what she'd seen, and didn't want to experience that kind of darkness firsthand. What was the old saying? The one about how if you stare into the abyss long enough it looks into you as well? Athena had no desire to wind up as looney and dangerous as Becca Greene. She quickly broke off contact with her consciousness before her madness could infect her as well.

"You don't believe me, do you? I suppose that's why they let me keep my memories. They knew I'd just sound totally nuts if I tried to convince anyone!"

"*I* believe you," Mark said firmly.

Athena shot him a disapproving look.

Mark continued undaunted. "I had a cousin who used to live in those apartments and he was convinced that other kids went missing in the woods sometimes. That whole place feels *wrong* doesn't it? I could feel it whenever I went to visit him."

"Yes! Yes! It feels horrible near those woods! It's like this oppressive feeling of dread that just hangs in the air all around there," Becca affirmed, delighted to know that someone knew exactly what she was talking about and believed her.

"Now Mark, remember we're supposed to maintain our journalistic neutrality," Lars admonished, leaning a bit too heavily into the charade that they were his interns. It occurred to Athena that he was enjoying playing the game. He shifted in his chair and addressed Becca.

"So what do you think was going on? What was this creature and what were these Men in Black doing there?"

Becca was silent for a few moments, gathering her thoughts. "I don't really know. I've had plenty of time to think about it, nothing *but* time to think about it! I'll tell you what I think it all means: I think that first monster, the one that attacked me and Dylan and all those students was like some kind of an experiment gone wrong. One of those Men in Black said something about how it couldn't be killed. I think they keep it out there in the woods, that it's been there for decades. Maybe it's kept there by one of those invisible fences like they use on dogs? I think they use it to test out their other experiments. That other monster was called a test subject, I think he was an experiment too, like a super soldier. Maybe they made him with alien DNA or something? The Men in Black are supposed to have alien technology from crashed UFOs aren't they? They sure had some fancy laser guns on them when I met them, like something outta *Star Wars.* I never really believed in any of this stuff until this happened to me, but I've been trying to learn more about it from books in the jail library since I've been locked up. I'm trying to understand what happened to me, and I guess to distract myself from thinking about what happened to Dylan. Every time I close my eyes I see him being ripped apart, screaming for me to leave him and run. Sometimes I wish that thing *had* gotten me, then we could be together again and people would remember me as a victim instead of a monster to be hated."

Athena didn't need to be psychic to tell that her wish to die was sincere, and for the first time since meeting her, she felt pity for the woman. She wondered if they had her on a suicide watch? Then she remembered all the people this woman had killed and decided she didn't care. She did at least seem to regret murdering her fiancé. She wondered what kind of a frenzy had overtaken her to cause her to do such a thing? Maybe they'd had a suicide pact and she'd gotten cold feet at the last minute? Obviously Becca didn't understand it herself, otherwise she wouldn't have had to make up such an elaborate story to hide the truth from herself.

Before coming there today, Athena had done a little research on the case and as she thought back on it, she thought she'd found a hole in the woman's story - not that the whole story wasn't like one big yawning chasm of bullshit.

"You said that you had no idea that the students were out there that day, right?"

"Yeah. I never saw any of them alive."

"But I recall reading that the details of the expedition were published on the website of the TOTOG Foundation, the group that sponsored the dig, and when the authorities seized Dylan's laptop they found that he'd been accessing that page. How do you explain that?" Her question earned her an impressed look from Lars.

Rebecca Greene shifted uncomfortably in her chair. "I don't know what was in his search history. I trusted him. If he knew anyone else was in the woods that day he never mentioned it. We're dealing with the Men in Black here, they can plant whatever 'evidence' they want. I've heard they put all kinds of crazy stuff in my own Google search history, things I never actually looked up, like 'how to get away with murder' or 'how does it feel to kill somebody.' It's all lies!"

"What about the pickaxe that has fingerprints from both you and Dylan all over it?" Athena continued to press her.

"I already told you, it's all manufactured evidence. They're out to get me! I'm their scapegoat. They can make it look anyway they want it to look!" Becca was obviously getting angry at this line of questioning.

Lars decided it was time to try and smooth things over. "Surely you can understand why it's hard for us to take your story very seriously. Is there anything you can tell us, anything we can look for that might prove your version of events is the true one?"

She shook her head. "Without sending you out there to get killed by that thing yourselves? No. All I can tell you is to talk to our friends and family. They'll tell you we're not the kinds of people who are capable of doing something that horrible."

Athena sat back and folded her arms. How many times had she heard stories from the friends and acquaintances of those who'd committed atrocities about how well behaved and quiet they were? It was a total cliche. If this was the best she had to offer, she'd better *hope* that her attorney entered an insanity plea on her behalf.

Lars asked her for a list of friends and family that she thought might be willing to talk to him. Even though his tape recorder was still going, he hastily typed the names into the notes on his iphone. It wasn't long after that when the guard announced that the visit was over. Lars looked visibly irritated, as he'd barely had a chance to ask any of the questions he'd had in mind. He promised to write to Becca so she could answer them later on.

Right before the guard ushered her out of the room, Becca paused long enough at the door to fix them all with a serious look. "Don't go into those woods if you know what's good for you, otherwise it might be the last thing you ever do."

It was meant to be a grave warning, but Athena found it so over the top in its delivery that she had to suppress the urge to giggle.

They were silent as they were led out of the building, each of them trying in their own way to process all that they'd just seen and heard. Athena was the first to break the silence as soon as they climbed back into Lar's SUV.

"Can you believe that load of horseshit she was trying to feed us?"

"Actually, I can," Mark replied from the back seat.

"Uh, oh! It looks like your plan backfired, Athena. Mark is a true believer!" Lars teased as he started the car up and began to cautiously pull out of his parking space.

"My plan? I don't know what you're talking about!" Athena fibbed, stubbornly hanging onto her charade.

"No, her plan worked - I *do* want to go on her Jersey Devil hunt now, just not for the same reasons that she wants to. I want to help that poor lady out. Maybe if we can prove that there's some sort of monster lurking around there we can exonerate her."

Athena was flabbergasted. "What, you're suddenly not too scared? If you believe in her cockamie story that means that you have to also believe in a monster that can't be killed and instantly regenerates dismembered body parts."

"*Somebody's* gotta help her. I don't see anyone else trying to do it. I'll bring my gun, it'll be fine."

"Wait, what? You've got a gun?" Athena was too shocked by this revelation to point out how ineffective such a weapon would prove to be against such an adversary - if that sort of thing was real, which it definitely was not as far as she was concerned.

"Sis, I'm Black and I'm Gay and we don't live in the most progressive part of the great Garden State. A man's gotta protect himself. You know what some of the local yokels call Gunning River Road, don't you?"

"I do," she answered grimly. Gunning River Road was a road in Barnegat where some of the few Black families in town had lived decades ago, and were sometimes terrorized by the more racist town residents. So much so that anyone who grew up in Barnegat knew that the word "gunning" was often substituted for "running," and the word "river" was replaced by the infamous n-word, by those insensitive enough to find humor in the suffering of others. People liked to pretend that this was all ancient history, but the undercurrents of this dark past were still very much there, rippling just under the surface of the bland, placid looking residential tracts.

"I've got a .44 Magnum, just like Dirty Harry. It might not kill it, but that thing would probably knock down a charging lion. I figure it could give us enough time to get away."

As plans went, Athena didn't think this was a particularly smart one. Assuming that this monster existed outside of the feverish imagination of Rebecca Greene and they managed to escape it, what did Mark plan to do with any evidence of its existence that he might've managed to obtain? Wouldn't the Men in Black just suppress it? Of course, she didn't bother to call attention to any of this. For one thing, she didn't believe Greene's story, and for another, her brother wanted to come along on her investigation now, which had been her goal in coming here in the first place. Did it really matter *why* he was coming? She just hoped he didn't accidentally shoot somebody's foot off while playing Dirty Harry out in the woods next weekend.

Lars risked taking his eyes off the road long enough to cast a quizzical look in Athena's direction. "I must say, Athena, I'm surprised you aren't more open-minded about her version of events. After all, you are someone who's infamous for talking to ghosts. Lots of people would consider some of the claims you've made over the years to be as crazy as her story is."

"Listen Lars, just because I believe that one strange thing is real doesn't mean that I have to believe in *every* outlandish idea under the sun. I've been seeing and talking to spirits ever since I hit puberty. I know they're not just figments of my imagination because they've told me things that I couldn't possibly know, things that I was later able to verify through research. Believing in ghosts isn't all that weird, anyway. Lots of people around the world are religious or spiritual or what have you. They believe that we're more than just animated bags of meat, that when we die some part of us lives on. It isn't much of a leap to believe that sometimes that immortal part of us gets stuck here and doesn't quite make it to the afterlife. If you believe in the soul, or in some kind of a God then you have to allow for the possibility that some ghost stories are true."

"But you want to go out into the woods to find a monster, and she basically corroborated your theory that there's a monster out there!" Mark argued.

Athena buried her head in her hands. "No, my theory is that there's a *ghost* in the woods that people are mistaking for a monster. Not some kind of a flesh eating zombie! It's completely different!"

"Is it?" Lars countered as he steered them past the gate and back onto the main road. "She said that it was the size of a boy, and was deformed. Your theory is that there's the ghost of a deformed child in the woods. Sounds pretty similar to me!"

"Hey, who's side are you on anyway?"

"I'm a reporter. I'm not on anyone's side, except perhaps for the side of truth," he said with such cornball sincerity that it almost sounded campy to Athena's ears.

"Granted, there is a slight *superficial* similarity between her description of it and some of the ones I've been sent of the deformed child that's been seen. But what she described is a killer. Nobody has ever been killed by the Jersey Devil."

"That we know of. Perhaps any such deaths were covered up by the Men in Black?" Lars suggested.

"Don't tell me you're buying all that talk about the MIB too?"

"I'm not buying anything. I'm merely trying to remain objective. Besides, her story is weird, and I like weird. That's why I hang around with you guys."

"Gee, thanks a bunch!" Athena replied sarcastically.

"You're welcome! You have to admit that the crime she's accused of is weird too, almost as weird as her story. Think about it: a couple with no prior criminal history decides to go out into the woods and murder a college professor and his students. Somehow the two of them managed to stalk and kill them all by themselves, using only a couple of pickaxes as weapons, which is in and of itself, a very strange choice for a murder weapon. Then they turn on each other and one of the killers murders the other one? The whole thing smells fishy."

"Maybe so," Athena grudgingly admitted, "but it's no excuse to go off believing in her version of what happened. But alright, I'll play along for a minute. Let's assume everything she said is true. Why would anyone keep such a dangerous creature out in the open where anyone could happen upon it and get gobbled up? It doesn't make any sense!"

"Okay, you've got me there. I can't think of a good reason for that. If they are using it to field test the capabilities of a type of genetically enhanced soldier like she suggested, surely they could do it in a less dangerous way?"

Mark had been silently stewing all this time, but now he'd heard enough. "Sis, you're the most stubborn person I've ever met! Are you ignoring what your own powers are telling you about her just because it doesn't perfectly fit into your little pet theory about the Jersey Devil? You're a psychic! Couldn't you sense that she was telling the truth?"

She turned around in her seat to face her brother. "Being a psychic doesn't make me a human lie detector. All I can tell is if someone believes what they're saying - which she definitely did. But that doesn't mean it's what really happened, not if she's delusional. In my humble opinion, that lady was delusional with a capital D! And paranoid as all get out to boot! All that shit about the Men in Black was just too much! The woman is like a walking, talking, conspiracy theory. It's a textbook case of paranoia."

"Is the idea of the Men in Black really that outlandish? The government is covering up shit all the time. Besides, when you were telling me about your first case with the JSPS, the one where you met

Miranda, didn't you say that wizard friend of yours Clark Kismet implied that there was some kind of a group like that that covered up evidence of magic?" Mark inquired.

"Oh! A wizard friend? I've never heard this story before! It sounds interesting!" Lars interjected.

"It *is* pretty interesting. It's crazy that I've never written it down or talked about it on the website before. I guess I've been reluctant because it has to do with Miranda's past, and I'm not all that comfortable putting all her personal business out there in public for everyone to see and gossip about," Athena clarified. This was all true enough, but she was also too anxious to bring up the topic of publishing the details of that case online to her best friend. Sometimes it was best to just let the past stay buried.

"Anyhow, that wizard is *not* my friend. He's a real weirdo. He tried to recruit me into his little coven. I'm not into joining cults," she added, a little too defensively.

In the rear view mirror she saw Mark smirking. "Irregardless, you still carry his business card around in your purse - I've seen it! You even laminated it!"

Athena grimaced. Mark knew that his frequent use of the term "Irregardless" was like scraping nails on a chalkboard to her. It wasn't even a real word! It just made him sound dumb, and he wasn't dumb. She'd lectured him about it plenty of times in the past and she believed that he now did it just to needle her.

"Number one, what were you doing rooting around in my purse? And number two, it's not even a functional business card! It just has his name and his old job title on it. No address, no phone number–"

"Duh! That's because it's a magical business card, obviously! Didn't he say you could contact him anytime you needed by holding it and thinking of him?" Mark asked.

"Well maybe so, but that's not why I keep it, I keep it for sentimental reasons. That was our first case, you know? When we all became friends. And you never answered my question about going through my purse!"

"Chill out. I was just looking for some gum. You always keep gum in there."

"Well, that's true. Gotta have my Juicy Fruit." Chewing gum was Athena's main vice in life. It had to be sugar free, of course, to preserve the perfect smile that she saw as her best physical attribute. The mention of gum reminded her to take out a stick and pop it in her mouth. She began smacking it loudly and making "mmm, mmm" sounds. If you asked the people around her, they'd tell you that the gum itself wasn't her vice so much as all the irritating sounds she made when she chewed it!

"So you believe in magic, but the Men in Black is a bridge too far for you?" Lars couldn't resist calling out the inconsistencies in Athena's world view.

"I believe that *some* magic is real, because I've seen it performed right in front of me, real life *Harry Potter* shit! But I also know that most of it is bullshit, like 90% of that stuff my mom peddles in her shop. Again, like I said before, just because I hold one unusual belief, that doesn't obligate me to believe in the entire universe of weirdness," she explained wearily.

"I repeat: what's so unbelievable about the Men in Black?" Lars continued to press her.

Athena vacantly stared out the window for a spell before replying. "Well, the first two movies were lots of fun, although the CGI hasn't aged very well. The animated series was da bomb, but nobody really remembers it anymore. The third one felt kinda uninspired. I dunno man, the magic's just gone," she joked.

She heard Mark groan from the backseat, which made her smirk in satisfaction. Lars just chuckled at her appraisal of the *MIB* franchise.

"Seriously though, I don't deny that there are any number of smartly dressed government agents poking their noses into things at any time, but the idea that there's one big agency trying to cover up all the weirdness in the world seems a bit too convenient. It's all tied up in that UFO shit, and 90% of that is sketchy as hell. All the evidence of the MIB is totally anecdotal."

"Yeah, but all the evidence of your deformed ghost boy is anecdotal too, yet you're still hell bent on searching for him," Mark answered.

"Touché!" Lars added.

"Yes, it's all just based on eyewitness accounts and that's exactly *why* I want to obtain something a bit more solid to back up my ideas."

"Well, it will certainly be interesting to see what, if anything, we find this weekend." Lars smiled.

"You still wanna come? Lizzy Borden back there didn't scare you off with all her warnings about not going into the woods?" Athena asked a little incredulously. Lars had been giving her the impression that he was swallowing Becca's story as much as Mark was, despite his claims of objectivity.

"Are you kidding? I wouldn't want to miss it for the world!" Lars asserted, visions of Pulitzer Prizes swimming in his head.

Chapter Seven:
On a Dark and Lonely Highway

Brenda gunned the engine of the Camaro, enjoying its powerful vibrations as she hit another deserted stretch of route 72. At this time of night there was precious little traffic in either direction and she risked getting her speed up as high as 100 MPH before letting go of the gas pedal and seeing how long it took her to coast back down to a more legal and reasonable speed. It was a dangerous game to play, but not necessarily because she was all that concerned about getting a speeding ticket or hitting another car - what made it so insane was all the deer that were out there sometimes.

But tonight she hadn't seen any of her antlered friends and decided to tempt fate. It was undeniably thrilling and it helped her stay awake on the long trip between Camden County College and her home in Forked River. She was studying to become a Veterinary Technician at night and trying to hold down a day job at the same time; she needed all the help she could get to stop herself from falling asleep behind the wheel on these long, late night drives where it was all too easy to fall under the hypnotic spell of the seemingly endless road and the rows of short, twisted, scrubby little pines that lined it.

She took another sip of liquid adrenaline from her trusty WaWa travel mug. The coffee was lukewarm by now, but still tasty as ever. She watched the speedometer slowly go down as she set the mug back in the drink holder. 90...95...80...85...75.... She let it get down to 70 before giving it any more gas.

She cruised for a while between 75-80 MPH and waited for a nice straight stretch of road before trying to crank it all the way back up to 100 again. She decided it was wise to give the engine a bit of a rest before taxing it like that once more. Not for the first time, she thought about how much her dad would kill her if he knew how much of a strain she was putting on the old car, let alone the danger she was putting herself in. Just as she was thinking of this, she saw her headlights cut out, felt the vibration from the engine cease, and no longer heard the radio playing.

"What the hell?!" she exclaimed, fighting down the panic as the car continued to fly forward, propelled by its fading momentum through a darkness so complete that she felt like she was in outer space. She slowly applied the brakes, getting her speed down as she maneuvered to where the shoulder of the road should be - she could barely make it out in the blackness of the night, only the characteristically white sands of the Pine Barrens stood out under the weak moonlight to guide her.

She brought the car to a full stop on the side of the road, cursing herself for messing up a perfectly good car by pushing it too hard. In the back of her mind she wondered why the car battery seemed to be dead too, if the problem was caused by her overburdening the engine? She didn't know a hell of a lot about cars, but she thought that if it was an engine issue then surely the battery would still be giving her the lights and radio? She tried restarting the car, but the engine wouldn't turn over. Wasn't there something called an alternator that could cause this problem? She strained to recall her father's less than exciting attempts to explain how cars worked and came up with a blank. His lectures might not have seemed all that interesting at the time, but right now she would've found it to be the most interesting topic in the world!

A shiver went down her spine. She didn't want to be stuck here alone on this dark and isolated road. She'd always gotten a bad feeling when she'd driven through this area in the past, and sometimes even thought she'd glimpsed sinister, shadowy forms darting between the trees around here. She pulled out her phone to give her dad a call and was dismayed to see that it too seemed to be dead. That really confused her. She'd been charging it the whole time she was in her last class and was certain it had been at 100 percent when she'd unplugged it. She hadn't even used it since leaving school.

How could this be happening? What could possibly drain both her car and phone batteries like this? A thought that was as exciting as it was frightening entered her mind. Didn't UFOs sometimes cause this exact kind of loss of power? She heard a rustling from somewhere in the inky expanse of trees to her right and her butt cheeks tightened. She'd heard about how these aliens loved to put probes into people's asses. Well, no man from another planet was about to put anything up there, she didn't care how cute he may be, she didn't do "butt stuff!" With a grunt of effort, she leaned over and fumbled to open her woefully inadequately named glove box. Her fingers were the ones doing all the probing now, desperately searching for the can of pepper spray she kept inside. If some aliens showed up, she'd see how much they liked getting blasted in those big, black eyes of theirs!

The rustling sound grew louder. It was now much more of a crashing than a rustling. Whatever it was, it was big! And it was getting closer! Her heart leapt in her throat and she scanned the nearby woods, amazed at how quickly her eyes had adjusted to the darkness. Brenda clutched the pepper spray close to her chest, feeling her heart hammering away.

That's when she saw it - a large form emerged from the woods about 100 feet away from the front of her Camaro. It began slowly, almost nervously skirting the edge of the forest, moving sideways with a curious gait that reminded her of an ostrich.

It was moving towards her!

As her eyes continued to acclimate to the gloom, she could make out more details. The long, thin legs, thick upper body and tiny, almost vestigial hands - or were those claws? Whatever they were, they made her think of the comically stunted arms of a T-Rex, but she didn't feel like laughing right now. She would've screamed, but her whole body was petrified with fear. The creature's tail was long and forked at the end with long spikes that continued down its length and up its back. At the shoulders were bat-like wings which were tucked into its sides. At the end of its long neck was a horse-like head, topped by a pair of curling horns. It seemed to be covered in a rusty red, fine, feathery kind of down, like you'd see on a newborn chick. As it moved ever closer, she could see yellow, reptilian eyes regarding her. It snorted loudly, and a plume of smoke escaped from its large, flared nostrils.

For one long, terrible moment, her eyes were locked with the thing, until it seemed to lose interest in her and hopped out into the middle of the road. It looked up into the sky and spread wide its impressive, leathery wings, which must've been twenty feet across. Then with a great flapping sound it lifted off the ground and hovered there for a moment. Brenda's headlights suddenly cut back on and out of the corner of her eyes, she saw her phone light up as notifications started rolling in. She quickly snatched it up, unlocked it, and snapped a photo just as the hovering beast shot up into the sky only to instantly disappear into the clouds.

After restarting her engine and sighing in relief that her car was still working, Brenda examined the photo she'd just taken. It was barely more than a dark blur against the cloudy sky, but she thought you could still make out the general shape of it. The shape of the Jersey Devil, for surely that's what it *had* to be! She was no expert on the subject, but she'd seen a thing or two about it on TV, just like she had with the UFOs. She was kind of fascinated by all that paranormal stuff. She'd even thought about getting involved in hunting for that kind of thing herself. She'd talked to some nice local people who did just that when she'd gone to that comic book convention with her ex last year. What did they call themselves? The Jersey Shore Paranormal Group or something like that? She'd taken one of the magnets from their table at the convention and she was sure it was still on her fridge. When she got home she'd give them a call.

She was sure they'd *love* to hear all about this!

Dennis Arden was smiling ear to ear as he hung up the landline phone they still maintained as a hotline to the JSPS and walked out into the living room to tell Athena what he'd just heard.

Athena was sitting curled up on the couch, stroking their fattest and oldest cat, Chairman Meow, while shouting out answers to questions on *Jeopardy!*. It was frightening how many of her answers were correct. Dennis often pestered her to go on the show, but the idea of playing a game on TV horrified her. She was convinced that her anxieties would cause her to completely freeze up. Dennis wasn't so certain. He'd seen her steamroll the competition when they played Trivial Pursuit with Miranda and her family. "That's different, I'm comfortable around them. They're almost like my own family at this point," she would always tell him when he brought it up. Dennis had eventually come to accept that he'd have to give up his dream of being able to brag that he was married to a *Jeopardy!* champion, but in his heart, he'd always see her as an unofficial champion.

He felt that she was far stronger and more capable than she often gave herself credit for. Hadn't she just interviewed an accused mass murderer a few days ago? Dennis would've found such a thing terrifying, but Athena just took it all in stride like it was nothing. Mysterious monsters he could handle, it was the human ones that gave him the willies. He had to hand it to his wife, once she set her mind on something she didn't let up until it was within her sights - anxiety issues be damned! He loved this strength of hers, although the upshot of it was having to contend with the often infuriating stubbornness that accompanied it.

He threw himself onto the couch beside her. "You'll never guess who I just got off the phone with!"

"You're right, I won't," she replied, then, in response to Alex Trebek's latest clue, she shouted "What is The San Andreas Fault!" which, of course, was the correct "question."

As they went to a commercial she turned to look at him. "Okay don't keep me in suspense, what's up?"

"I just talked to some lady who saw the Jersey Devil last night. I mean the classic, winged version with a horsey head and everything!"

She rolled her eyes. Athena was the undisputed queen of the eye roll. "Ya know, drugs are a terrible scourge upon our nation. Did you tell her to lay off the 'shrooms?"

Dennis chuckled at her endless sarcasm. "This case is actually really interesting, she lost all electrical power to her car and cell phone right before it appeared."

That did seem to catch Athena off guard. She made the scrunched up face that she often did while concentrating and smacked on her chewing gum a little louder. "I think I've read about something like that happening in a few other scattered cases, but it's unusual."

"Aha! So you do find it interesting!"

"Well, *intriguing*, is perhaps a better word for it. Although I'm still quite skeptical about it. There's simply no good reason for a creature like that to really exist. See, I was afraid this would happen when we posted that last meeting online. All the kooky people would come out with stories like this to refute my hypothesis.”

“She said that she didn’t even see our last meeting,” Dennis told her.

“Hmm, I don’t know if I should feel hurt about that or not. It’s a pretty crazy coincidence though isn’t it? Here we are planning to go look for the ghost that is surely the *actual* basis for the Jersey Devil legend this very weekend, and someone claims to have seen the version that I say is just a bunch of folklore last night?”

“It gets better. She got a picture of it.”

Athena raised an eyebrow. “Really? Did you ask her to post it to our website?”

“She doesn’t want to share it online, but she’s willing to show it to us when we go out there to interview her.”

“So you agreed to meet with her?”

“I figured we could do it before we head down to Leeds Point on Saturday.”

Athena sighed. Her eyes found the “I want to believe” poster like the one Fox Mulder had in his office on *The X-Files,* which was hanging on their living room wall, framed between a pair of *Star Wars* posters. Her husband did indeed want to believe.

For Athena, it wasn’t so simple. She never chose to be able to see and speak to the dead, it was something that was thrust upon her by some weird quirk of her genetics. She might’ve chosen differently if she’d ever had that luxury. As it was, she just tried to make the most out of the “gifts” she’d been born with to help other people find closure and peace of mind. She had little use for or patience with all of this cryptid business. However, she knew how much it meant to her husband and she wanted to please him. For whatever reason he *needed* to believe in this stuff. One look into those baby blue eyes of his and she knew she couldn't let him down. He'd always been there for her ever since they were kids, and she tried to return the favor whenever possible. And the whole aspect about the electricity cutting out *was* kind of fascinating after all.

"Alright, I guess we'll go see what she has to show us," she agreed somewhat grudgingly.

Chairman Meow purred away contentedly in her lap.

Chapter Eight: Eyewitness News

Saturday arrived before any of the members of the JSPS knew it. That morning, the group met up in the parking lot of the big WaWa at the end of West Bay Ave as Athena had planned. She'd chosen that location because it was conveniently close to the ramp for the Garden State Parkway, and of course it also gave everyone a last chance to gas up their vehicles and grab a few snacks before heading out.

Athena was disappointed to see that aside from the addition of Lars, only her typical stalwarts had chosen to show up for the expedition. Lars was already waiting for them when she and Dennis arrived in his work van, which was now filled with a mix of camping supplies and the sundry technological devices typically deployed on their investigations. Miranda, Tyler and Mark showed up not too long afterwards. They hung around for a little while to see if anyone else would show up before heading north to Forked River to meet with Brenda, the young woman who'd allegedly had a frightening encounter with the Jersey Devil himself just a few nights ago.

Athena was pleasantly surprised when, just as she'd told everyone to climb into their respective vehicles, she spotted Kim and Beverly pull into the parking lot. Kim and Beverly ran the Atlantic County branch of the JSPS. They were the ones who had been gathering stories of a deformed boy seen in the woods which had been instrumental in Athena forming her theories about the true nature of the Jersey Devil.

They were driving in Beverly's old Honda Civic, which was a battered relic of the 1980's. She rolled up to Athena and Dennis, leaning her head out the window. She was a rather plump, but pleasant looking middle aged woman who fought to pull her long dirty blonde hair out of her face as she came to a halt next to Athena.

"Sorry we're late. We got caught in traffic. I would've called or something but I was driving and Kim was on her phone the whole time," she explained breathlessly.

Kim leaned forward to peer out Beverly's window. She was a tall, thin woman with short dark hair. "I just got off the phone with a couple of guys who saw The Boy last week. They claim it chased after them on their dirt bikes."

"The Boy" was what the pair had dubbed the phenomenon they'd been investigating.

"Wow!" Athena was quite pleased by this latest news. "Any chance we could talk with them today and find out exactly where they had their encounter?"

"I'll give 'em a call back right now and let you know," Kim replied.

"Okay, sounds good. We're all about to head down to Forked River to talk to someone who had a sighting a few days ago. Dennis will text you the address."

Dennis nodded dutifully and produced his phone from his back pocket to do just that. Shortly afterwards the small convoy moved out to interview their first witness.

Brenda lived in a small ranch style house in a large housing development that was built around a trio of small lakes. In the few days that had passed since her first call to the JSPS, Dennis had persuaded her to tell her story on video, since he could alter her voice and blur out her face later on. So when they arrived at her home, Mark helped him get his camera and tripod out of the van and volunteered to run the camera while Dennis and Athena questioned Brenda in the living room. Lars was looking on, notepad and pencil at the ready. The others all sat at the nearby dining room table where Brenda's mother worked overtime, quietly asking everyone's preference for refreshments and delivering them with uncanny promptness. Brenda's father had retreated to the den to continue watching his game on the TV as soon as he'd seen that his home was being invaded by a small army of investigators.

Brenda was a pleasant looking, heavy set girl in her early twenties with short, light brown hair and twinkling eyes. She nervously recounted her story at Dennis' gentle prompting.

"I totally locked eyes with that thing for a good minute. It felt like it was looking right into my soul. It was the creepiest feeling that I've ever experienced in my whole life! But I also felt like it didn't mean any harm. It was more like a lost and confused animal. The strangest thing is how steam was coming out of its nose, even though it was a warm summer night."

Dennis nodded enthusiastically. "According to some sources, the Jersey Devil can breathe fire."

Tyler couldn't resist an opportunity to show off his vast knowledge on the subject. "There are stories of him causing rivers and lakes to boil with his fire, then eating the fish he just cooked," he called from the dining room.

"Yeah, it's not too hard to imagine that thing breathing fire, it really reminded me of a small dragon," Brenda agreed.

"Technically, a dragon with only two limbs it can walk on would be classified as a wyvern," Tyler added.

"Dude, we know, we've all played D&D," Athena replied, for once exasperated with Tyler's know-it-all attitude. She didn't need Tyler Lambert to lecture *her* on the difference between a dragon and wyvern! Athena smiled to herself at her happy memories of playing Dungeons and Dragons at the old location of the Barnegat Library with Dennis and a few other friends. She was the only girl in the group, and it was the first time she'd been allowed to hang out with Dennis outside of school. Those were such simpler times. She forced herself out of her reminiscence to concentrate on the matter at hand. Something was bothering her about Brenda's story. Well, actually the whole story seemed wacky to her, but one detail in particular confused her.

"You say that the power returned to your car and your phone *before* it flew off?"

"Yeah, just a few seconds before it decided to fly off everything came back on."

"Well then, it couldn't have been the creature itself that caused the power loss. Presumably it was farther away from you when the power loss first occurred. It sounds like it was probably somewhere off in the woods running parallel to the road when your engine cut out."

"That sounds about right," Brenda told her.

"There is the possibility that the creature *did* cause the power loss, but when it decided that Brenda was no threat, returned the power," Miranda interjected.

Tyler regarded her with an impressed look. "Are you suggesting that the ability to control the flow of electrical power is some sort of a defense mechanism that it has?"

"I suppose I am."

"Interesting." Tyler smiled.

"No, *intriguing*," Athena corrected. She just liked the sound of the word "intriguing" better.

"I've seen other weird stuff along that same stretch of road. I drive through there almost every weeknight. Like shadow people and things like that," Brenda blurted out.

Athena raised a skeptical eyebrow. Even though she knew that sometimes ghosts appeared in the form of "shadow people," she also felt that many of the stories told about such beings were a little out there. Some people believed that they were people from an alternative reality that sometimes crossed over into our universe. But as far as Athena could tell, there wasn't anything approaching a shred of actual evidence to back up such an outrageous claim.

"You, um, don't have any kind of a history with drugs or alcohol, do you?" Athena asked.

"Jesus, baby!" Dennis shot his wife a scolding look. Didn't she know how hard it had been to persuade this girl to agree to tell her story on camera? Now she was insulting her in her own home!

Athena threw up her hands in a gesture of blamelessness. "Hey, you know I have to ask these kinds of questions! It's part of the vetting process. Gotta make sure the eyewitnesses are credible and all that!"

Now it was time for Dennis to roll his eyes. He thought of reminding her that he'd already asked all those questions over the phone days ago - and far more tactfully - but thought better of it. The last thing he needed to do was get into a silly argument with his wife on camera. Lord knew he'd already have enough editing to do on this footage to disguise Brenda's identity as he'd promised.

"Believe me, I know how crazy this all sounds. But if I hallucinated the whole thing, then tell me what *this* thing is!" Brenda said as she held her cell phone in front of Athena's face.

On the screen was the picture she'd snapped that night. As the screen hovered a few inches in front of her face, Athena looked down her nose so she could see it more clearly, wearily thinking that she really needed to just bite the bullet and get bifocals since it was becoming harder and harder to see things properly up close through her glasses.

Bypassing her glasses didn't improve the current situation, however. The image on the screen looked just as blurry and unimpressive to her as it had a moment earlier. It was little more than a slightly darker smudge against a dark sky. She didn't know what to say. She knew she'd already put her foot in her mouth once and could tell Dennis was silently fuming at her, but honestly that picture was a piece of shit!

"Interesting," she said, refusing to dignify it with an "intriguing" as it clearly didn't warrant such an accolade. "Would you be willing to share that photo with us so we can analyze it further?" There! That was nice and diplomatic wasn't it? Pretending to have any real interest in such a crappy shred of "evidence?" Whoever said that Athena Arden was socially awkward? She was *dominating* this situation, like a boss!

"Sure, analyze it all you want to, it's the real deal. I have nothing to gain from making this up, I don't even want my name or face attached to this story."

"Thanks, we really appreciate your cooperation," Dennis assured her, gently kicking Athena in the shins.

"Oh, yeah! *Definitely*! Thanks so much for being willing to share your story with us," she purred insincerely.

Not much later, everyone was gulping down the remnants of their last batch of refreshments, Dennis and Mark were packing up their equipment and the group was about to head back out on the road. They all gathered around Dennis' van parked in the driveway, awaiting their marching orders.

"Where to next, Sis?" Mark inquired, slamming the back door of the van. "Didn't she give us the location where she had her encounter? Do you wanna check that out first before heading south?"

Athena shook her head, some of her long brown hair escaping the confinement of her somewhat disorderly bun. "Nah, I think that kid's whole story is pretty sketchy. I think our time is better spent talking to those guys who say they were chased by The Boy. Kim said they were willing to meet with us today, and maybe even show us the spot where it happened. Besides, they live closer to the neck of the woods I want to be in, out near Leeds Point."

This pronouncement brought no disagreement from Mark, who was more eager to investigate The Boy since he hoped any evidence they might gather of its existence could help exonerate Rebecca Greene.

Dennis was considerably less enthused about the fact that they weren't doing more to follow up on

Brenda's tale, which he found to be *very* credible, but he didn't want to contradict Athena in front of the whole group. He'd wait until they had a little more privacy to plead his case.

"Don't you think you were a little too dismissive back there?" Dennis asked as they pulled out of Brenda's driveway.

"No way, that picture is awful!" Athena asserted.

"Maybe so, but we're still going to get it analyzed aren't we? I mean, we did promise that we would," Miranda reminded them. She was tagging along in the van, riding in the back with all the equipment.

"I suppose so, might as well. Bruce is always way too happy to take a look at any new photographic evidence we collect. The guy must get pretty bored."

Bruce was an expert at detecting the signs that a photo or video had been digitally altered. Years earlier he'd volunteered his services to the JSPS at no cost. He seemed to genuinely enjoy doing such analysis.

"But don't hold your breath for a good outcome. Even if it wasn't photoshopped, I'll bet it's still a fake. She probably just taped a cutout silhouette of the Jersey Devil to her windshield," Athena added.

"I really don't think she's trying to pull one over on us. Didn't you sense her sincerity?" Dennis argued.

Athena pulled a face. It was true, she hadn't sensed that Brenda was a liar, which was why she'd wondered if the girl had hallucinated the entire encounter. However, it didn't make sense for someone who was so earnest to try to hoax them. Maybe Athena *was* being unreasonable here? Yet it was still hard for her to swallow such a strange story - she felt like she couldn't give up quite so easily. "Yeah, but– "

"*But* you just can't stand anything that contradicts your theory about the Jersey Devil. What about maintaining an open mind?" Dennis countered.

"There's a difference between keeping an open mind and falling for every crackpot story out there," affirmed Athena. She let out a long breath and looked over at her husband apologetically. "I guess I do get a little carried away sometimes though, while trying to maintain reason."

She knew that her father, who had worked as a high school physics teacher before retiring, didn't really approve of all this paranormal stuff she was involved in. Sometimes she wondered if she was always taking the skeptical approach as some kind of misguided way of pleasing him? She knew this was a silly impulse; her dad might not endorse the path she was on, but she had no doubt that he loved her all the same. Yet she couldn't help but feel that a part of her that was still a little girl hungering for his approval. When it came to this particular part of her life, she'd never get it, so why bother? Unfortunately, dismissing such feelings was easier said than done. But there was more to it than that; it wasn't as if she didn't have her own healthy appreciation for the power of reason and science. She just needed to figure out how to balance that with an understanding of the importance of intuition and faith. It was something she'd been struggling with for more years than she cared to count. She was constantly stuck between these two seemingly opposite worlds.

"Maybe we can take a look at the spot where she had her encounter tomorrow on our way back home?" she offered diplomatically. "I just didn't want to try and squeeze it in today, we have a pretty full itinerary."

Dennis grinned. It was a rare day when he was able to get such a concession out of his strong-willed wife.

Kim had sent everyone the address where they'd find their next eyewitnesses. Soon the small convoy of explorers of the unknown was besieging the front yard of an isolated two story house in the wilds of Galloway Township. The pair of eyewitnesses in question were already outside when the group arrived, sitting on the front steps and drinking a few cool beers under the hot August sun. They were a pair of young men in their twenties named Jim and Dave. Brothers, although Athena couldn't figure out which one of them was the older one. She found herself wondering if perhaps they were fraternal twins.

"Our mom doesn't really want anyone coming inside the house, she thinks it's kind of a mess. Do you mind if we do this outside?" Jim, the slightly taller one asked.

"Fine by me," Dennis told them. It was a pleasant enough day, not too hot and not too cold and he didn't mind getting a little extra vitamin D.

The next few minutes were spent retrieving the camera from the van and setting it up on its tripod on the front lawn. Once again, Mark ran the camera while the others stood or sat around. Just as before, Lars had his notepad and pen at the ready, his face an impenetrable mask as he waited to hear this latest strange account. Unlike Brenda, the brothers had no issues with appearing on camera to share their story with the denizens of the world wide web. The brothers had their beer in a cooler on the front porch and offered the whole team some, but only Tyler took them up on it. He was never one to turn down a good beer.

Dave, the slightly shorter, darker haired and noticeably fitter brother was the more talkative of the pair, and he started the story off.

"Me and my brother are into exploring abandoned places. We take videos and post 'em on our Youtube channel sometimes," he began.

"Oh! Hey! That reminds me! Maybe you could post a link to our channel on your website?" Jim interjected. Dave gave his brother a dirty look at being interrupted and took another swig from his bottle of Heineken.

"Sure, just text us the link after the interview," Dennis said, hoping they couldn't sense his irritation at the fact that he'd have to edit this part out.

Dave set down his beer on the steps and continued his tale. "Anyhow, we decided to check out these abandoned apartments a few miles from here."

"The Deercrest Apartments?" Mark asked from behind the camera. Now it was Dennis' turn to dish out a dirty look.

"Yeah, that's the place! How did you know?" Jim inquired.

"It seems to keep coming up in connection with sightings of this entity," Athena explained. "I believe its territory is nearby."

This was news to Mark. His sister hadn't shared this latest theory with him yet. He wondered if she was starting to take Becca Greene's story a bit more seriously.

Dave was eager to carry on with his story. "We rode over there on our dirtbikes. There are some trails through the woods that lead right up to it. We spent the better part of the day going through the buildings. There's four or five of them, all pretty big, and all empty. The place is in surprisingly good shape. I was surprised that we didn't run into any squatters there, sometimes we do."

"I'm not surprised. That place was fucking creepy, you'd have to be outta your Goddamned mind to wanna live there!" Jim interrupted again. "Oh shit! Is it okay to swear on camera?"

Dennis couldn't help but laugh at the fact that the kid had just sworn again in asking the question. He also noticed how he slurred his words and contemplated just how many beers the brothers had been drinking out here before they arrived.

"It's alright, we're all adults here," he assured him, still chuckling.

"*Well,*" Dave said pointedly, eager to get things back on track, "after exploring the buildings and shooting some video inside them, we decided to try and find the old summer camp around the lake. It was getting pretty dark, so we just wanted to scout it out for a future video. I had to twist the arm of my chickenshit little brother here, he didn't wanna go near the place."

Athena nodded eagerly, more because she was happy that she finally had an answer to her earlier musings regarding the ages of the brothers. Then her face scrunched up in confusion. "Wait, what summer camp?"

Lars finally broke his silence. "There was a summer camp on the shores of Deercrest Lake which operated up until the mid 1970's. It's been closed since the camp counselors who were preparing to open up for the season were all found murdered. The killer was never found."

Athena was floored by this revelation. "What? That sounds like the plot to a *Friday the 13th* movie! Why haven't I heard of this before?"

Lars shrugged. "It was a long time ago. It's actually quite difficult to find much information on it nowadays." He smiled at her wickedly from over his notepad. "Or perhaps the Men in Black are covering that up too?"

She couldn't tell if he was joking about that or not. It was always so infuriatingly hard to tell what Lars truly believed about any of this stuff, even with her psychic abilities. She tried to digest this new information. "So the latest bunch of murders around the lake weren't the first ones?"

"Yeah, the rest of the world might've forgotten about those murders in the seventies, but us locals never forgot. That's why I didn't want to go there at night. The whole place is supposed to be haunted. And now, with this latest bunch of killings, I was sure the place would be crawling with ghosts!" Jim told her as he fumbled to pop the top off another beer.

"The murders this summer happened on the opposite side of the lake, dumbass! I kept telling him that, but he was still acting like a big scaredy cat. I didn't care. I wasn't scared, I don't believe in ghosts or any of that shit. At least I *didn't*. But now....now I'm not so sure...." Dave's voice trailed off and a haunted look stole over his face.

"What did you see out there?" Athena demanded.

"Nothing, at first. Eventually we found the remains of the old camp cabins. They were a total mess. Most of 'em had collapsed roofs. It was really late and too dark to film anything, so we decided to go home and come back some other time during the day. On the ride back we got a little lost. Just when we'd found our way back to the right trail, the one that would bring us back to the apartments, this *thing* came charging from the bushes and started chasing after us."

"What did it look like?" Dennis asked.

"Like a fucking walking nightmare!" Dave swore.

Jim tried to give a more helpful description. "We had it in our headlights for a good minute before it started chasing us, so we got a really good look at it. It was small, like the size of a kid who's maybe like eleven or twelve years old. It sorta reminded me of a zombie, but *worse.* I swear, it's skin was literally *crawling.*"

"And bubbling! How the hell does anyone's body do that?" an astounded Dave shared.

"Bubbling? What do you mean by that?" Athena couldn't imagine it.

"I dunno, it's like the surface of its skin was always moving and these little bubbles of flesh would form and pop and all this pus would come spilling out. It was really gross," Dave elaborated. Tyler choked on his beer and almost spat it out at this latest description. Everyone looked at him for a second and he smiled back awkwardly.

"It was so fucking weird. It's like parts of its body were rotting away and sliding off and other parts looked all fresh and pink and new. That's how I knew it wasn't anyone trying to prank us. I don't see how someone could've faked something like that. It was like nothing I'd ever seen before, like nothing I could even dream of! It would've cost millions of dollars to make a costume like that, if it's even possible. No, whatever the hell that thing was, it wasn't human!"

"We tried to get the fuck out of there ASAP, but the damned thing kept following us! It was really fast, even though it was limping like the Hunchback of Notre Dame. It was *supernaturally* fast. It wasn't as fast as our bikes, but I'm amazed at how well it was able to keep up with us, and how long it followed us. It only really stopped after I almost ran over that guy."

"What guy?" Athena felt like she could barely keep up with them. They kept throwing new wrinkles into their story.

Dave gulped down his beer and looked right at her. "There was an old VW bug out on the trail ahead of us. I thought someone had abandoned it out there, but then this guy jumped out and started shouting and waving his arms around. My brother damn near ran him down by accident. We kept on riding past him, there was no way we were gonna stop with that monster chasing us!"

Dave looked down. What did Athena sense from him? Guilt? Shame? All of those things, along with a toxic dose of self loathing hit her like a wave, threatening to drown her. She struggled to regain her composure, like a ship that had almost capsized in a tempest righting itself. Dennis noticed the sudden shift in her demeanor and instinctively rubbed the small of her back. She smiled up at him appreciatively.

"It was a while after we passed that guy before I looked back over my shoulder again. The thing was gone. There was no sign of it. I...I'm afraid that it stopped and got that guy. I tried going back there a few days later during the day with my shotgun. The car was gone. But there was a big dark spot in the dirt near where I think it used to be. Like a giant bloodstain. We got away, but that dude wasn't so lucky, I'm sure of it. We wouldn't be alive today if he hadn't...distracted it." He looked down again, too consumed by emotion to go on.

To Athena's surprise, Jim threw an arm around his brother and hugged him. "You can't blame yourself, man. I keep telling you! It's not our fault! I don't know what that guy was doing out there at that time of night anyway." He looked at Athena and Dennis. "I thought this guy right here was crazy to go back out there again looking for him, shotgun or no shotgun! What would a shotgun do against something like that anyway? Something that's body looks like it's always regrowing?"

Dennis was temporarily speechless. They all were. It wasn't a good thing to be when you were supposed to be conducting an interview. "So, how did you find out about us?" he asked lamely. It was the best he could come up with.

Jim was the talkative one now. Dave seemed to have lost all interest in the interview, lost in the dark tangle of his own feelings. "I was looking up stuff on the Jersey Devil on the internet. I figured maybe that's what it was. I don't know much about what the Jersey Devil is supposed to look like, but that thing sure seemed like a devil to me! That's when I saw your video, the one where you talk about how you think it's a ghost. Well, this thing *was* sort of like a deformed kid, but I dunno, it seemed too real to be a ghost. And if it really did kill that guy? Can a ghost do something like that?"

"It's possible, but very, very rare. We've been doing this for over twenty years and I've only ever met one ghost that I think was powerful enough to hurt someone that badly," Athena admitted, then a new idea hit her. "Isn't it possible that the man you saw escaped? His car was missing when you went back, someone had to move it. Maybe he just jumped back into his car and got away too?"

Dave looked up at Athena for a moment with something like hope in his eyes. Was it possible that he'd never even considered that possibility?

"Or the Men in Black got rid of it," Mark suggested.

Athena saw Lars tilt his head over in Mark's direction and she no longer had any doubts about where his sympathies lay, all his claims of being unbiased be damned! She was surprised the two didn't share a high five.

Dave scratched at his scraggly beard. "Why do you guys keep on bringing up the Men in Black?"

"Don't worry about it. It's kind of a running joke." Athena shot her brother and Lars an accusing look before continuing. She looked at Dave and spoke to him in a gentle tone, "Would you be willing to bring us out to where you saw the entity?

He shook his head. "I don't plan on ever going back out there, and neither should you."

Jim on the other hand, was all too eager to be of aid. "If you're really crazy enough to give it a try, the coordinates to the old campground have been geotagged. That's how we found it. We first ran into that thing within a mile of the camp."

Dave gave his brother a dirty look, then met Athena's eyes. "Don't go out there. It's not worth it. That thing is probably still around there and it's dangerous."

"Don't worry, I'm well armed!" Mark bragged.

Dave just shook his head some more and looked down. "Well good luck to you then - you're gonna need it!"

Chapter Nine: The Devil's Birthplace

Athena Anderson Arden watched the rows of gnarled pines flying past her through the passenger side window of Dennis' van. Her gum was beginning to lose its flavor and she was beginning to question the wisdom of her decisions. After hearing Jim and Dave's story, Mark and Lars had been eager to abandon their original plan to visit the alleged birthplace of the Jersey Devil and instead go to the old campground at Deercrest Lake. Athena, being the creature of habit that she was, had been loath to alter her itinerary, but hadn't completely closed the door on the idea, promising to mull it over. Now she was sitting here, staring out the window and doing just that. The harder she mulled, the more she felt like she was slowly sinking into a quagmire of her own making. She had felt so confident in her assumptions about this case before meeting Jim and Dave, but now that bravado had evaporated like morning dew on a blade of grass. The look in Jim's eyes haunted her, and what she'd felt in his mind terrified her. It was the same level of fear and dread she had sensed oozing from Becca Greene, but had quickly dismissed as the product of the woman's own delusions. Jim was harder to disregard; he hadn't been accused of any atrocity. He was just an innocent young man who had seen *something* that had traumatized him, and he had someone else to back up his claims.

She decided to air her doubts to get the opinions of the two people she trusted most in the world on the matter.

"I'm starting to think maybe we shouldn't go anywhere near that campground. I'm heavily leaning towards just sticking to our plan to investigate the woods around the old Leeds house and leave it at that."

Miranda was the first to balk at this. "I've known you for something like 22 years and you never stop surprising me, Triple A! You have no problem calling bullshit on the story of a perfectly sober young lady who wants to remain anonymous, but now you're getting spooked by a couple of kids who were literally getting wasted right in front of us? Those guys are just looking to get more viewers for their YouTube channel and they obviously think they can do it by creating a buzz about themselves on our website!"

Athena twisted in her seat to look back at her best friend. "So you think they made the whole thing up?"

"I think there's a better chance they did than Brenda did. At least she had some proof. These kids admitted that they watched your presentation in the last meeting. I think they're just feeding you what they think you want to hear."

"No, that one brother, the one named Jim, was really messed up by what he saw. I could *feel* it. He completely hates himself for abandoning that guy from the car to the entity. He blames himself for his death. But that's not all, too much of what they said about the entity matches up with what Rebecca Greene told us. She gave us details that haven't been released to the public. Lars hasn't even written his article yet, let alone published it. There's no way they could know these things unless they witnessed the same creature. I'm beginning to wonder if maybe she isn't so crazy after all? If she's telling the truth, it would be suicide to take the team out there."

Dennis finally piped up. "You just called it a creature for the first time ever. So now you're starting to question your own theory?"

"I don't know, maybe. Maybe I've been too pig-headed about this whole situation. I'm really starting to think that there's definitely something out there, and whatever it is, a ghost or some kind of monster, I'm not sure we're equipped to protect ourselves from it."

"Mark's got his hand cannon, and all of us have these." Miranda pulled a necklace from her generous cleavage, revealing a bright white crystal dangling from its end. These were crystal necklaces given to the founding members of the JSPS years earlier by the wizard Clark Kismet during their inaugural case. Athena had saved them all from the ghost of Miranda's father by channeling her psychic energy through the crystals and blasting him with it. Athena had purchased more of the necklaces from Clark's occult shop for the newer members of the team and insisted that they always wore them when going out on an investigation. It was standard equipment, right along with their matching JSPS t-shirts.

"Mark might have his gun, but I doubt he could hit the broad side of a barn with it. He'll be lucky not to shoot off his own foot if he has to use it. And that kid Jim had a shotgun the second time he went out there and *still* thought it wasn't enough to stop the entity! If it *is* a ghost, I'm afraid that it might be even more powerful than your father was. Even if it isn't, the truth is that I'm not sure I still have it in me to do that trick with the crystals again. It was a lifetime ago, and I'm so, so *old* now. I really don't even know how I ever did it to begin with!" For the first time in forever, Athena was actually questioning her decision to refuse Clark's offer to train her to use her powers properly. Had she been too rash in turning the wizard down?

Dennis automatically put a comforting hand on his wife's thigh. "You're not old, you're just deliciously seasoned!"

She smiled over at her man. "You're sweet, but seriously, I don't want to be responsible for leading us off a cliff here. What do you think we should do? Technically, it is *your* group after all."

He laughed at her comment. "It's only ever *my* group when you start to feel overwhelmed by some aspect of it. It's a partnership. Always has been, always will be." He took a deep breath before giving her his unvarnished opinion on the matter.

"I believe it's possible that both sets of witnesses we spoke with today are telling the truth. The Pine Barrens are *huge* - over 1 million acres - there's plenty of room for all kinds of weird shit to be hiding out there. Why can't there be more than one kind of strange thing prowling around? Both cryptids and ghosts? Like you said once, whenever someone runs into something unusual in these woods they call it the Jersey Devil. It's become a catch-all term for anything weird in the woods. I think both stories are worthy of investigation. Besides, I thought it was always a part of our plan to have Kim and Bev show us some places around here where The Boy has been sighted? We'd be doing just that if we went out to the camp. As to the possibility of us walking into too much danger, I don't believe there's any danger that we can't handle or you can't protect us from. Your brother has his gun and I've got my trusty nunchucks. I think we'll be okay."

That last comment earned him a snort of laughter from Athena. Dennis always kept a pair of nunchucks under the seat of his van "in case I run into some unsavory characters on a job." In addition, he kept a matching pair in the top drawer of his bedside table to defend the house with his questionable kung fu skills. Athena often made fun of this, but she couldn't deny that she felt a bit more secure whenever they heard something go bump in the night outside the house and Dennis reached for his nunchucks to walk the perimeter of their property in his sweatpants. It was as much a ridiculous flex of his masculinity as it was sexy. Or perhaps the ludicrousness of it all is what made it seem so sexy to her? Athena did have some pretty peculiar tastes.

Dennis carried on, "The most fair thing is to put it to a vote beforehand, let the whole team decide."

"You're a true champion of democracy," Athena replied. "Okay, we'll put it to a vote when we arrive." She was touched by Dennis' confidence in her, yet at the same time it almost felt like a heavy weight around her neck. Sure, she had a few unusual powers, but she was hardly some kind of a superhero who could save them all if need be, no matter how much he might believe in her.

"I knew you'd see it my way." Dennis grinned as he looked at his phone in its holder stuck to the windshield. The suction cup that was supposed to keep the holder secured there had an irritating habit of popping off, but it had done an admirable job of remaining in place on this excursion so far. "Well, we're about here." He pulled over to the side of the road, watching the line of cars behind them obediently following suit in his rear view mirror.

The team was now within walking distance of the alleged site of the old Leeds house where the Jersey Devil was rumored to have been born. It had been their plan to see if Athena sensed anything at this location which might help her make contact with the restless spirit she had decided was the basis for the legend. It had always made sense to Athena to start their quest for the Jersey Devil at the place where it all began.

The team slowly left their individual vehicles and stretched their legs. Dennis opened up the back of his van and pulled out a pair of compact, hand held cameras. Mark was at his side in no time flat, asking about what other types of equipment they should bring. Before he could answer, Athena spoke up.

"Whatever you do, don't bring the spirit box!" She looked at Dennis and crossed her arms. "I don't know why you insist on bringing that silly thing with us, you know how I feel about them."

A spirit box is a device used by some paranormal researchers which scans a narrow band of radio frequencies. It is believed that spirits can manipulate these frequencies to send messages to the living. Well, believed by lots of people other than Athena. She saw no evidence that spirits could affect radio waves other than the wishful thinking of some of her fellow investigators.

"I also know that other investigators who you respect use them and have gotten interesting results," her husband parried back.

"I'm sorry, I can't get past the fact that the guy who invented them originally created them to talk to space aliens, not ghosts! And then you went and bought one directly from him!"

"Hey, Frank is a nice guy and his boxes are the best," Dennis said defensively.

"He's a crackpot! The only thing that machine is good for is generating auditory pareidolia." Athena shot back. "Auditory pareidolia" being the phenomenon of the mind hearing random sounds and interpreting it as words.

"People say the same thing about EVPs, but we still try to capture them," Dennis pointed out.

"Yeah well, they're not completely wrong. Most EVP *are* illusions of the mind. But sometimes the EVPs are really clear and are obviously directly responding to us."

"And that's true of spirit boxes too! If you just give them a chance, you'd see that."

Mark sighed. He'd seen them have this exact same argument a dozen times in the past year since Dennis had bought the box.

Athena took a breath, thinking about how her own stubbornness might be turning into an obstacle to them lately, and relented - somewhat. "Fine! Take it out of the van, but we're not posting any video of us using it to the website. We have a reputation to protect."

Dennis picked up the box which looked like an old time radio and set it down a few feet away where the cameras were piled on the ground.

"What about the REM pods?" Mark asked.

"Sure, go ahead and grab a few. Also, make sure everyone has a recorder on them to pick up any EVPs."

Mark whispered conspiratorially to his sister. "Have you made up your mind about going to the campground yet?"

"We're gonna vote on it. I figure we'll do it before we all head out to what's left of the Leeds House."

"We've gotta help that lady, Athena. I *know* she's innocent! And you know that those guys we talked to back there ran into the same monster she did, you can't deny it!"

She regarded her not-so-little little brother for a moment. She was finally starting to see him for the man he was becoming, unafraid to stare injustice down wherever it reared its ugly head, no matter the risk. And to think she'd originally been worried that he'd be too scared to come out here! All that initial fear had vanished and been replaced with a steely resolve.

She wondered why he was so determined to see that Rebecca Greene got the justice he believed she deserved? Did he see her as another victim of the hopelessly flawed justice system which had so desperately failed his own people time and time again? He couldn't do much for them aside from marching in the occasional Black Lives Matter rally, or blasting people on Facebook who made racist comments, but here at last was an opportunity to finally do *something* substantial for someone the system was throwing away. Was this what was driving him? She wasn't sure, but she appreciated this new aspect of him. Who was she to deny him? Yet she was also responsible for the safety of the whole team and she couldn't let *them* down either.

"I know. I'm starting to think that maybe you're right. But if that's true, going there could also be impossibly dangerous for us. We have to let the whole group decide, it's the only fair thing to do."

He nodded. "You're the boss, sis."

She rolled her eyes and spat out her gum in a manner which her mother would doubtlessly call "unladylike." "No I'm not! Why does everyone keep saying that?"

The other members of the team were now all gathered at the back of the van to see if they could help carrying any equipment. Athena decided now was as good a time as any to switch the JSPS from a benevolent dictatorship to a democracy. So long as they didn't bring up the merits of spirit boxes for a vote, she was quite comfortable with this transition of power.

The vote broke down the following way: Athena, Miranda and Tyler all voted against going to the camp, whereas Dennis, Mark, Kim and Beverly voted in favor of going. Lars wasn't entitled to a vote as he wasn't officially a member of the JSPS, but it was obvious that he had been in favor of going. So it was that the group resolved to visit the storied shores of Deercrest Lake. Athena hoped they hadn't all just sealed their fates. She worried if perhaps she hadn't done an adequate job of making them understand the sort of danger they might be walking into? Either they had failed to grasp the gravity of the situation, or they were placing too much confidence in her brother's gunslinging abilities and Dennis' acumen with nunchucks.

But first things first, they had the birthplace of the Jersey Devil to investigate. Athena hoped that they'd pick up some fantastic new lead here that would lead them away from Deercrest Lake and make the rest of the team forget all about going there.

They walked single file along a narrow wooded trail that started near where the convoy had pulled over. After a short hike, they arrived at a sight that Athena had seen before in videos on YouTube, but never in person. Dennis had been here once before though, nearly a decade earlier, with a Jersey Devil investigation team that was sadly now defunct. Back then, there hadn't been a fence around the place, but now a chain link barrier walled off the fieldstone foundation of the old house from the rest of the forest. Some of the others who had been unaware that a fence had been put up were obviously disappointed to see this. Or perhaps the roughly rectangular hole in the ground which was all that remained of the house was just an inherently disappointing sight?

"We can't even sit in there to do an EVP session!" Miranda noted bitterly.

"The hell we can't! These boots were made for climbin'!" Tyler said, pointing to his Doc Martens.

"Tyler! Don't you dare!" Athena commanded. "Respect the wishes of the property owners. We're gonna take a video of ourselves here, remember? We don't wanna get ourselves in trouble!"

Tyler thought about telling her about the various "No Trespassing" signs they'd ignored, but knew the futility of arguing with Athena Arden.

"Well, let's get to work. If some of you want to explore around here and see if you can pick up any EVPs, go for it. I'm going to see if I can sense any spirits." She watched as most of the group wandered around the fence or deeper into the woods armed with their digital recorders and meters that could detect fluctuations in the local electromagnetic field. Mark walked off with one of the groups to take video of anything they might encounter. Dennis walked off with his treasured spirit box under his arm, eager to play with it.

For the moment, Athena was all alone. She found a moderately comfortable tree stump to sit on near the foundation of the house and closed her eyes. She took several deep breaths, smoothly entering a meditative state. She was an old pro at this. It came very easily to her as she often used meditation and breathing techniques to deal with her anxiety issues as an alternative to taking a regimen of medications.

She stretched out her awareness. Images flooded her mind of people dressed in colonial period costumes. These images lacked the "flavor" of glimpsing a real event psychically, so she decided that this merely a byproduct of her own imagination. Next, she felt a kind of desperate longing; a questing, probing feeling that was associated with this place, like a search for meaning. She realized that what she was feeling was the collective hopes and expectations of all the other paranormal investigators who had come to this same spot over the decades, all looking for the same thing she was looking for - answers to the mystery of the Jersey Devil. She felt their awe at the idea that they might be at the house where the legendary creature was birthed, standing in the same basement where he might've been confined, and inevitably the crushing disappointment when this place failed to deliver upon whatever questions had first brought them there.

Is anybody out there?

She put the question out into the air around her.

If so, come forward now and speak with me.

She lingered there, trying to feel the telltale signs of another mind brushing up against her own.

There was nothing. Nothing but the creaking of the boughs of trees in the warm summer breeze and the occasional scurrying of squirrels in the underbrush, or the chirping of birds in the branches above her. Although she felt the warmth of the sun on her face, there was a coldness about the place, a hollow emptiness that she didn't often feel when out in nature.

It was almost as if the soul of the land itself had been ripped out. This revelation filled her with unease. It was something that she wasn't sure she could explain properly to someone who didn't share her abilities. The more she probed it, the more certain she became that there was something fundamentally *wrong* with this forest. Wrong. Not dark, not evil, just *wrong*. Broken. Yes, perhaps broken was a better word for it. How could a place be broken? It made no sense, and yet she felt it to be true, felt it with every fiber of her being. Although she could sense the plant and animal life all around herself, it was at a low ebb - lacking its normal vitality. Some important spark was missing. Almost like a living death. She had no idea what it all meant, but the idea of it chilled her to the bone.

Her eyes snapped open and she allowed herself to breathe normally again. She rose from her improvised seat with a grunt. She hoped the others had come across something more interesting than she had. She came across Bev and Kim first. Bev was rewinding her recorder, then holding it up to her ear to see if she'd captured any EVPs. One look at the frown on her face told Athena all she needed to know.

"Don't sweat it. I didn't sense anything in this place. Well, no spirits at any rate," she told them. "Have you seen my husband?"

Kim pointed in the opposite direction from which Athena had just come. "I think I saw him head down that way."

"Thanks." She smiled at them as she moved past them.

She heard her husband long before she found him, or rather she heard his spirit box. In a loud, echoey voice she heard the words "Chicken Legs!" and saw her husband standing in front of the box scratching his head. "Chicken legs? What the fuck is that supposed to mean?"

Tyler was standing nearby. He pulled a strand of his long, greasy black hair out from in front of his glasses. "It means that silly thing is just picking up random, meaningless radio broadcasts - or the spirits want you to pick them up some KFC."

Athena stepped into the clearing where they were gathered. "Hey! Nobody gets to bust my husband's chops like that except for me! Although of course, you're 100 percent right about that thing."

"Rosebush," the spirit box nonsensically proclaimed with all the solemnity of a sage in its spooky voice.

Dennis smiled at her. "Hey baby! As you can see, we're not having much luck with this thing. Although I'm wondering if the skeptical attitude of Mr. Lambert here might be affecting my outcome."

"Oh, I'm sorry, I forgot! Was I supposed to click my heels together three times and wish for that hunk of junk to channel a ghost?"

Dennis ignored Tyler's snark. "So have you had any better luck?"

"No, I'm not sensing any spirits at all. Although I did pick up something weird about this place, it's hard for me to put my finger on what it means."

"It means that this probably isn't even the site of the real Leeds house! There's no proof that it is. Several other locations have been proposed. We should probably check those out too if we can get to them."

"Spoon...tile!" the spirit box announced. Dennis leaned down to switch it off and scooped it up. He sighed, "As much as it pains me to agree with Tyler, I have to. This location is a total dud so far. We should find someplace more promising to investigate."

"Someplace like the old campground!" Lar's always ready for prime time news announcer voice boomed from somewhere behind Athena. She spun around to see him crashing through the underbrush towards him, Mark trailing behind. Lars was wearing shorts which showed off his skinny, almost luminous white legs and a loud Hawiian shirt. She realized it was the most casual outfit she'd ever seen him dressed in during the many decades she'd known him.

"I second that motion!" Mark agreed from behind Lars. Athena popped a fresh stick of Juicy Fruit into her mouth. These two seemed to be thick as thieves lately. United by a common cause, she supposed.

"I guess I must surrender to the inevitable. Let's find the girls and head over there."

"What?" Tyler objected. "Why not look into some of the other sites associated with the birthplace of the Jersey Devil? If he really is a ghost, it makes sense that he might return to his former home sometimes."

Athena gave Tyler a sympathetic look. "It does make sense, but the other location is also where the most recent sightings have occurred. It's the most logical place to go."

Tyler shook his head, "I can tell that you don't really want to go. You know those dudes' stories weren't credible!"

"I found their story to be quite sincere, actually. But you're right, I don't really want to go. The truth is, I'm a little scared of that thing. I'm not sure we can protect ourselves if we do run into it."

At this, Mark pulled his gun out of its belt holster and spun it around on his finger by the trigger guard a few times. "Never fear, sis! I'm the fastest draw in the wild west!"

"Jesus Christ! Put that thing away before you kill somebody!" Athena barked.

"Relax! The safety is on, I know what I'm doing!" he protested as he returned it to the holster.

"Remember how Becca Greene said she saw someone chop that thing's hands off and they grew back right away? I'm not sure that guns are gonna do us much good if her story is true."

"Becca Greene?" Tyler sputtered out a hollow laugh. "Don't tell me that now we're taking the story of a mass murderer at face value!"

"*Alleged* mass murderer," Lars reminded him calmly.

"She's innocent!" Mark affirmed.

Athena held up her hands, pleading for peace. "Either way, the group voted to go to the campground this weekend and I have to respect that. We're ghost hunters first and foremost. If a bunch of people really were murdered at the campground in the seventies, and another group was slaughtered nearby more recently, we might make contact with some of their spirits. So we'll at least have something to show for this investigation even if this business with The Boy turns out to be nothing but a bunch of hooey."

Athena had spoken, and her word was tantamount to law within their little circle of friends. It wasn't much later before they found themselves all loading the equipment back into the van and driving off towards the abandoned campground that haunted the still waters of Deercrest Lake as surely as any ghost might.

Chapter Ten: The Crucible

"**N**ow *that* is intriguing!" Athena said as she spotted a pair of large columns of gleaming white stone, capped by another stone which stood over the trail like a gateway. "Nobody ever said anything about there being a mini Stonehenge out here."

"It is pretty cool," Dennis agreed, pausing to turn on his camera to film the group walking towards the mysterious stone structure.

They'd already driven as far as they dared along the dirt road which once led up to the camp. It hadn't been maintained in decades and could only take them so far, although it showed signs of someone trying to clear it recently. Now everyone was walking towards whatever remained of the old summer camp. They'd yet to see any hint of the camp so far. As they approached the strange stone gateway Bev spotted something on the side of the path.

"Hey, check this out!"

It was a sign so faded that they couldn't make out what the name of the camp had been. They paused for a moment to try and decipher it. Kim leaned down to brush it free of pine needles. Despite her efforts, the first word appearing in front of "Camp" remained as inscrutable as ever.

Lars knew what the place had been called, of course. He'd come across the name during his research. "It was called Camp Massingw," he said as he looked down at the sign lying on the ground.

"That's an interesting name. Is it Native American?" Miranda asked him.

"Indeed it is. Massingw was a forest spirit that the native Lenni Lenape people worshiped. He's tasked with maintaining the balance of nature, and is the protector of the forest and its animals, especially deer. Apparently, this place was considered sacred to him."

"Weren't those archaeology students here looking for native artifacts?" Miranda inquired.

"Yes. The Lenni Lenape used to camp on the shores of this lake. There might've even been an entire village near here at one time."

"I'd heard this lake was man made," Mark commented.

"No, it's been here a very, very long time," Lars said wistfully, an odd look in his eye, as if he were peering into the past. "It used to be much bigger. We're probably standing in what used to be part of it."

Athena found this difficult to imagine since they could see nothing of the lake at all from their current position. "Damn, global warming really is a bitch, isn't it?"

Lars laughed. "It has nothing to do with that, it's just time. Time is the real bitch."

Athena thought about all the little aches and pains she'd had since hitting her forties and found herself smiling in agreement. She also realized that this was the first time she could recall Lars ever using anything close to a cuss word. Wearing shorts *and* cursing! He was really letting his hair down this weekend - or Athena was just corrupting him. She didn't think that was it, though. This was just an aspect of his personality he'd never felt comfortable sharing until now. She was pleased that he was opening up to her a bit more. It was funny you could know someone for most of your life and still never truly know them. We all hide behind so many masks, and keep so many secrets - even from ourselves.

Athena was right up to the standing stones now. As she passed underneath it, she reached out her fingertips to touch its rough surface. The moment she reached the other side she felt a sickening feeling deep in the pit of her stomach. It was like the feeling she'd gotten when she was meditating, only now it was a thousand times more powerful. A feeling that there was something horribly wrong with the land she'd just entered. She doubled over and almost threw up.

Dennis was still filming everything. He instantly noticed the change in his wife and rushed towards her, putting his strong, calming hand on her shoulder. "Are you okay?"

She looked up at him gratefully, standing herself up straight. "Yeah, I'll be alright. I just got hit with a really strong bad feeling."

"Hmm. Now that you mention it, I don't feel so hot myself all of the sudden," he told her.

The others had gathered around them, concerned about their leader's welfare. There were a few murmurs of agreement from among them. It seemed as if everyone was suddenly feeling very uneasy. Athena's skeptical nature made her want to immediately dismiss it as nothing more mysterious than the group responding to her suggestion, but she could also feel the disquiet within them. Some of them were in a near panic all of the sudden.

"Well, I'll just take this as a sign that we're on the right track." She smiled with forced cheerfulness.

Mark took his gun out of the holster. She didn't know if this made her feel safer or more worried. She ultimately decided that the two feelings roughly balanced each other out.

The group continued on the trail in silence, each consumed by their own feelings of dread as they moved through the eerily quiet forest. Soon they came upon the rotted log cabins that had once been Camp Massingw. The lake was clearly visible now, as well as the remains of a pier. Athena was struck by how still the waters were, shining like a great mirror in the distance, yet the placid scene brought her no comfort. The dark, vacant rectangles where the windows of the cabins had once been glared out at her, and she could sense unquiet spirits stirring within.

The group reached a clearing that the cabins seemed to be clustered around and took stock of the situation. "Do we want to split up and try to see if we can make contact with anything in these cabins?

"Split up? That's the classic horror movie mistake! There's only one of me. I can't protect us all if we run into something truly nasty if we're in different groups," Mark scoffed.

"Ah, but you aren't our only defender! So easily you forget the power of my flashing nunchucks!" Dennis replied in what Athena supposed was intended to be the raspy voice of an aged martial arts master. To illustrate his point, he whipped his nunchucks from his back pocket and did a little routine with them which she had to admit was somewhat impressive looking - especially for someone who she knew had not a single minute of proper training. Never underestimate the power of repeat viewings of Bruce Lee movies and endless hours spent in front of the mirror, she supposed.

"Not to insult your manly skills, but there's a more practical reason not to go into those cabins. They don't look particularly structurally safe. I don't see anything wrong with wandering around them, but I wouldn't go inside, personally. I'm gonna plop myself down and try to make contact. I've already sensed a few spirits. We're definitely not alone out here." With that announcement, Athena unceremoniously sat herself down in the dirt and shut her eyes. A moment later she opened them again, clearly irritated that everyone else was still standing around her. She sighed.

"What are you guys all waiting for? Skedaddle! I can't concentrate with everyone staring at me. Go explore, reach out to some of these spirits, just try to stay within viewing distance of one another." She closed her eyes again and was gratified by the sounds of feet shuffling away from her, yet one pair of feet remained.

"You don't mind if I stick around do you? Someone's gotta keep an eye on you." It was Miranda's voice.

"Hey, suit yourself," was Athena's casual response, but inside she was pleased by the loyalty of her best friend. Or perhaps Miranda was just too spooked to go near those creepy old cabins. Athena certainly couldn't blame her. There was something unbelievably disquieting about them.

Athena got her breathing under control and the images began to flood her awareness. Terrible, graphic images of people being methodically stalked and killed, their blood being collected in an old mason jar. She could sense the mind of the killer and was for some reason surprised to realize that she had been a woman. A woman driven by an all consuming grief - and an equally powerful, single-minded desperate hope.

A mother. She had been a mother. Athena felt it to be true. She wasn't even a mother herself, yet she couldn't help but wonder how any mother could rob so many other mothers of their own babies. Then she stopped speculating. Long ago she'd decided that there was no sense in trying to understand the mind of a madman - or in this case a madwoman - you only risk going a little nuts yourself.

In her mind's eye, Athena saw some of the spirits of her victims. Miranda would've been upset to know that they were standing right behind her. They were a man and a young woman. Both were covered in blood from the multiple wounds the killer had inflicted on them decades earlier. Strange symbols were carved into their foreheads and arms. She didn't sense that they had been a couple in life. They were drawn to Athena like a moth to a flame, unable to resist their curiosity about these visitors, yet still too traumatized from their deaths to feel particularly chatty. For Athena these events had happened a lifetime ago, but for these two ghosts, it was as fresh as if it had just happened. She could feel their dead eyes boring into her, until they gradually receded, fading away into the spreading afternoon gloom.

Athena let out a long breath and slowly opened her eyes to return to the world as most people experienced it. Miranda was standing over her expectantly. Athena stood up with a grace that surprised her, and brushed the dust from her behind.

"Are you alright? You don't look so good."

"Hmm. Maybe I'd better schedule an appointment with my beautician, then?"

Miranda folded her arms. "C'mon, be real with me Athena." This was her standard response when she was done drinking from her friend's bottomless well of snark.

"Sorry. Yeah, I saw some really unpleasant things."

"What sort of unpleasant things?" Lars asked from behind her. He seemed to be leading the rest of the team back to where Athena and Miranda were standing. Dennis was right behind him, filming the whole thing.

"I saw the murders." She shook as she said it, her body responding to the horrors her mind was trying to minimize.

Lars raised an eyebrow. "All thirteen of them?"

"Thirteen! Holy shit! There were really that many? No, I only saw a few of them, but that was enough, believe me!"

Lars continued to press her. "The killer was never caught. You didn't happen to get any insight into who was responsible?"

"It was a woman. A mother. She was really sad about something, yet oddly hopeful too. And driven, incredibly driven," she revealed.

Lars looked flabbergasted by this information. "There was a woman who was a suspect. Her son had drowned while attending the camp a few years earlier. She sued the pants off of them and they were forced out of business. The murders happened after someone had purchased the property and was trying to fix it up to reopen. The whole work crew sent out here was slaughtered. This woman disappeared before the police could question her. They never did find her, but she was the prime suspect. Other people argued that one woman couldn't have killed all those people by herself. They pointed to the ritualistic way the victims were killed and blamed it on some sort of Satanic cult."

He chuckled to himself. "It was the mid seventies. *The Exorcist*, *The Omen*, and *The Amityville Horror* were all huge hits at the box office. People started imagining sinister cults lurking around every corner. It was the beginning of what we call 'The Satanic Panic' nowadays."

Athena nodded enthusiastically "The victims did have weird marks carved all over their bodies - I saw it!"

"Yes, that matches the police reports," the journalist confirmed.

"I don't know if she was part of a cult, but she definitely acted on her own."

"This really is way too much like *Friday the 13th*! I can't believe it really happened!" Tyler exclaimed.

This appeared to rustle Lars' feathers somewhat. "I assure you, it's all too real, although finding any record of it is unusually difficult. This only happened about forty years ago and I've had better luck researching stories from 140 years ago!"

"C'mon though, a woman's son drowns at a summer camp and she goes on a murder spree when they try to reopen the place? It's almost exactly like the plot of the first movie. It's uncanny. Too uncanny to be a coincidence! They must've based the movie on this story."

"I suppose it's possible it was the initial inspiration for it," Lars conceded. "The story was never very widely circulated, despite its sensationalism. I think the local police were embarrassed that they never caught the culprit and stopped cooperating with the press. The press eventually lost interest. Well, except for me. I'd heard rumors about it growing up, but always assumed it was nothing but folklore."

"Fun fact!" Tyler suddenly announced. It was obvious that he'd stopped actually listening to Lars some time ago and had just been waiting for a pause so he could show off his vast, yet mostly useless knowledge. Groans could be heard rippling throughout the group. Tyler was full of facts which he thought were fun, yet rarely were. Either he didn't hear the groans or didn't care, as he verbally plowed on regardless.

"*Friday the 13th* is set in New Jersey! They filmed the first movie at a Boy Scout camp up in North Jersey. If you look at all the license plates, they're Jersey plates. Even the remake from a few years ago was set in New Jersey. Jason Vorhees is as much our own personal state monster as the Jersey Devil is! I wish we'd do a better job of claiming him! I mean, he's one of the most iconic horror movie monsters of all time."

Dennis couldn't resist a good nerdy topic. "Ya know what I wish we'd do a better job of claiming? Batman! Gotham City is supposed to be in New Jersey, south of Atlantic City! Our state is home to one of the coolest, most popular superheroes and we don't claim him! It should be on our welcome signs: 'Welcome to New Jersey - home of the Batman!'"

"You guys just wanna claim all these cool fictional characters as residents of the state because it makes it seem a little less boring and uneventful to live here than it already is!" Kim wryly observed.

Tyler shrugged. "Yeah, so what's wrong with that?"

Athena rolled her eyes over this whole topic. It was time to refocus the group on why they were here in the first place, otherwise the conversation would likely go on in this vein for hours. Well, it would *feel* like hours to her, even if it wasn't!

"So, did anyone capture any evidence? I felt the presence of a male and a female ghost nearby, but neither one of them wanted to talk to me. I feel like they're not the only ones out here."

"Bev caught a pretty cool EVP. And I saw some shadow figures over by that cabin," Mark said, pointing with his gun at a particularly sad looking cabin whose roof had completely caved in.

A chill ran down Athena's spine as she looked where her brother was indicating. Indeed she could feel someone watching them from within. She recognized the cabin from her vision, too. The death in that cabin had been a particularly nasty one involving a pitchfork through the neck.

"Wait 'till you hear this one! It's really clear too!" an enthusiastic Bev said as she rewound her digital recorder and cranked up the volume to maximum. The others all crowded around to listen.

"Get out!" a hoarse voice rasped. "Go before it's too late!"

"Holy shit!" Athena gasped. It was indeed as clear as Beverly had boasted. It was hard to imagine that it was saying anything else or was just some random background sounds. Even the typically uber skeptical Tyler was temporarily speechless.

"Play it again!" Dennis demanded.

Bev complied. The group was, if anything, even more astounded the second time they heard it.

"That's some great evidence! Good job! At least one of these ghosts was willing to talk to us!" Athena complimented.

"Did you hear anything at the time or only on playback?" Miranda asked.

"Just on the playback. But I could see something moving around in there through the windows," Bev explained.

"I saw it too," Mark added.

"Damn. I wish I hadn't left my spirit box in the van," Dennis lamented.

"You still haven't given up on that hunk of junk yet, huh?" Athena admonished.

"Well, if it's ever gonna pick up anything, it's gonna be here! This place is quite the hotspot!"

"It sure is!" Athena agreed, and before she knew what she was doing, she found herself marching towards the cabin in question. The others soon followed her lead. She wondered what she was thinking walking over to this cabin? She knew that what was inside was going to be quite unpleasant, but she couldn't help herself. This was the one spirit in the whole camp that might be willing to speak with her - she couldn't let the opportunity go to waste.

As soon as she reached the rotting, moldering old log cabin, she called out. "Is there anyone in there who wants to come forward and talk with us? We'd love to hear your story!"

She nearly jumped right out of her skin as a pale, gore-streaked face loomed at her from a window only a few feet away. The pitch fork was still dangling from the man's neck. She could even see the points protruding through the back. Not for the first time, Athena wondered why so many ghosts appeared exactly as they did in their last moments of life. Was it just to terrify the living, or a visible sign of how they were literally stuck in their trauma?

"You see something, babe?" a concerned Dennis asked.

"He's right there! In the window!"

Dennis squinted, then trained his camera on it. He switched it over to FLIR mode (a type of thermal imaging) and made a face.

"The camera isn't picking him up. I can't see anything either."

Athena smacked her gum loudly in irritation. Sometimes it was so frustrating being the only one who could see these kinds of things so clearly.

"I can see a shadowy outline," Mark said. Athena wanted to believe him, but also couldn't rule out that he was just responding to her suggestion.

"Go. Leave this place," the gruesome thing in the window wheezed at her in its sandpaper voice. "There's nothing here for you. He's still here. He can never leave. We see everything he does. He'll get you too if you stay." The ghastly shade's watery eyes burned into her.

"Who? Who are you talking about?" she shouted in desperation. But the ghost was already floating backwards into the darkness it had emerged from.

"Wait! Come back!"

"Go!" The voice was so loud that they all heard it. The front door of the cabin was suddenly blasted off its hinges and flew several feet through the air, nearly hitting poor Miranda before crashing to the ground beside her.

Athena sprinted to her friend's side. "Jesus! Are you okay, Mira?"

Miranda nervously pulled back a strand of her long brown hair. "I somehow managed not to pee my pants, so that's a win, right?"

"That was amazing!" Tyler gushed, "Please tell me you were still filming?"

"Oh yeah, I got the whole thing on camera!" Dennis quickly rewound the footage and listened. "I even got the voice!" He rewound it a little further back. "Oh wow! I even got it talking to Athena! All the parts of the conversation we couldn't hear with our ears. Guys, this is the best evidence we've ever gotten!"

Athena grimaced. While she was happy for Dennis, she was afraid that in their excitement, everyone was forgetting that a door was just thrown at them and came within an inch of taking off poor Miranda's head.

"This all well and good, but I'm inclined to take that spirit's advice and vamoose. We're obviously not welcome here. We wanted to check out the area where those kids ran into The Boy before it gets too dark, didn't we?"

"With all due respect, are you nuts? Dennis is right - this is some of the best evidence we've ever collected in all our years of doing this!" Tyler protested. "Why go chasing after some silly monster that probably doesn't exist when there's a real, measurable phenomenon right here?"

"We can always come back later, Tyler. Besides, I think the two things are connected somehow, I can *feel* that there's a connection." Athena surprised herself as she said this. She hadn't been consciously aware of this feeling until she spoke it out loud. But there it was, and it was a real, tangible intuition.

"And we always respect the wishes of the spirits. It's always been our policy. If they really don't want us in their space, we listen to them," Miranda reminded him.

"I know, I know." Tyler knew when he was beaten. It seemed par for the course lately.

So it came to pass that the team was walking down a trail beyond the haunted, huddled, dilapidated remains of Camp Massingw.

At the moment, they no longer had the excitement of an investigation to distract them from the bad vibes that permeated the entire area. The oppressive air which hung about the place continued unabated. Normally there would've been all manner of playful banter amongst them at a time like this, but instead they trudged on through the darkening woods, lost in their own grim thoughts.

They came upon another set of standing stones, this one slightly smaller and set off to the side of the trail rather than forming an arch over it. Athena sensed a strange energy emanating from it, just as she had from the other one. She could almost see this energy forming a wall that cut through the forest and stretched on as far as she could perceive. A word popped into her head and she spoke it aloud.

"A fence post."

"Huh?" asked a bewildered Dennis, who was walking right behind her.

"Nothing, nothing it's probably nothing." But as she said it she knew that it wasn't, she just didn't understand what it meant yet.

They pressed on.

After walking in silence for a while longer, Dennis spoke up. "I really don't think we should try to camp out here tonight."

Athena craned her head back to regard him. "I agree, this place is way too spooky, even for us."

"No, that's not why - well it's not *entirely* why. I'm sure you've noticed there's an unusual number of new-looking 'No Trespassing' signs around since we left the camp."

"Sure, but we haven't let that stop us before."

"There's more than signs. I've spotted a few cameras high up in the trees. Real hi-tech ones. Solar powered with a battery backup and wireless transmission," he informed her in hushed tones.

Leave it to my husband to find some high tech gadgets even in the middle of nowhere! Athena smiled to herself.

"Whoever put up those cameras is serious. I don't want us to get ourselves in any legal trouble. Those kids were able to zip in and out of here quickly without getting caught because they were on motorcycles. I don't think we'd be so lucky if whoever owned this property decided to show up. I say we do a quick investigation at the spot where they saw the creature and head back to our cars ASAP."

"Sure, we can go check out the place where Brenda said she had her encounter tomorrow if anyone is still up for it." Athena tried to sound casual, but inside her head was churning with anxiety over what Dennis had just shared with her. She began to wonder if there was something to all this talk about the Men in Black after all?

She should be excited. Here she was, finally out on the investigation which had been delayed for an entire week and it was a beautiful day. Her brother was with them which was what she had wanted. They had just captured on video the best evidence they'd ever come across, and all the spectral activity in this area meant she might be on the verge of proving her theory that the Jersey Devil was a ghost. Yet she felt nothing but an awful dread clawing at her mind.

Eventually, after studying his phone, Dennis announced that they should be in the area where the two brothers had run into and been chased by the entity they were calling The Boy. He couldn't be completely sure because he'd lost signal on his phone quite some time ago, but he still had the information pulled up on his screen from before losing signal, and had estimated they should be in the right spot by now.

"We're definitely in the right place, look at that!" Mark said, gesturing with his gun like a pointer.

Athena looked in the direction he was indicating and saw a large dark spot in the otherwise pristine white soil. She walked over to it and saw that it was brown and about four feet across. "Just like those two described. If this really has been stained by blood, that's a helluva lot of blood!"

Dennis joined her at the edge of the mark and began filming again. "Hey, what's this?" He leaned down and pulled something from the ground. He made a grossed out face as he studied it. "Ewww it's a bone! You don't suppose it's human do you?" He held it out. It was a small piece of bone that reminded Athena of a finger joint.

"Let me see that!" She snatched it out of his hand to take a better look and immediately regretted doing so. The moment she touched it, her body was wracked by unimaginable pain and horrific images. Her mind was inundated with emotions. Deep despair and confusion, but above all rage and hunger.

A hunger which could never be satisfied.

She convulsed from the agony of it and dropped the bone like it was hot. "His name was Dustin and he was eaten alive!" she exclaimed and was surprised to feel hot tears running down her face. She didn't know how she knew it, she just knew it.

Dennis already had his arms around her, doing his big teddy bear thing. The feel of them stopped her shaking at least. She could still feel that terrible hunger she'd just sensed, she could feel it nearby. In a flash of insight she understood that it could sense her too, whenever she tapped into her psychic abilities out here it was like sending up a flare, a light in its darkness which it was instinctively drawn towards. Yes, *it*. And whatever *it* was, it was no ghost. Ghosts don't eat people alive. They were all in terrible danger! They had to leave now!

"We've gotta go! Head back to the cars now! It's still out here! It's close!"

"What's close?" Miranda asked.

"The thing that did this!" She gestured to the large spot in the ground that was stained with Dustin's blood.

"We're just turning back already? So we walked all the way out here for nothing, then? I *told* you we should've stayed at the camp!" Tyler whined.

Mark smiled. He pointed at Tyler's slight beer gut, for once thankfully not with his gun. "I wouldn't complain, you needed the exercise, hon!"

"Ha, ha!" He clapped his hands mockingly. "*Very funneeeeeeeeeeee!*" Tyler's voice went up several octaves as *something,* some dark, horrible shape erupted from the bushes behind him and dragged him back screaming into the foliage.

"Holy shit!" Mark screamed and fired off two rounds into the woods Tyler had just disappeared into.

"Stop! You might hit Tyler!" Dennis shouted. He was already pulling the nunchucks from his back pocket.

"What the hell was that thing? Holy shit! *Holy shit!* What just happened?" Bev hollered in a panic. Kim patted her on the back, trying to calm her. It wasn't working.

"C'mon! We've gotta go after it!" Athena ran towards the spot where Tyler had been standing mere moments earlier.

"Go after it? Are you nuts? Aren't you scared?" Bev challenged.

Athena paused in mid stride and looked straight at her. "I'm terrified! But this is the JSPS and we never leave a man behind!" With that she crashed off into the dark and tangled underbrush.

Part Two

Chapter Eleven:
Lots of Running and Screaming

"She's fucking nuts!" Bev swore. "'We don't leave anyone behind!' I'm a middle-aged paranormal investigator not a Goddamned marine! I'm out of here!"

Kim nodded along enthusiastically, "Yeah, didn't she say something about someone getting eaten alive? I say we get the fuck out of Dodge while that *thing* is busy chowing down! I'm sorry, but there's no point in trying to help that poor guy, he's toast!"

"Fine! Go! Get to safety and call 911 as soon as you've got some signal!" Mark shouted at them as he ran to follow Dennis, who was already disappearing into the woods ahead of them.

Bev and Kim needed no further encouragement. They ran back the way they'd come with surprising speed for a pair of middle aged ladies.

"Hold up! I'm coming too!" Miranda called after him.

Mark paused and twisted at the waist to glance back at her. "Don't be an idiot! You'll just get yourself killed! You don't have any weapons!"

"Yeah...well...I have to help! Those are my two best friends out there, I can't just leave them! We're a family!"

Mark sighed. Off in the distance he could hear Tyler screaming at the top of his lungs. "Whatever! Suit yourself! I've gotta catch up with them!" He noticed that Lars was still lingering. "What about you?"

"Are you kidding? This is the scoop of the century, I'm not missing this!" He was actually smiling. Mark liked Lars. He even thought he was kind of cute. But at that moment he wanted nothing more than to wipe that callous grin off the reporter's face with his fists. Instead, he ran after his sister and brother-in-law before he was tempted to follow through on that impulse. Maybe it wasn't too late to save Tyler...if he could just reach him in time!

Miranda quickly picked up a few stray rocks she spotted on the ground around her and thrust them into her jeans pockets, keeping the biggest one in her hands. She knew it was lame, but it was better than nothing.

"Smart thinking!" Lars commented approvingly as he bent down to imitate what she was doing.

"Thanks, let's go!" She ran off in the direction where Athena, Dennis and Mark had gone.

It was the same direction where all the awful screaming was coming from.

What the hell am I doing? Athena thought as she crashed through the foliage. Despite all her brave talk a moment ago, she was fully aware of how stupid what she was doing was.*I mean, when I catch up with it, what am I gonna do? Wave a crystal at it?*

She was thinking of the crystal pendant she always wore, which was a great defense against a purely psychic assault, but completely useless against a physical threat. Yet she couldn't in good conscience just abandon Tyler to his fate. He was her responsibility, and basically family. She knew she'd never be able to live with herself if she didn't try everything possible to save him. Her heart broke a little with each fresh scream coming from somewhere ahead of her. She'd never heard such an awful sound before, but she tried to remind herself that so long as she kept hearing those cries it meant he was still alive, that there was still *hope.*

"Triple A! Wait!" It was her husband's voice. She looked over her shoulder to see a red-faced Dennis bounding towards her, his ridiculous nunchucks bouncing in his hand with each step, one of them occasionally hitting him.

"Both of you wait for me!" Mark called as he caught up with Dennis. With his arrival, Athena finally stopped, surrendering to the logic of letting the guy with the gun take the lead.

"Where...are the...others?" She wheezed out the words. She'd been so lost in the chase that she hadn't realized how out of breath she was until then.

"Bev and Kim are going back to the cars, Lars and Miranda should be somewhere right behind me," he reported breathlessly.

Athena grimaced at the news. "No! Miranda is a mom! She needs to get out of here! This is too dangerous for her!"

"I tried to tell her, but she wouldn't leave you guys."

Athena opened her mouth to argue, but before she could get a word out, another scream split their ears. Then there was nothing but silence - the death of hope.

"No!" Athena wouldn't accept it. She wouldn't give up. She sprinted in the direction of that final scream, the others following closely behind. Mark caught up with her and overtook her, his gun held out straight in front of him. She didn't argue.

Athena's foot crunched on something. She looked down to see that she'd just smashed Tyler's glasses. She quickened her pace. Then she saw Mark come to a sudden stop and stiffen. She came up beside him - that's when she saw the most awful thing she'd ever seen in her life.

It was the sounds which got her first. The sickening wet sound of slurping, chewing, and vigorous chomping. Then she saw the source of it, a bloated mass of filthy flesh which somehow seemed to be constantly moving in an obscenely undulating way. It was straddling what was left of Tyler. The thing had long, stringy hair that was matted and caked with bloody bits of meat. The hair thankfully obscured its face so all she could see was one bulging, bloodshot eye, burning with a feral madness...and its teeth. Those teeth! Rendered black and yellow with age and broken into jagged points. They seemed to burst from its mouth in places, somehow growing out of its mottled, crawling skin.

Tyler wasn't moving. Half of his face was gone, exposing the bright white skull beneath. The thing looked up at them and seemed to smile.

"Oh God! *Oh God!*" She heard Dennis near her shoulder. They were both pushed forward as Miranda and Lars collided with them.

"No!" Miranda screamed.

"Good lord! It's true! It's all true!" Lars exclaimed.

"GET OFF OF HIM YOU FUCKER!" Mark shouted. He followed this immediately with several shots at the thing.

Athena looked on with a kind of twisted fascination as each of the shots found their target, all hitting it in the same spot.

He's actually a good shot, she found herself thinking in an oddly detached way, and immediately realized the shock of everything was causing her to dissociate. Damn the knowledge she'd picked up from all those psychology books she read to try and cope with her anxiety!

The well-grouped gunshots all landed in the thing's bloated, misshapen arm, near the bend of its elbow. At this range, the high caliber shots almost tore the arm off at the joint - it was only connected by a stretched out membrane of skin. The monster howled in rage.

Then, before their astonished eyes, they saw the damaged flesh rise up and spread itself over the wound. It was growing back!

A new sound registered in her mind, a clicking sound. She saw that her brother was breathing heavily, his eyes wide as saucers and he was repeatedly squeezing the trigger, but nothing was happening. He needed to reload, but was too traumatized to realize it yet.

She heard an odd sort of gurgling sound coming from the creature and understood that it was *laughing* at them. She saw it tense up as its shattered arm finished knitting itself back together. It was coiling up as if to jump at them.

To jump at Mark, who was the closest to it.

Before she even knew what she was doing, Athena felt herself stepping forward, pushing Mark out of the way. "No!" she shouted at the thing.

The monster leaped at her.

She could feel the heat of its breath, smell the fetid stench of its grisly flesh. She shut her eyes and screamed. Then she heard a loud TWACK!

She opened her eyes in time to see a nunchuck savagely smack the side of the creature's face. Dennis' weapon of choice didn't seem quite so ridiculous now. He swung his weapon at it again, but this time the monster caught it before it could strike him. Athena watched with horrified fascination as it tore the nunchuck from her husband's hand and bit right through it!

"Run!" she screamed. Up until then, everyone else had been frozen in place, watching the whole horrific scene play out - spellbound by it, like people driving past a particularly terrible highway wreck. Her shout shattered their stupor and they all tore off back the way they'd come.

The thing that called these woods its home was hot on their heels.

Athena ran like she hadn't run since she was a little girl. She ran until it felt like her lungs were on fire and her heart would burst out of her chest. She knew it was all futile. She knew with a sickening kind of certainty that it would only be a matter of time before it got another one of them.

The devil always got his due, didn't he?

Chapter Twelve:
More Running and Screaming -
Now with Puking too!

As she ran, Athena's hands found the small purse she had slung diagonally over her torso. She thrust a hand inside the unzipped top of it, and her fingers found a slick piece of laminated paper bouncing around inside near her beloved pack of gum. She grabbed the card and fervently wished, wishing like she'd never wished before, to see the one person she knew who might be powerful enough to get them out of this situation alive.

There was a blinding flash of light from somewhere ahead of her. She instinctively threw up her arms to shield herself from it. When she looked up again she was met with an odd sight: a tall, lanky, pale man with long brown hair and a beard which went down to his waist was now standing before her, dressed in nothing but a pink towel wrapped around his waist, reading "Myrtle Beach, NC". The man looked equally confused and irritated. Then his sparkling gray eyes fixed upon Athena just as her momentum sent her crashing into his damp body. He looked quite different than he had the last time she'd seen him, but there was no doubt that this was Clark Kismet.

"Oh Athena, of all the places you could've ever gone, this is the one place you absolutely, categorically *never* should've gone!" he scolded her in a soft, lilting voice with an odd accent that sounded vaguely British. He glanced beyond her and his eyes bulged and he roughly shoved Athena behind him. In a loud, commanding voice he chanted something which sounded disconcertingly like baby talk.

Athena peered out from behind him just in time to see a glowing green barrier of energy appear in front of him and the thing which had been violently chasing them slam into it. Clark looked distressed as he saw the thing rapidly pick itself up off the forest floor and dart to the left. He chanted some more strange words and gestured with his long fingers. Athena watched as the barrier grew longer, wrapping itself around the creature to form a complete circle of mystical energy. Clark then gestured as if he was pushing something up with both hands, and the barrier grew taller until its walls towered over them. The monster contained within howled and snarled in a rage, snapping its teeth at them impotently.

Clark smiled and clapped his hands together. "There! That'll hold you for a while!"

"For how long exactly?" Athena asked, ashamed of how tremulous her voice sounded in her own ears.

"Oh, about twenty minutes, give or take a few seconds."

The others had either heard the commotion or seen the flash of light and were all making their way over to where Clark and Athena stood, a mere two inches from the thing, which was leaping over and over again, trying to jump over the emerald energy barrier.

"What on earth?? Who *are* you? What is *that*?" Lars pushed his way forward and poked the barrier with one finger, sending small ripples through it.

"This is Clark Kismet," Athena explained.

Lars' mouth hung open for a moment, but he quickly recovered. "Oh! Your wizard friend! I...I never imagined that such things were possible, I mean, not *really*," he babbled. "How did you do it? How did you get here?"

Clark waved at the approaching members of the JSPS. "Hello there, Dennis! Have you lost weight? Looking good, m'man! And Miranda! Still hanging out with these two, I see?"

Miranda and Dennis both waved back numbly, still too shell-shocked from their ordeal to do much more.

Clark saw Mark walking towards them. "And you must be the baby brother! All grown up now! Pleased to meet you!"

"Errr...yeah, hi," an obviously dazed Mark mumbled.

Athena looked up at the wizard. "Look, I really appreciate you saving my bacon, but we can all exchange pleasantries later! That thing just *ate* one of my friends! Our cars are more than twenty minutes away from here! We've got to get moving!"

Clark's face fell as he heard her news. "Oh no! I'm so sorry to hear about your friend. I had really hoped this kind of thing would've stopped happening after I bought those apartments and shut them down. We have plenty of time to get away though, I can simply teleport you back to your vehicles once I pull their location out of your mind." He extended his bony fingers to touch Athena's forehead. "Ah, I see them now. Not too far away, thankfully! Now let's all link hands and we can be away from this dreadful place!"

"Teleportation! Are you serious?" Lars was astonished.

Clark stood up straighter, making himself appear even taller than he was, and in a grave voice said, "My good sir, I'm always serious!" It probably would've been a more effective statement if he wasn't dripping wet and wearing nothing but a beach towel.

"Whoa! Not so fast! We have to bring Tyler's body with us! For his family to bury," Athena interjected.

"Tyler? That would be your unfortunate friend?"

Athena nodded.

"Well, take me to him and I'll teleport him along with the rest of you."

Athena started to walk around the energy shield Clark had erected, trying her best not to look at the terrifying thing held within the transparent barrier. It was still trying to find a way out, and it was still covered in Tyler's blood. Clark followed her, then he let out an impossibly loud shout, right in her ear. Her heart leapt in her chest at the sound, then again as the monster threw itself up against the barrier right near where she stood.

"Are you okay?"

The wizard sucked his teeth. "I stepped on a rock! Big one, too! That's it! I'm levitating until I can get myself a good pair of shoes!" With that he chanted some more of his nonsense words and his bare feet lifted a few inches off the ground.

"Amazing!" Lars exclaimed.

Athena rolled her eyes. "C'mon."

As she led the way back, she found herself nervously thinking out loud, "I don't know how we'll ever explain all this to the authorities, or to Tyler's family. Oh, God! What have I gotten us into?"

"We can blame it on a bear attack. Leave it all to me, I'll take care of it, my dear," Clark said mildly.

Dennis made his way up to Athena and threw an arm around her. "You can't blame yourself for this, babe."

She looked at him with eyes red from tears she hadn't even noticed were there. "Can't I? I'm a fucking psychic, and I ignored my own instincts! I ignored all the warnings!"

Dennis wouldn't hear any of it. "We all did! None of us knew how much of the stories to believe! We thought we were just chasing a ghost like we usually are. We all voted to come here–"

"*Tyler* didn't want to come! If I'd just paid more attention to him, maybe he wouldn't be...maybe he'd still be...." She started sobbing loudly now, completely surrendering to the wave of grief she'd been holding back while she'd been focused on survival. Athena being Athena, the sorrow was mixed with an unhealthy dose of anxiety over everyone seeing what an ugly crier she was.

She continued to lead the way as she fought to get her tears under control. It wasn't much later that they came upon the spot where Tyler's corpse lay sprawled out in a pool of his own blood.

"Oh dear," Clark frowned as he floated towards the body.

Some of the others were sick as they got a better look at their friend's remains. Dennis let go of Athena and ran off into the bushes to throw up.

With a look of disgust, Clark lifted one of Tyler's gnawed-on arms by the hand. He held out his other hand to Athena.

"Right then! Everyone take somebody's hand and let's form a chain," the mage commanded. The others all obeyed without question.

More bizarre words were chanted by the wizard, there was a rush of wind, another brilliant burst of light, and Athena found herself surrounded by a confusing kaleidoscope of colors.

Then they were gone.

Chapter Thirteen: A Time to Catch Your Breath

Athena's stomach felt like it was filled with butterflies. There was another flash of pure, white light and she found herself wobbling on her feet near where they'd all parked. Clark released her hand. She watched his face turn several different shades of green, and for a moment she was sure he'd toss his cookies all over the place, but he seemed to get the impulse under control.

"Don't worry. He can't get to us here. Even when my spell wears off. The megaliths in these woods create a magical barrier he can't get through. We're on the other side of it now, so we're all quite safe," Clark announced, loud enough for all of them to hear.

"You seem to know a lot about this place and that thing. Care to explain?" Lars probed.

"I do, unfortunately. But now isn't the time for long-winded explanations. We may be safe here, but I suspect you're all eager to get back to civilization."

"Damn right I am!" The outburst was accompanied by the sound of a slamming car door. They all looked over to see Bev marching towards them.

"I thought you'd be gone by now." Athena smiled at her thinly.

"We couldn't back out! That damned SUV is blocking us in!" She angrily waved a hand at Lars' Mitsubishi Outlander. Indeed, the cars were all parked in a row, one behind the other, and the trail was too narrow here for them to easily maneuver around each other.

"What's going on? Who is that?" Bev demanded, pointing at Clark. "Omigod! Is that...Taylor?" Her face crumpled up in horror as she spotted the ruined body still oozing blood. It lay on the ground right before her, where Clark had dropped it when they'd rematerialized.

"Tyler," Dennis corrected her, but she was already turning her head away and making telltale retching sounds.

Kim was now out of the car too, rapidly striding towards her friend, who was busy wiping the remaining nastiness from the corners of her mouth.

"Did you get through to 911?" Mark called to her.

"The signal is still too weak!" Kim complained.

"The magical barrier generated by the megaliths is interfering with your cell signal, even at this distance. You'd have to get quite high up over this area to escape the effect," Clark explained. Athena recalled the cameras mounted high atop the trees that Dennis had pointed out earlier.

Whoever put those there knew about the barrier, that's why they're mounted so high! she realized with a start.

"I'm afraid we'll have to drive the body to the hospital ourselves," Clark stated.

Mark looked Clark up and down for a moment. "I've got some clothes in my car that might fit you. I brought 'em because we were originally planning on camping out here."

Clark smiled at him. "Thank you, that would be wonderful. I'm afraid Athena caught me at an inconvenient time. The enchantment I had placed upon that calling card summoned me here instantly, no chance to throw on anything! I was beginning to think she'd never use it."

Mark walked over to his car and began searching through it while Clark stood nearby. Athena followed them.

"You don't seem all that surprised that I still had it after twenty years," she observed.

"Twenty-two years, actually. No, I'm not surprised. I also put a spell on it which compelled you to always keep it near you - and to use it if you were ever in mortal danger. Although I *had* hoped you'd reconsider my offer to become my apprentice and contact me sooner. No calls, no Christmas cards, I was really beginning to think you didn't care at all!"

"Don't be silly!" Athena laughed nervously. "I've always been grateful to you for helping us out on our first case. And we've run into each other since then, a few times."

"Awkwardly bumping into each other on a couple of occasions while grocery shopping at Acme doesn't count!"

"There was that time I picked up all those crystal pendants for the new JSPS members at your shop," she reminded him.

"That was ten years ago!"

"Was it? Well, anyway you look great. I really like the beard, it makes you seem more wizard-y."

She meant it. He did look good for his age. Perhaps *too* good. As she studied him closer she didn't see any gray hairs, big wrinkles or other signs of aging. Aside from the beard and decidedly longer hair, he looked very much as he had when she'd first met him during the summer of '94. This was odd because he'd been at least as old as her mother was back then. By Athena's calculations he'd have to be somewhere in his sixties by now, yet he still looked like he was in his late thirties or early forties at the latest. Hell, he looked younger now than she, Dennis, or Miranda did! It wasn't fair!

"Well, it's very kind of you to say so, but I'm afraid that I've let myself go a bit lately. I've been too preoccupied with...other matters to deal much with petty concerns such as my personal hygiene. Why, I only took a shower today because Jasmine was honest enough with me to tell me I was beginning to stink!"

"Jasmine? Don't tell me you've got a special lady in your life now?" she was teasing him, but part of her hoped it was true. Clark had always had a bit of a crush on her mother, which Athena had found irritating since she hadn't wanted her mother getting too involved with someone as odd as Clark. Although, to be honest, none of her mother's boyfriends would ever be good enough in Athena's eyes. Not as good as Dad had been. She hated to admit it, but despite all his strangeness, Clark *was* better than some of the losers her Mom had seen over the years. Maybe it wouldn't have been so bad after all if they had wound up together?

Clark looked mildly repulsed at the suggestion that Jasmine was a romantic interest. "No, Jasmine is practically a child! She's one of the kids who works at my occult shop."

"Here you go, try those on." Mark had emerged from his back seat and was handing a neatly folded stack of clothes to the wizard. "You can change in my car, we won't peek!"

Clark thanked him and disappeared into the vehicle. Athena and Mark turned their back on him to give him whatever privacy they could.

Mark looked down at his sister, his eyes red from the tears he was holding back. "I can't believe he's really gone. He could be a real pain in the ass sometimes, but he was like a...brother."

Athena squeezed his arm. "I know. I'm still trying to make sense of it all myself."

"Athena! Can you help me over here?" Dennis called out to his wife. She glanced over to see him carrying the big blue tarp he used for work from his van over to where Tyler's body was laying. She walked over to join him.

"You're gonna wrap him up in that?"

"I figured it's the best way to get him to the hospital without him bleeding all over my van. I'm not sure why we're taking him there anyway, there's not anything they can do for him at this point."

"Because a healthcare professional has to legally declare him deceased," Clark answered. The wizard had just climbed out of Mark's car wearing a pair of shorts and an old JSPS t-shirt that they no longer sold on their website. Somehow, he managed to look more preposterous in this ensemble that he had while wearing nothing but a beach towel.

"Here, let me help you with that." The wizard then did another of his strange chants and the lifeless form of Tyler floated off the ground and landed where Dennis had spread out the tarp.

Okay, now he's just showing off! Athena thought, although she was grateful that she didn't have to touch those cold, bloody hands.

Clark wandered over to where they stood over the body and studied it critically. "Hmm, I may have to alter a few details to get them to believe this was caused by a bear."

The wizard chanted a few words over the corpse and it began to glow. The others soon gathered round to watch the gruesome spectacle as the wounds on the body shifted slightly, changing in often-subtle ways. "I rather think that should do it. Don't want to overdo it. Fortunately, dead tissue is a little easier to work with than the living kind."

"How is he doing that? And how the hell did he get here anyway?" an awestruck Bev asked nobody in particular.

"He's a wizard and I summoned him here," Athena told her. She could tell that Bev was about to tell her that such things were impossible, but was also quite aware that she had already seen two impossible things today - in fact one of them was unfolding right in front of her now.

Clark then muttered a few more unfamiliar words, and the awestruck group watched as the tarp wrapped itself around the body tightly, then levitated off the ground and into the already open back of Dennis' van at a gesture from the wizard.

"That's cool and all, but what good is all that power if you can't use it to bring him back?" Mark commented bitterly.

"Dude! Show a little gratitude! He saved our asses back there!" Athena chastised him.

"No, it's okay. Mark's reaction is quite understandable under the circumstances," the mage looked at Mark sadly. "There are certain things which are beyond even my power, and that's how it should be. Trying to tamper with such forces is what brought about all this trouble to start with."

A cloud passed over the sun and the whole forest grew a little darker. "Are you sure that we're really safe standing around out here like this?" Bev asked nervously.

"So long as the megaliths are still in place, yes."

"Do you mean those big stone things that look like Stonehenge?" Kim wondered.

"Yes."

"We passed them on the way in, they're still there." Athena informed him.

"Good, good. Well, let's get our stories straight, shall we? It's a good idea to do so before we head off to wherever the nearest hospital happens to be," the wizard suggested.

"That would be AtlanticCare, we can show you the way. It's only a few miles from here, on Jimmie Leeds Rd," Kim offered.

"Leeds? How appropriate," Athena said. "We came out here looking for the Jersey Devil," she replied in answer to Clark's puzzled expression.

"Oh. *That* old chestnut. Remind me to tell you all about the *real* Jersey Devil someday. Your family has a rather interesting connection to it, in fact."

Now it was Athena's turn to look confused. "What? We do?"

Clark patted her on the hand. "Some other time. Right now we need to focus on how we'll explain all of this to the authorities. You know, there was a time when I'd just call my friends in the ABC and they'd handle all of this, but my sources tell me that the current leadership of the group isn't quite so trustworthy as they once were. A pity, really. I had a hand in founding it, me and Sara, right after the last World War. It's a terrible thing to live long enough to see your own creations go awry."

Athena frowned. Clark was rambling about things that none of them understood, and he was telling *them* to focus! And now he was talking about founding something right after World War II ended? How was that possible? Exactly how old was he?

She hated to encourage him in this, but her curiosity got the best of her. "What's the ABC?"

"Oh, it's the organization that inspired all the stories about the Men in Black. They cover up the activities of my Order of magic users, the Temple of the Old Gods, as well as the doings of all the other secret Guilds."

"I *told* you the Men in Black were real!" Even under the current grim circumstances, Mark was unable to resist saying "I told you so" to his big sister. She decided to take the high road and ignore him. Out of the corner of her eye she spied Lars pulling out a small notepad and furiously scribbling notes.

"Yeah, well your sources are probably right about them being untrustworthy. They framed an innocent woman for the last batch of murders that monster carried out to hide its existence," Athena revealed, now fully accepting that everything Becca Greene had told them was true. She wished she'd figured that out sooner instead of letting her pride blind her.

"You mean the creature has killed again recently?" Clark looked extremely horrified by the news.

"You didn't know? It was all over the news a couple of months ago! It got a professor and all his archeology students."

"No, I didn't know. I already told you, I've been *very* preoccupied lately, lost in my own world. Too lost in it, apparently! Dear, oh dear! Things are really starting to get out of hand!"

"Why can't you just kill that thing? Or move it somewhere where it can't hurt anyone?" Dennis wanted to know.

"Both things are impossible. I'll explain it all later," the wizard promised. "Yes, it's probably all for the best if we don't involve the ABC. Even if they were still as honorable as they once were, they'd probably alter all your memories. I've had lots of time to ponder the ethics of that lately and I have to say I no longer agree with such tactics. After all, in the end what are we but collections of memories?" Clark was waxing philosophic again, as he was wont to do. He seemed to have temporarily forgotten all about the dead body they were standing only a few feet away from.

Bev cleared her throat loudly. "Aren't we supposed to be working on getting our stories consistent? Megaliths or not, I'm pretty eager to get the hell out of here before it gets much darker!"

"Yes, yes. You're quite right my dear, quite right! We'll tell them that a bear came out of the woods and dragged him off. But not here. I don't want them poking around this deeply into these woods. Our story will be that it happened right on the edge of the forest at the old Deercrest Apartments, near the playground. Have you all got that?" They all nodded.

"We'll just pretend that I was with you at the time. I own the Deercrest Apartments and some of the land nearby. We'll tell them that I'm a member of the JSPS, so I granted permission to investigate on my property and was participating myself."

He paused for a moment to catch his breath. "We only went a few feet into the woods near the playground when the bear came out of nowhere and pulled Tyler away. We chased after it hollering and screaming and eventually scared it off, but it was too late. If they're a little skeptical, I have ways of *persuading* them if need be, but I hope it doesn't come to that. I'm trying to lead a more ethical lifestyle these days. I hate messing around in people's minds unnecessarily."

"I guess it's gonna have to do," Athena said wearily. Part of her was scared that despite Clark's assurances, they were still in danger.

All she wanted was to go home and try to begin to process the crazy events of the past hour and her grief over Tyler's sad fate. Instead, it looked as though she was going to spend most of the rest of the day in a hospital and lying to the police. It killed her a little inside to know that Tyler's killer was still out there right now and could kill again. She chafed at the injustice of it all.

What she *wanted* to do was tell the authorities the truth, to bring back an army to exterminate that thing so it could never hurt anyone ever again, but for whatever reason, Clark seemed to believe that possibility was completely off the table. He was probably right, considering what had happened to Becca Greene.

She had to trust that he knew what he was doing. It was just hard for her to put all her trust in someone who was so flighty and weird, but what choice did she really have? It was especially hard to trust him because Clark seemed to have *experience* covering things up like this. He'd already admitted to co-founding the Men in Black or the ANC or whatever they called themselves, not to mention altering people's memories and minds. He could probably do it as effortlessly as he had changed Tyler's wounds. On top of all that, it was strange to suddenly discover that he knew more about her family history than she did and owned some of the nearby land!

She couldn't help but wonder what other secrets he was keeping from her.

Chapter Fourteen:
In the Garden of Athena

As Athena had feared, a good portion of that evening had been spent exactly as she had anticipated: sitting around in an emergency room and answering a plethora of pointed, uncomfortable questions from the police, once they'd finally arrived.

In the end, the police seemed to have accepted their version of events. They were all allowed to leave. Fortunately, Mark had known the name of one of Tyler's brothers and what town he lived in. The police had promised to contact him and let the family know what had happened to Tyler. Athena was grateful she was off the hook when it came to that responsibility. She couldn't begin to figure out how to tell them the awful news. She also couldn't help but feel like they'd believe she was responsible for his death. She wouldn't blame them if they did. Despite all of Dennis' attempts to convince her otherwise, she believed it herself.

This entire expedition had been her idea! She'd received so many warnings from both the living *and* the dead - and had chosen to blithely ignore them all. For what? To prove that one thing that most sane and rational people think of as impossible - a cryptid - was in fact something they'd just as easily dismiss as fantasy - a ghost? She knew damn well that any "proof" they would have gathered would never convince them. She was trying to prove it to *herself*. To satisfy her own vanity over how clever she was - the one woman in the world smart enough to finally solve the mystery of the Jersey Devil.

And now a man, a good man she'd known for almost a decade, one of her most reliable teammates, was dead.

His killer was still free. Free to kill. And it likely would kill again if anyone got too close to where it roamed.

And there wasn't a damned thing they could do about it.

No, she couldn't face Tyler's family. Not tonight. She couldn't look them in the eyes and lie to them. If anyone deserved the truth, it was them. But how could she convince them of the truth without being able to show them what had killed Tyler?

In all the excitement, nobody had bothered to take a picture of the thing or film it. Even when they'd had it trapped behind Clark's magical wall, they hadn't thought to take a picture. They'd just wanted to get away from it, to forget that anything so horrible, so fundamentally twisted and wrong was real. The last thing they wanted was a reminder of its existence.

Maybe it wouldn't have been so bad to have their memories altered like Clark had mentioned. Perhaps it would've been a blessing? Otherwise, she feared these terrible memories would continue to haunt her forever.

Clark had offered to take them all out to dinner as soon as the police finally told them they were all free to go. Even though she hadn't eaten in many hours, Athena had no appetite. She'd just seen a human being eaten alive. Twice! Not only Tyler, but that other guy, Dustin, whose death she'd seen in her mind. Not to mention all the murders she'd psychically witnessed at the camp. The whole ordeal was enough to completely destroy her appetite for some time. Who knew that seeing lots of murders was the best diet plan out there?

Yet despite her lack of appetite, here she was, along with everyone but Kim and Beverly (who had been all too eager to go home), sitting in a restaurant with Clark Kismet. She wasn't there for the food, she was there for the explanations Clark had promised. She still didn't have the first clue as to what The Boy actually was, why he was there, or why he couldn't be killed or removed. Even if she hadn't been such a fatally curious person, she thought she'd still want to have some idea as to what had just happened to her.

The restaurant was actually called "The Athenian Garden." It seemed that even under the grim circumstances, Clark hadn't lost his strange sense of humor. But why should he be upset? He hadn't known Tyler, hadn't seen him eaten by a fucking monster. Clark claimed the restaurant's name was just a coincidence.

"But then again, there really is no such thing as a coincidence - and yet there is. We prefer to call them synchronicities," Clark had said in his typically cryptic way.

The Athenian Garden was a Greek restaurant in Galloway Township that he apparently frequented, having picked up a taste for authentic Greek cuisine after spending many years living on a Greek island called Elysium. Or so he claimed. The owners seemed to know him and were happy to see him.

The six of them were seated at a pair of large wooden tables which had been pushed together. Athena had studied the menu with complete disinterest. It was so strange to be in this place, full of people happily chatting away when just a handful of hours earlier she'd been trapped in a scene from a horror movie. When the waitress appeared she ordered nothing but a salad, and only because Dennis insisted that she had to eat something.

As the waitress left the table with their orders, Athena looked at Clark, who was seated directly across from her, expectantly. "Okay, you promised us answers. So start spilling the beans. What was that thing?"

Lars produced his digital recorder and set it on the table. A little red light burning on its surface indicated it was on.

Clark raised an eyebrow. "You can't record this conversation," he said flatly. All the joviality that was usually in his voice was gone; she'd rarely heard him sound so deadly serious.

"I'm a reporter, this is what I do!" Lars' protest sounded a little petulant to Athena's ears. On some level he must've understood that the argument was already over before it had begun. This was Clark's world now and they were all just living in it.

"Not today, not now. This information cannot leave this table."

The journalist reluctantly switched off his device and removed it from the table, bitterly mumbling something under his breath all the while. Athena could've sworn he was pouting.

Clark nibbled an appetizer for a moment, then began speaking. "As some of you already know, for many years I was a part of a secretive group of mages that call themselves The Ancient Order of the Temple of the Old Gods. Well, technically I'm still a part of them. Once you join you're never *really* out. You're just removed from what they'd call 'active duty,' yet even in retirement they like to find little things for us to do for them. The group tries to maintain a monopoly on the use of the most powerful kinds of magic. I served the group in many capacities over the decades, but one of my jobs was Inquisitor."

"Nobody expects the Spanish Inquisition!" Mark quipped, quoting a notorious line from a classic Monty Python skit.

Athena was surprised he could joke around at a time like this, she knew he was really upset by Tyler's passing. She supposed everyone dealt with grief in their own strange way. She was fortunate enough not to have lost many people that were close to her in her life. Both her parents were still alive and in good health. There had been the odd great aunt or uncle that she barely knew here or there, but the biggest personal tragedy she'd suffered had been the loss of her grandfather on her mother's side and her grandmother on her father's side, both of which had passed when she was in her teens. They'd been old and sick for some time; that constant reminder of their mortality had softened the blow somewhat. This was the first time she'd seen someone relatively young and healthy, whom she'd known well, unexpectedly cut down in the prime of his life. Even though she knew for a fact that death wasn't the end, she still had no idea how to handle it all.

Clark chuckled at the reference. "The Spanish Inquisition. Yes, unfortunately we were behind that, back when we played a more active part in your world.

Our modern Office of the Inquisition is related to the Catholic Church's version. Fortunately, we're a tad more benevolent these days. We monitor and try to recruit those who happen upon the secrets of High Magic or have potentially dangerous psychic abilities."

Athena perked up at that last sentence, regaining some of her old fighting spirit. "Is that what you were trying to do with me all those years ago?"

Clark looked down at the food in front of him, unwilling to meet her gaze.

"We've been watching your family for quite some time. You and Mark both have ancestors who were part of the Temple. I even knew one of them, long ago." The wizard looked wistful as he said it.

Mark was floored. "I do too? But I'm her half brother. All the psychics are on her mom's side of the family."

"No, not all of them. One of the most powerful witches I've ever known was actually on your father's side. She was a great, great, great aunt of his. I may be off by a great or two. She died without producing any children, and there ended your family's relationship to the Temple. Despite producing some promising psychics, Athena's mother's side of the family has never been a part of the Temple."

"So you were secretly spying on me? For how long?" Athena demanded.

"I wasn't! I swear! When I decided to retire to the shore, I chose this area because I liked it, and also because they like to have a few mages around here to keep an eye on The Scar."

Miranda put down her drink. "The Scar? Is that what that monster is called?"

Clark laughed. "No, The Scar is something completely different. It's, well, a scar left upon the fabric of reality from an epic battle that happened here ages ago. Even before the Native Americans settled here. There was a war between magic users in your prehistory which very nearly destroyed this world. We call it the Great Magic War. That's why we used to employ such draconian measures to control who had access to magical knowledge - to prevent something like that from ever happening again. This whole area was once the site of one of the biggest battles of that war. This entire region still bears the scars from the terrible energies unleashed on that day. Like an old wound that will never completely heal, sometimes it opens up again and things pass through it. Things from other worlds."

"So *that's* what that thing is that we saw today!" Dennis ventured.

"No! Stop trying to figure it out for yourselves and just let me tell the story!" Clark was starting to lose his patience. Athena had rarely seen him lose his often infuriating cool like that. Clark appeared to be startled by his outburst too.

"I'm sorry, Dennis. I didn't mean to snap at you like that. I suppose we're all feeling a little under the weather after what we've been through today."

"It's no problem, man. Forget about it."

"Thank you for your understanding. As I was saying, in my retirement I was expected to help keep watch over The Scar. There's a Guardian of The Scar whose full time job is to protect people from whatever may come through when it opens up. They like to have a number of 'reservists' like myself on hand nearby in case they need some help. Every so often some of the things that come through The Scar are considerably *worse* than what you saw today. Athena and Mark's ancestor had been the Guardian of The Scar, back in the middle of the 19th century."

"And you knew her? Personally?" Athena asked skeptically.

"Yes, she was a good friend. That's when I first became familiar with this area. You remind me of her in many ways, Athena." There was that wistful look of his again.

"This was in the 19th century? The 1800's? Jesus Christ, Clark, how old *are* you?"

"Too old. Too old to protect innocent people from my failures." In that moment, as he said it she thought she could actually see the weight of all those years in his strange gray eyes. She couldn't help but feel a little sorry for him.

The odd mood that had settled over the table was unexpectedly interrupted, as sometimes happens, by the arrival of the irritatingly perky waitress with their food. Everyone tried to act normal until she was gone.

Shortly afterwards, as the others began digging into their food, Clark looked at everyone gathered around the table.

"Okay, I'm going to start over with my story. Everyone just enjoy your food and hold all your questions until the end. I'm afraid I may get too sidetracked otherwise."

Then he opened his mouth and spoke.

Chapter Fifteen: Clark's Story

It all began shortly after I had retired from the Temple of the Old Gods. This would've been around 1974, or was it '75? Anyhow, the precise date isn't important. As I've already mentioned, while I was down here I was expected to help out with any issues with The Scar which might arise, but aside from that, I was free to do whatever I fancied. I decided to open up my own occult shop as a way of keeping me in contact with the rest of the human race, since otherwise I can too easily get lost in my own world. It's also a great way to get some products out there which have truly effective spells cast on them that can help protect people from negative spirits and influences.

I was still in the process of getting my store all set up and organized when out of the blue, I received a phone call.

"Hello?"

"Clark! It's you!"

I recognized the voice on the other end straight away as an old colleague of mine, a wizard named Barnabas Crowe. We all called him Barney. Even before that name was applied to a silly purple dinosaur, it was considerably less threatening than "Barnabas Crowe" sounds. Good old Barney was a gentle soul, so that definitely suited him better. We'd worked together a few times many years ago as Inquisitors. Like myself, he was in retirement now and on "reserve Scar duty."

"You were expecting someone else?"

He laughed, "Hardly! I was just testing out the phone number that was given to me. I'm trying to do everything the 'normal' way these days. It's difficult to avoid the temptation of using a sphere to contact you."

The "sphere" is an enchanted polished stone we mages use to communicate with each other. Good old Barney had spent most of his life around other magic users, so mundane things like phones still held a strange novelty for him. But I digress.

"Is something up with The Scar already? Are we needed?"

"No, no. Nothing so dire. It's probably nothing. I'm likely a fool for bothering you with this."

"Nonsense!" said I, "What are friends for?"

"Well, I suppose I should just get right to the point. You see, I recently discovered that I had a copy of the *Vida Inmortal* in my possession. Must've forgotten to return it to the Inquisition's Library and just packed it up with all my other things. It's taken me years to unpack all my books, you know how I am. Apparently nobody else has noticed it's missing yet."

I couldn't believe what I was hearing! "You don't mean *La Vida Inmortal,* written by the mad Spaniard Ignacio Vilagra in 1459, the accursed volume containing the darkest secrets he learned at the feet of Mortus Locke himself, do you?"

"Is there any other?"

"But that's one of the most dangerous books on necromancy ever written! Thank goodness nobody has noticed it's gone! Look, if you need me to discreetly slip it onto a bookshelf the next time I'm in Elysium it's no problem whatsoever. I was planning on making a trip back there soon."

"Would that it were so simple, my friend! Would that it were so easy." He sounded so distressed, so lost. Alarm bells were going off in my head.

The book in question contained spells for prolonging one's life by draining the life force from others, and even spells that could raise the dead! Such things are typically forbidden by ancient international accords, yet Inquisitors sometimes need to interrogate the recently dead, and so we alone are allowed access to such terrible secrets. In the wrong hands such a powerful volume could cause a great deal of misery.

"What are you getting at? Don't tell me you've lost it!"

"Worse than that. I think it may've been stolen." My heart sank at the news. He couldn't hide the shame in his voice, which tempered my instinct to yell at him for being so careless.

"Do you have any idea who the culprit might be?"

"I'm almost certain it's my apprentice."

"You've taken on another apprentice?" It wasn't unheard of for someone in retirement to take on a new apprentice, but it was a trifle unusual. But then again, Barney was an unusual fellow, which was probably why we'd always gotten along so well.

Barney went on to explain that he'd recently taken on a woman by the name of Pamela as his apprentice. The woman had tracked him down. She seemed to know a great deal about the Temple of the Old Gods, which was itself quite atypical. She said she'd joined various occult groups in the past year or so, only to conclude that most of them were frauds or simply couldn't help her with what she sought. In her quest for an authentic magical experience, she'd somehow learned about the Temple and discovered that Barney had been a member.

Barney, as I said earlier, was nothing if not a kind-hearted fellow. This was the other reason why I liked him so much. He was really too nice to have ever been a very good Inquisitor; it requires a bit of ice in the veins at times. His superiors were likely relieved when he retired. Oh my! I digress again!

Anyhow, when this Pam woman confessed that the reason why she had made herself so obsessed with the occult was because she had recently lost her only child, a boy named Doug, in a tragic accident and was desperate to contact his spirit, Barney felt sorry for her. He resolved to help her. The woman had already acquired some potentially dangerous magical knowledge, the sort of stuff that would've gotten her burned at the stake in the old days. She showed no signs of abandoning her quest and would likely go on to learn ever more dire secrets in time. Old Barney felt that the best way to keep her from ending up on the radar of a less benevolent Inquisitor was to bring her into the fold - to redirect her obsession to something more positive.

So she became his apprentice. He promised that in time, they might try to seek out the spirit of her lost son, but there were no guarantees they'd be able to reach him. In the meantime, he wanted her to establish a firm foundation in the fundamentals of spell casting. And so they worked together, slowly and deliberately making her into a witch.

She had been there in the room that day when he was trying to organize his personal library and discovered a copy of *La Vida Inmortal* amongst his things. Barney, ever eager to share his knowledge, had made the awful mistake of telling Pam what the book was capable of. He actually told a grief-stricken woman that he had a book which could raise the dead!

Now at this point she had been his apprentice and constant companion for some months and he had begun to trust her like she was family. At the time, he thought nothing of it. But once he realized the book was missing and he was unable to reach her, it became quite clear what was going on.

He was growing more frantic as he explained his dilemma. "I drove out to her house in Vorhees, but she wasn't there. I'm afraid she may have gone out to the summer camp where her son passed away. He drowned in the lake there two years ago and they never found the body. I fear she may try to raise the body and reanimate it."

I tried to calm him, despite my own concerns. "Surely a novice couldn't successfully accomplish such a thing! Who knows how much of the body may be left after all this time? I wouldn't worry so much."

"She's quite talented. You don't understand the power of that book, my friend. If she makes contact with certain dark spirits which can be easily summoned using it, they can guide her through the process. It's almost like being possessed by them. They're hungry for the sacrifices needed to perform such a task."

The mention of sacrifices got my attention. "You don't think she's capable of murder, do you?"

"I think that woman is capable of *anything* if it means she'll see her son again. I never thought she'd steal from me either, yet she did! I'm afraid I've made a terrible mistake trusting her as I did. I'm just a foolish and lonely old man, desperate for a bit of companionship, and now people may die because of it!" I could tell he was trying not to cry.

"I need your help, Clark. I need to find her and I need to handle this quietly. You know what the Order would do to me if they ever found out about this. I know you've got strong connections within the ABC, you're friends with the Director. We may need them to help cover all this up without letting the Temple know. If we can't reach her before, before she..." His voice trailed off and he was openly sobbing now.

"There, there. Pull yourself together, man! I'll be more than happy to do whatever I can to help you and prevent a tragedy. Now let's think about this logically, shall we? I believe that the kind of spell you fear she's trying to cast would require a great many sacrifices. She's just one woman. It's quite likely that we can get to her before she can collect enough blood to cast the spell if we don't dawdle. You already know where she's ultimately headed, so that's something."

"I'm afraid she may be able to find everything she needs at that camp," he sniffled. "She sued the pants off of them after her son died. They had to shut the place down. She poured all her money from the lawsuit into her occult obsession, into finding a real mage that could help her. That should've been my first red flag. Anyhow, someone bought the property recently and is looking to remodel and reopen it. She complained about it all the time. She's convinced that the lake is too deep to be safe to let children swim in it. She wanted to stop them from opening it back up. There are probably workmen out there right now, and I fear they may be in terrible danger. With the dark spirits she can reach with the book guiding her, she may be able to overpower them. She may even be able to overpower *me*."

I couldn't believe it. "Do you really think so?"

"Yes! These are very powerful demons, Clark, very strong. That's why I need your help too; if they've taken control of her, I won't be able to handle her on my own."

We quickly made arrangements to get together. We met at my shop and Barney teleported us to the camp, as he already knew its location and time was of the essence. We materialized in a secluded circle of trees a few hundred feet away from the cabins.

As soon as we arrived I knew something was wrong. The whole place just kind of felt off.

I couldn't help but remark upon it. "Do you feel it?"

"Yes. It's as if the soul is being sucked right out of the land itself."

"What do you think it means?"

"I'm not completely sure, but I have a few unpleasant ideas– hello!" He jumped back as an upside down corpse swung towards him. Somehow, it was fastened to one of the big branches of the tree before us.

"Too late! We're too late! Curse me!" he cried out.

"We're certainly too late to help this poor fellow, but we might still be able to save some other lives. We mustn't lose hope!" My words were encouraging, yet I was filled with fresh misgivings as I studied the body still swaying ghoulishly back and forth. There were arcane symbols carved into his forehead which I recognized as M'bogish, the ancient language of the sorcerers. He'd also been disemboweled and his wrists had been slashed to aid in draining his blood. It was a horrific tableau.

"This is a ritualistic murder. You've read *La Vida Inmortal,* do you know the meaning behind these wounds?" I asked.

"It's exactly as I feared. If she collects enough blood from enough victims, the demons will grant her the power to bind a spirit to her son's body. Unless his ghost is still hanging around here, she could end up putting *anything* into that body. Based on how this place feels, I think I already know what she's using."

"A nature elemental!" I exclaimed as the truth dawned on me. "Why would she do such an idiotic thing?"

"Perhaps she plans to channel the regenerative power of the elemental to heal her son's body?" he speculated.

It sounded feasible, but there were bound to be dire complications. If she wasn't such a novice, she would've known that. It was the kind of thing that only an amateur or a maniac would even attempt to do, and unfortunately Pamela was both.

"How many victims would she need to complete the ritual?"

"Thirteen if I recall correctly. Perhaps she won't be able to find enough all the way out here?" he said hopefully.

I shook my head sadly. "The binding process must've already started, or else this place wouldn't feel so off. We must hurry before she completes the ritual. A nature spirit trapped in a human body - it could get quite nasty!"

As if on cue, the skies above us darkened. I looked up to see the clouds rushing by at a fantastic speed, producing a great gust of wind. A few bolts of lightning arced through the sky somewhere nearby, followed by an ear-splitting peal of thunder which shook the whole forest.

"This way!" Barney shouted to be heard over the rushing wind as he ran off in the direction of the lightning.

Chapter Sixteen: A Monster is Born

We rushed through the woods in the general direction of the occasional flash of lightning splitting the sky. It felt as if all of nature was fighting against us. It was nearly summer, yet there was a deadly chill to the gale force winds which battered us.

Along the way, we made another terrible discovery. I nearly tripped headlong over an outstretched arm belonging to another victim. This one was splayed out on the ground, another familiar symbol cut into her forehead, blood from that wound dripping down her face. Again, the wrists were cut open and the entrails pulled out. Later on we'd discover that there was a mix of local contractors and young people who had been hired to work as counselors at the camp that day. By some cruel twist of fate, there were exactly thirteen of them. I couldn't pause long to pay my respects to the unfortunate young woman, we had a job to do.

As we drew closer to the lakeshore, the storm died down and a horrible sight met our eyes. Standing on a pier that jutted out into the dark waters stood a surprisingly small wisp of a woman. Her long, brown hair was flying around her head and she gripped a thick, old book in her hands. A large glass mason jar lay at her feet. We both watched with a mix of disgust and disbelief as we saw what was hovering over the water and slowly moving towards her.

The mud at the bottom of the lake must've preserved the body to some extent, but even so I could tell that much of him had decomposed. The body was frantically trying to heal itself, flesh moving to repair the damage, but as soon as it was repaired it started to rot again. Even the powers of an elemental could only hold back the decay for so long.

On the pier, the woman dropped the book and held out her arms to embrace the sick parody of life that was now mere inches away from her.

"No! Pam! Get away from it! That's not your son!" Barney bellowed the words louder than I'd ever heard the normally soft spoken man speak before.

Other than a brief look over her shoulder at us, she didn't react. She was too enraptured by the opportunity to reunite with her son. The monster now landed right in front of her, and before our horrified eyes, bit into her neck. Her blood jetted out like a geyser and she slumped lifelessly to the boards. I'd swear she was still wearing a big smile on her face.

"No!" Barney screamed from somewhere beside me.

The thing had murdered its own mother. It was obvious that there was very little, if anything, left of Dougie inside it. Of course the child's soul would've left the body long ago, but if his brain had been preserved well enough, the elemental spirit which now animated his body would be able to access the boy's memories and make some sort of sense out of its situation. The fact that it didn't recognize Pamela or have any emotional attachment to her showed how far gone the brain was. Or perhaps it *did* understand what had happened and was just that angry with her? It's difficult to say for certain. Most nature elementals have very rudimentary, animalistic minds to begin with.

All that was for certain was that there was a very dangerous new kind of creature now before us. It was something which had no business existing - an abomination, a crime against nature - yet there it was. At first the thing didn't seem to see us as it continued to feed on Pam's body in a disgusting, ravenous frenzy. As I watched the repulsive spectacle, I theorized that just enough of Doug's brain was left that it was driven by the most basic of needs: the instinct to feed. Later on, when I'd had a bit of time to use magic to probe the creature, I discovered that there was more to it than that. It needed to feed to fuel its attempts to heal itself. When it didn't have enough to eat, its body started consuming itself, increasing the tremendous pain that it always bore. But again, I'm getting ahead of myself.

The creature *did* know we were there, and when it got tired of picking away at Pam, it started moving towards us, slowly but deliberately.

Barney was still so distraught, so inconsolable that he didn't even see it edging closer, preparing to lunge at us.

"I'm so sorry that this has happened to you." I was trying to address the elemental spirit within. "If there's any way to undo this, I will, I swear!"

If, in its present form it could even comprehend what I was saying, the thing was obviously unimpressed by my words. It sneered at me and leapt towards us.

I zapped it with a bolt of lightning, sending it shooting backwards into the dirt. Before it could recover, I enclosed it in an energy barrier like the one you saw me create in the woods. Once it was penned in, Barney and I combined our powers to magically "scan" it.

"It's hopeless isn't it?" Barney looked over at me sadly as we completed our probe of the monster.

"I'm afraid so. The blood magic of this spell is too powerful for anyone to reverse. The immortal spirit of this chunk of land is now forever tied to this wreckage of a physical form. It's a formidable nature spirit, but it isn't quite powerful enough to ever make this into a properly functioning, normal body."

Barney shivered. "Eternally stuck between life and death. What a terrible fate!"

"And it's in constant pain. Its mind is so confused, confined to that barely working human brain. It has little understanding of what it is or how this came to be. All it knows is pain and hunger, a terrible hunger which will never be satiated."

"Well, what are we going to do with it? We can't undo the spell, and we can't kill it, nor can we move it! A part of it will always be tied to this forest, drawing power from it. If we try to remove it from the forest it could destroy the whole place!"

I nodded grimly. "It's worse than that. Since we can't communicate with it, we don't know how big of an area this spirit is tied to. It could be just a few acres of woods, or the whole forest, or a good chunk of this state and some of the neighboring ones!

It was a real pickle of a problem. I asked Barney to find a nearby place where we could lock the thing up. He found a fairly secure basement in the largest building of the camp, where the business office had once been. We locked him up down there and took turns guarding him to make sure he didn't bust out.

Barney took the first shift while I contacted my friends in the ABC to do something about covering up the murders. I made certain that Barney's name and all mention of *La Vida Inmortal* would be excised from the

ABC's reports. I collected the accursed tome from where Pam had dropped it so that I could safely return it to where it belonged later on. The ABC did their usual thing, discouraging people from taking too much of an interest in the details of the tragedy, starting with the local authorities and the press. Everything was blamed on some unknown killer. Pam's involvement was hidden completely. The ABC purchased a good portion of the forest, including the camp, to ensure it would never open again.

We eventually concocted a plan to construct a series of megalithic structures around an area of a few square miles. It took a few weeks for the stones to be delivered from the quarry, with Barney and I maintaining watch over the monster the entire time. The stones, once enchanted by us, created a permanent barrier that would keep him in, and at the same time put out waves of negative energy that would discourage people and even some of the more clever kinds of animals from venturing beyond them. I didn't want to completely prevent animals from being able to enter its territory; I wanted it to be able to feed regularly on whatever wildlife it could catch, since feeding was the only thing that ever eased its pain.

I felt sorry for it, and I suppose I still do a little, despite all that it's done. The spirit that's trapped inside that body never asked for any of this. In a way, it's as much of a victim as all the people that have died. It's acting out of pure animal instinct rather than true malice. I also can't help but wonder how much of the memories of young Douglas still exist inside it? Is there a part of it that believes it's an eleven year old boy? So I resolved to do what little I could do to reduce its suffering. I made sure animals could wander inside so he could eat them. That's why there's no big fence or a wall around the place to prevent anyone from entering his domain.

There's an old abandoned farmhouse on the land that we confined him to. I made sure he knew where it was so he'd have a place where he could take shelter. In the winter, I'd deliver blankets, clothes and cans of food to the farmhouse. The creature is just barely smart enough to dress itself and use basic tools like a can opener. I became something of a caretaker for him.

Unfortunately, Barney didn't last much longer to help share my burden. The poor fellow died a year later, his grief over the entire ordeal eventually killed him. He blamed himself for all the deaths, right up until the very end. It's ironic - I went to such great pains to make sure that the Temple of the Old Gods never found out about this episode, I used all my high level connections and called in all my favors to protect him, only for him to pass away not long afterwards! I decided to maintain the secret after his death, though; he didn't have the greatest reputation amongst our people, and I had no wish to see it tarnished any further by this incident.

It worked for a while, our little scheme to keep the monster under wraps and under control. Or rather that's what I believed. This part of the state was far more rural and underdeveloped back in the 1970's. When we first put up the stones, we weren't very concerned about people coming into his territory, it was simply too remote. We didn't think anyone would ever go there.

Unfortunately, in the eighties, some fool built an apartment complex on the edge of the woods, less than a mile away from the beginning of the creature's territory. Curious and bored children who lived in the apartments sometimes went wandering too far into the woods and never came back. The ABC covered it up of course, but they never informed me, and it kept on happening! The third time a child went missing, sometime around the late nineties, word of it finally reached my ears. I felt terrible. I had no idea this had been going on. I offered the owner of the apartments a ridiculous amount of money for the property and promptly closed the place down.

Don't look at me like that! I'm not heartless! I also used my considerable wealth and resources to help relocate all the tenants. Then I just let the place rot. Good riddance to bad rubbish, I say!

I still check in on the creature, right before the start of the winter, around Thanksgiving. The old farmhouse has mostly collapsed and become uninhabitable, so the thing sleeps in an old chicken coop next to the house that's still intact. Dropping off supplies for it has become something of a grim holiday season ritual for me.

Clark ended his tale, and finally picked up the neglected fork sitting next to his equally neglected plate. "That's about all there is to it. Good thing too, I wouldn't want my dinner to get too cold. You may now ask me questions, if you have any, and I'll try to answer them...if you can stomach watching me talk with my mouth full!"

Athena's mouth hung open. "*If* we have any questions?!'"

She had about a million! The only problem was she didn't know where to start.

Chapter Seventeen: Q and A

Before Athena could articulate her first attempt at a question, Mark chimed in.

"Holy shit! That thing is almost like, like your *pet*. Tyler was killed by your fucked up pet!"

Lars shook his head. "No, it's more like he was killed by the real world equivalent of Jason Vorhees! How do you account for the uncanny similarities between all of this and the *Friday the 13th* movies?"

"Ah, I was wondering if any of you would pick up on that. That's down to the doings of the ABC. I believe they would call it a misinformation campaign nowadays. They make sure that enough of the truth penetrates the public consciousness to make the whole thing seem ridiculous. People hear a story about what happened at the camp and dismiss it as an urban legend because it's too similar to the plot of a well known movie, therefore it *can't* be true. It's quite ingenious, really. I believe one of the ABC agents gave the idea to someone out in Hollywood. Pam from Vorhees became Pamela Vorhees. Dougie became Jason. I don't think they ever intended for it to become quite the phenomenon it became in the eighties. I don't believe they ever intended for it to go beyond the first movie, but it was a hit and so that meant plenty of sequels which continued to further distort the truth."

Dennis leaned forward. "I know this is a weird thing to say, but I think Tyler would've felt a little honored to know he was killed by the monster that inspired Jason Vorhees."

Miranda nodded in agreement. "You're right, it is a weird thing to say, but it's also kind of true. He really loved all those old eighties horror movies. And at least he died doing what he loved."

Athena had heard enough. "He died doing what he loved? What's that? Getting eaten alive? I didn't know he was into that! No, no matter what you guys say this is a total shit sandwich and no amount of sugar-coating will change that. There is no silver lining here."

Her words stung everyone at the table, and a silence fell over it again.

Only Clark dared to speak. "Athena, I'm so sorry–"

"Sorry! You sure are sorry! You and those ABC people knew that thing was out there and you never bothered to put up a real wall around it to keep people out, because why? Because you feel sorry for it? What about all the people it's killed? Where's your compassion for them?"

Clark decided not to let her bait him, ignoring the worst of her barbs and responding in a calm tone. "Actually, I found out that the ABC *did* put up a fence after the first child went missing. They even topped it with barbed wires. You know what happened? People just cut holes in it! So they electrified it. Then they found sections that had been knocked down by repeatedly battering it with a wooden baseball bat. People hate nothing more than something designed to keep them out, and they always figure out a way to get around it. So they decided to get rid of the fence altogether; it was attracting too much attention. Kids from the apartments were daring each other to get through it."

Athena shook her head, it all still sounded like nothing but a bunch of lame excuses to her.

Lars raised his butter knife in the air like a kid in the classroom trying to get the teacher to call on them. Clark acknowledged him with a nod.

"Why couldn't you put a spell on those megaliths to keep regular people from getting in?"

"Unfortunately, magical barriers that are strong enough to stop physical objects typically can't exist for very long. Oh, there's examples of ones from antiquity that could do the job, but the secret of how to create such things has been lost for millennia. The megaliths only work on the creature because part of it is an elemental spirit. The barrier binds the spirit, which is itself irrevocably bound to a material body, thus stopping both."

Dennis had a question now. "Earlier you said something about Athena's family being connected to the real Jersey Devil. Could you explain that?"

Athena shot her husband a dirty look. How could he still care about learning the secret of the real Jersey Devil at a time like this? Tyler was *dead*, didn't any of them understand that? Nothing else seemed to matter right now but that. She'd had enough of monsters to last her a lifetime! To hell with the Jersey Devil! To hell with all cryptids!

Clark took a few more forkfuls of his dinner and washed it down with some Dr Pepper before launching into his explanations. Yet as Clark began to speak again, Athena felt her ears prick up and hated herself a little for her own interest. But how could she not be curious? It had to do with her own family history.

"The creature that is most often called 'The Jersey Devil' is what my people would call a 'war wyvern.' Smaller than a great dragon, but larger than your average wyvern. A wyvern, of course, is simply a scaled down, if you'll pardon the pun, version of a dragon."

The wizard smirked at his little joke before continuing. "A dragon with only two legs. Well, to be fair, two big legs and a pair of cute little wee ones like on a Tyrannosaurus rex."

Athena rolled her eyes. "Jesus! We know what a wyvern is, Clark, we're nerds!"

"Speak for yourself!" Mark joked back. For a second, it was almost as if everything was normal again.

"Why does everyone always think I don't know what a wyvern is?" Athena mumbled, then recalled the last time she'd had this thought. It made her think of Tyler, and her heart sank a bit.

"Hmm. Well excuse me for underestimating your knowledge of creatures most people believe to be mythical. Now where was I? Oh yes, as the name implies war wyverns were created by magic users to be used as living weapons in war. In this case, the most terrible war your world has ever seen, The Great Magic War. The same war that created The Scar. All of the war wyverns were killed in the war, except for a handful that escaped by flying through The Scar during the battle that first ripped it open. They still come back here, migrating between this world and the one on the other side. They come mostly to mate and lay their eggs where predators from the other world can't reach them. Sometimes they even nest as far south as Maryland, where they're called 'Snallygasters.' The natives used to see them sometimes, deep in the Pine Barrens. They called the Pine Barrens 'Popuessing,' which means 'Place of the Dragon.'"

"Damn!" Dennis was excited by these revelations. "I'll bet that's what Brenda saw! How did these wyverns get ever mixed up with the Leeds name?"

"That's an unfortunate bit of slander perpetrated against Daniel Leeds. He published an almanac that angered his more conservative neighbors because it contained horoscopes and astrological charts. His neighbors called him a devil, or said he was working with the devil. When his daughter-in-law gave birth to a deformed baby, they took that to be proof that his family was cursed. In time, this idea became mixed up with the occasional sightings of the wyverns. They were said to be the deformed child, all grown up and escaped from the basement where his family had confined him. Or they claimed it was a demon conjured up by Leeds himself, whom some people believed to be a wizard. The wyverns were called 'The Leeds Devil' for a long time before the name morphed into 'The Jersey Devil.'"

Athena couldn't hide how impressed she was with this latest infodump from Clark. "So there *was* a deformed child! Hey, was Leeds a wizard or was that all a lie?"

"Nothing but lies. Oh, Leeds might've made a fine wizard, if we'd been recruiting outsiders. Unfortunately, our ranks were still limited to certain bloodlines back then. And we also didn't take kindly to anyone who was skirting the edges of discovering dangerous magical knowledge like he was. Our witch burning days were thankfully behind us, but my people had a hand in Daniel Leeds' persecution. As usual, the first people to shout 'witch!' were in fact, the only real witches around."

"What does this have to do with our family?" Mark wanted to know. "Are we Leedses?"

"Not so far as I know. No, your connection to the wyverns comes through your ancestor, the witch Marlena Anderson. When the old Guardian of The Scar, the Piney wizard Jerry Munyhon passed away, I sent Marlena to the Jersey Shore to replace him. She had been betrothed to a pirate. Unfortunately, her lover lost his head in a botched boarding party and Marlena never really moved on. In fact, she conjured up her lover's spirit and they carried on their relationship despite the fact that one of them was now a ghost! That's why her branch of the family died out; you can't have a baby with a ghost."

Athena was baffled. "Okay, so we have a weird great, great, great aunt who liked to get freaky with ghosts. I still don't see what this has to do with the Jersey Devil."

"We magic users sometimes take on a familiar - usually a magical beast that we have a particular affinity for which can aid us in spell casting. Marlena took one of the local war wyverns that came out of The Scar as her familiar. Sometimes she was a little careless and was seen by the locals walking along the beach or in the woods in the company of The Leeds Devil and a pirate ghost!"

"The Lady in White!" Athena exclaimed, the story had temporarily stirred her out of her doldrums.

"Huh?" Miranda asked.

"It's one of the legends tied to the Jersey Devil," Athena answered. "A beautiful blonde woman in a long, white dress was sometimes witnessed by people walking with the Jersey Devil, or a headless pirate ghost, or with both of them! It's something I always dismissed as folklore because it was so strange. So you're telling me that The Lady in White was not only real, but is my relative?"

Clark nodded as he polished off his dinner. "Yes, she was a good woman and a better friend. I miss her dearly." The grief was evident on his face for a moment, then passed away like a cloud over the sun.

"So, in a way you could say that the Jersey Devil is *your* family pet. Or rather one of them was. You might have even inherited her affinity for the beasts. She could see into their minds and join with them, controlling them and seeing through their eyes. Perhaps if you'd agree to become my apprentice, we could find out - together?"

Athena was taken aback by the sudden offer. She thought that ship had sailed long ago. She didn't realize the offer was still open. She hadn't really regretted her decision to reject him all those years ago, but she wasn't sure she'd make the same decision now that she was a little older.

After all, she thought, *if I'd been fully trained in how to use my abilities, then maybe Tyler would still be alive.*

She couldn't help but blame Clark for Tyler's death, but she blamed herself just as much. She wasn't really all that mad at him, she realized. He had come when he was called and saved their lives. You couldn't ask for much more than that, could you?

"You'd still take on an apprentice, trust someone like that despite how badly it went when Barney took one on?" she asked disbelievingly.

He smiled. "I'm not Barney. I've had other apprentices. My last one went on to run the entire

Temple of the Old Gods until fairly recently." The fatherly pride was evident in his voice.

"I'm flattered, man I really am. I'm surprised you'd still consider me after how I turned you down last time, and how old I am now. I'm a lot more open to the idea now than I was then, but I'm gonna need a little more time to think about it. Right now, what happened to Tyler is all I can think about. It's hard to think about the future. It's hard to imagine that there even *is* one without him around."

Clark sighed, but not in a disappointed or huffy way. He was sighing in sympathy. "Of course, I understand. Take as long as you need. I want you to know that I really am sorry about your friend, and the fact that we have to lie about what happened to him. I intend to make sure that this creature doesn't kill anyone else. I don't have a plan yet, but I will come up with something. This has to end. Tyler will be its last victim, I promise you."

Something about the way Clark said it made her a believer. He'd never been so serious before.

"When you do come up with something, I want in." she swore.

"Naturally. In the meantime, watch out for the ABC. They might very well figure out that something is up and come calling. If they do, just stick to our story about the bear no matter what, do you all understand?"

Everyone around the table agreed.

The rest of the dinner passed amiably enough. Mark, Miranda and Clark even ordered desserts. Clark paid for the entire meal, reminding the ones who felt obliged to insist on paying for their own food that he was filthy rich. They all promised to stay in touch, and everyone went their separate ways.

On the ride home, Athena wondered what the future would bring, or if there even was a future for the JSPS anymore. She'd seen the ugliest side of the paranormal now, and she wasn't sure she could go on prodding the unknown anymore - sometimes, the unknown bit back.

Chapter Eighteen:
A Funeral and an Interrogation

Safely tucked away behind the cover of the tinted windows on her jet black Cadillac, Agent Method watched the funeral of Tyler Lambert with intense interest. A small crowd was shivering in the light afternoon drizzle, the lucky ones huddled under umbrellas. It was an appropriately dreary day for such a dreary occasion. She was examining it all through the lenses of a pair of high tech binoculars strapped to her head which also happened to be recording everything. The voice of a priest reading passages from the Bible droned on, playing through the speakers of her company car thanks to numerous concealed directional microphones built into the vehicle.

She was particularly interested in one of the couples attending the funeral, Athena and Dennis Arden. According to their website, they were the ringleaders of the ill-advised expedition to find the Jersey Devil which had ultimately cost Tyler his life. She had identified them by cross referencing the footage from the cameras located in the Danger Zone with the ABC database. Athena had come up almost instantly because she already had an open file with the ABC. As someone with unusually powerful psychic abilities she'd been monitored since birth by the retired and semi-legendary wizard Clark Kismet, who seemed to have some sort of a personal interest in Athena's family. All of Kismet's reports on her insisted that she was harmless and "only interested in squandering her considerable talents on chasing ghosts," as he had rather critically phrased it.

It was difficult to piece together what had actually happened last week. By the time the ABC finally got their asses in gear and made it out to the site, the JSPS was already gone. There hadn't been a magic user working that weekend that could teleport a team in as soon as trespassers were detected, so they'd been forced to travel by car. Ideally, there was always supposed to be a magic user on duty for this very reason, but persistent staffing issues prevented it.

The cameras hadn't picked up everything due to a combination of the thick foliage obscuring things and much of the action happening just out of their range. The creature didn't appear in any of the footage, but it was very fast and good at hiding, so that wasn't so unusual. All that the cameras showed was eight individuals entering the Danger Zone, one of them being Tyler Lambert. What was so odd was that the cameras only showed two of the JSPS team ever leaving the Danger Zone. Also, at one point, a ninth individual was captured on video. He was a lanky, pale man dressed only in a towel with a long beard that made it impossible to positively identify him, but Method had her suspicions about who he was.

The cameras had also picked up two flashes of light so bright they nearly damaged them. Such a brilliant burst of light was usually only caused by someone magically teleporting. Teleportation could explain where the mystery man had come from and where everyone else disappeared to. Judging by his previous association with both Athena Arden and the creature,

Agent Method believed that the JSPS had been aided by none other than Clark Kismet himself.

The same mystery man showed up again in the security video from the ER where they took Tyler. Thankfully, he was fully dressed by then. In the footage, he can clearly be seen speaking to the police. Oddly, the only mention of him in their report was that he was the owner of the property where the incident supposedly occurred, and he had granted the JSPS permission to investigate there. There was no mention of the police actually interviewing him. Method wondered if he used sorcery to keep his name out of the report as one of the witnesses, or simply the more down-to-earth magic of bribery?

It was all strange enough to get her to use her influence to examine the body before it was released back to the family. She'd scanned it with one of the ABC's many technological miracles. The device had confirmed that while the wounds were consistent with an animal attack, there were also traces of magical energy lingering on the body which could indicate that the corpse had been magically tampered with.

To her, it was quite obvious that the JSPS had blundered into the Danger Zone, Tyler had been killed by the creature, and Clark Kismet had rescued them and for whatever reason was attempting his own cover up instead of coming to the ABC. This infuriated her because after her partner had narrowly survived being mauled by that *thing* (he was still on the mend), and after finding the pitiful remains of Dustin McCloskey, she'd sworn to make sure there would be no more victims. She was currently compiling an exhaustive report on all the attacks over the years to try and persuade her superiors to put up a high concrete wall around the entire Danger Zone. The more deaths she could cite, the better her chances of success - she hoped. But she couldn't include Tyler's death unless she could prove he was a victim too. Plus, it just bothered her that she *didn't* know what had happened when a large group of civilians trespassed into an area that was partially her responsibility to monitor.

Agent Ember had told her to back off when Method confided her suspicions that Kismet was involved.

"*The* Clark Kismet?" she'd asked, dumbfounded. "Surely you don't mean the wizard who is considered to be, along with Sara Berry, one of the founders of this organization?"

"That's exactly who I mean."

"Stay out of it. His name still carries lots of weight in certain circles. We don't need that kind of trouble."

"But what about the truth?"

"What about it? Truth *isn't* our business."

"But what if these people start talking about what they saw in those woods? One of them is a reporter! That *is* our business!"

"We don't know that they saw anything unusual while they were out there–"

"There was plenty of desperate running around and screaming going on in the video. Those people were obviously reacting to something dramatic - and we know that one of them ended up dead!"

"Yes, in a completely different location outside of the Danger Zone! If anything out of the ordinary did happen and Kismet is handling it, I'm content to leave it all in his hands. Remember, he helped write our standard operating procedures. If he's not involving us, he must have his reasons, and we should respect that. For the last time, forget about it - and that's an order!"

That had been that. Or so Ember thought. But what Ember didn't know couldn't hurt her. And Ember had no idea that Method was spending the leave time she'd requested going to funerals for people she didn't even know.

Method had to admit that Athena looked pretty upset. She wondered if the woman blamed herself for what happened? It was a sentiment she could relate to. Method had come to blame herself for each new death that happened. Nobody else seemed all that concerned with preventing these tragedies so long as they were sure they could cover up the true cause of them. That attitude and the way the organization had treated Becca Greene made Method ashamed of her line of work. Her curiosity had drawn her to this job, but the gee whiz factor was wearing off and now she was the keeper of all kinds of dirty secrets she felt she was better off not knowing. She joined up to protect people from all the unpleasant things out there that are too scary for the public to know about, but lately she felt more like she was doing nothing but covering up the tracks of the deaths caused by her own organization's apathy and bureaucratic incompetence. But what could she do? Once you were in, you were in for life. This wasn't the kind of job one could just walk away from. She knew too much.

Method wished she could tell Athena that she would've had no way of knowing what she was walking into. She hoped her husband and her friends were telling her that, although she knew that there was a world of difference between hearing something like that and actually believing it for yourself.

She envied Athena for one thing, the fact that she could share her troubles with her husband. Method was married to a wonderful man, but she had to keep so much of what she did from him and she hated that. It was difficult having an entire dimension of your life that you couldn't share with the one person that you're supposed to be able to share everything with.

Things were beginning to wind down. The priest was finishing up his eulogy, which was peppered with the usual platitudes about death that had always failed to bring Method any comfort. She was disappointed to note that Kismet wasn't there. She'd been hoping he'd show. She supposed it wouldn't make much sense for him to do so if he was trying to hide his involvement in this entire affair.

As the crowd gathered around the open grave began to break up, she fired up her car. She wanted to be ready to tail the Ardens to whatever their next destination might be. She looked on as Athena and her husband said their goodbyes, then squeezed into Athena's humble little car. Method tore the strange binoculars off her head and began her pursuit. As she followed them at a discreet distance, she wondered if they'd be heading to Tyler's wake or straight home instead. She hoped they'd just go home. If they did, she planned to approach them and interrogate them herself.

She didn't have long to wait before it became obvious that they weren't headed towards the VFW hall where the wake was being held. She wondered if the reason for skipping the occasion was because they found it too difficult to face Tyler's family for that long, or if they were just too emotionally exhausted to deal with it? She recalled the tight, distraught look on Athena's face that had marred her otherwise beautiful features, and wondered again why she was doing this. Why couldn't she just give these poor people their space? Even if they did confess what they knew, would adding one more death to the roster of victims really make much of a difference in persuading her bosses?

She knew that it wouldn't. Appeals to her superiors' compassion were typically fruitless. If she had any hope of convincing them to do more to protect the public from that thing lurking in those woods, she'd have to demonstrate that it was ultimately more cost effective and efficient to prevent the attacks than it was to simply sweep them under the rug.

So why couldn't she just let it go? Why was she openly defying orders? She guessed it was down to her damned curiosity again. She simply couldn't stand not knowing exactly what had happened. How did Kismet know they were in trouble? How much had he told them about the creature? She was called "Agent Method" for a reason - namely because she was so methodical and by the book when it came to her duties. It was driving her nuts that there were so many likely witnesses to the creature's existence, so many potential sources of information leaks, and nobody in her office was doing a damned thing to plug those leaks simply because the great Clark Kismet might be involved! It flew in the face of everything she'd been taught about the right way to do this job. Shouldn't someone at least confirm that Kismet was involved? Shouldn't someone verify that they didn't see the creature and Tyler was really killed by a bear instead of simply ignoring the whole thing because it *appeared* to be taken care of? This kind of unprofessional sloppiness would come back to bite them all in the ass unless someone took care of it.

It was all down to her. Sometimes you have to break the rules to do your job the right way. The others might not care enough about any of it, but she did. She took a great deal of pride in doing things the way she'd been trained to do them, back when the ABC still stood for something. If she could just gather enough evidence she was sure she'd be vindicated and nobody would care about her disobedience.

She guided her car into a position in front of a house a few doors down from the Arden residence and parked. She still had a pretty good view of their house from here thanks to the curvature of the street. She looked on as Athena glided out of her car with practiced ease while her giant of a husband struggled to clamber out. She decided to give them a moment to get settled in the house before bothering them. The truth of the matter was that she was actually feeling a little nervous about talking to them, which was unlike her.

As she sat there in her work vehicle, Method scrutinized her feelings to better understand them. She wondered if her hesitation stemmed from Agent Ember's dire warnings about getting involved with anything to do with Kismet. Or perhaps it was because she usually conducted such interrogations with a partner by her side? Even though Agent Fresh hadn't proved to be of much help in such scenarios in the past, it still felt weird to be doing this by herself. The more she mulled it over, she concluded that it was none of these things. The truth was that she had started to empathize with Athena too much. She saw something of herself in the older woman. She recalled watching the video on their website of the meeting where they'd announced their intentions to begin searching for the Jersey Devil. She'd been impressed by the woman's intelligence (even if her theories were completely wrong) and her enthusiasm for it all. It made for a startling contrast to the crushed shell of a person she'd just been spying on at the funeral. Like herself, Athena was a person whose passion for something had been drained away by the harsh realities of life, or rather, death. A part of her wished she could just leave them alone to grieve their friend in peace instead of harassing them like this, but her devotion to what she saw as her duty was too great to allow that to happen.

She pushed down her humanity and put on her stony face of professional detachment. She had a job to do. She pulled back the sleeve of her black sports jacket to reveal her wrist computer. She activated an app which would put out an ultrasonic signal that tended to make people more pliant and open to suggestion. This program always came in handy during an interrogation. She was protected from its effects by an earbud she was wearing. She slid her trademark sunglasses on, checked her long red hair in the rearview and climbed out of the car.

She went over her cover story in her mind as she walked up to the front door and rang the doorbell. There was a bit of a wait between the bell and the sounds of someone fiddling with the handle on the other side. So much time, in fact, that she almost turned around and walked back to her car. When the door did open, she was greeted by a bleary-eyed Dennis. The redness around his eyes revealed that the big man had recently been crying.

"I'm sorry, miss, but now really isn't a good time." He muttered the words in such a low tone that it took her a moment to unscramble it.

"Mr. Arden, I'm with the American Bear Commission. I'd just like to ask you a few questions about the recent tragedy so we can help prevent any further incidents. I promise I'll make it brief." She flashed her shiny silver ABC badge and put on her most inviting smile.

She could virtually see the ultrasonic waves taking effect on Dennis as his expression softened. "The American Bear Commission?" he asked dazedly.

"Yes, we're a minor federal agency which monitors the effects of taking various species of bears off the endangered species list in recent years. We advise state game commissions on crafting hunting policies." She was particularly proud of this lie. She thought most people might fall for it, even if their brains weren't being bombarded with inaudible sounds that made them more gullible.

"Hon, who is it?" Athena's voice inquired from somewhere inside.

"Some lady who says she's with something called the American Bear Commission," he replied in his increasingly drunken-sounding voice. Method wondered if she had the setting on her suggestibility app turned up too high. Then she recalled that people who were in the throes of certain emotions were more susceptible to the ultrasonic waves. Grief was one such emotion.

"Come on in," he slurred.

"Why, thank you Mr. Arden." She smiled at him again as she pushed her way past him and into the house, batting her eyelashes, forgetting that he couldn't see them through her dark sunglasses. She wasn't above a little flirting if it got her what she wanted.

"Call me Dennis." He grinned back.

"The American whatsit? Wait! Holy shit! ABC! Don't let her in, she's one of the MIB!" Athena shouted from another room, then she emerged from the hallway and saw the tall, pretty redhead dressed all in black standing in her living room and looking around appraisingly.

"Oh, fuck," she muttered.

"Hello, Mrs. Arden. I'm sorry to disturb you at such a sensitive time. I just have a few questions for you and your husband, it won't take long." She hoped that now that they were only a few feet away from each other that the high frequency waves would soon calm down Athena, who appeared to have already been warned about the ABC, no doubt by Kismet.

"I like the decor. I see you're big *Star Wars* fans. I am too. I love science fiction." She wasn't lying this time, although *The X-Files* was really more of her jam. It was always far more fun to watch these kinds of stories than to actually live them.

"Have a seat. Can I get you something to drink?" Dennis asked Method.

Athena shot him an acid look for his misplaced hospitality. She felt like he'd just invited a vampire into the house.

"Don't mind if I do. I'll take a glass of water." Method sank into a recliner.

Athena sat down on the couch opposite the intruder. As if sensing her distress, Chairman Meow leapt into her lap to comfort her. Athena stroked her furry friend and narrowed her eyes at the ABC agent.

"Is bottled water okay? Believe me, you don't want to drink the tap water in Barnegat!" Dennis' voice came from the kitchen.

"That's perfect, Dennis, thank you."

"Oh, I didn't realize that you were on a first name basis with my husband, miss...hmm...that's funny! I don't recall catching your name?"

"That's because I didn't give it. It's alright, you don't really need to know it." Behind her icy grin, Method was starting to panic. Surely Athena should be feeling the effects of the sound waves by now?

"I like to know who I'm talking to in my own home. I guess I'm kind of old fashioned like that." Athena smiled back with pursed lips.

"You can call me Agent Dougherty, if it will help put your mind at ease." Method liked to use "Jane Dougherty" as an alias when the situation required it. It was her idea of a joke since it sounded so much like "Jane Doe."

"Sure. Whatever," Athena said skeptically.

Dennis reappeared and handed an opened bottle of water from Acme to Method.

"Thanks, Dennis," she purred at him as he took a seat beside Athena on the couch.

She took a long swig of water, hoping that it would buy her some extra time for Athena to fall under the spell her wrist computer was trying to weave.

"Ah. That really hit the spot!" she announced after nearly draining half the bottle.

"Geez, your future must be really bright," Athena suddenly said. Dennis immediately got the reference and snickered.

"Pardon?" Method was genuinely caught off guard by the seemingly nonsensical remark.

"Your future's so bright you've gotta wear shades. It's an old song from the eighties. What's up with the Ray-Bans?"

"They're prescription. I have a high sensitivity to light."

"Uh huh. Sure."

Method had to fight down her rising panic. Athena seemed impervious to her powers of suggestion. She supposed psychics had a higher resistance to the device.

"So you said you had some questions for us?" Dennis reminded her.

Athena gently nudged him in the ribs with her elbow.

"What?" he asked in confusion. She just shook her head at him.

"Yes, I do. How well do you know Clark Kismet, the owner of the property where the incident allegedly occurred?"

"Clark? Oh he's great! We go all the way back to '94!" Dennis answered with a childlike glee. Athena really jammed her elbow into him full force this time.

"Owww! What was that for?"

"Shut up! What's wrong with you?" she whispered. Before he could respond, she turned to face Agent Method and plastered a phony smile on her face.

"My mother used to own a small New Age store in town years ago and she used to buy her so-called magic crystals from Clark. He had a crush on her and they went out on a date once. It didn't go anywhere, but he remains a friend of the family," she answered hurriedly. "But I'm sure you knew that already."

"Hardly. Tell me, according to the police reports, the bear suddenly came out of the bushes and hauled your friend Tyler away. That's pretty unusual behavior for a bear that's confronted by a large group of people. Did you perhaps notice a cub around which the animal might've been trying to protect?"

"I think Tyler had some beef jerky in his backpack, it probably smelled it and that's what the bear was really after," Athena dutifully recited.

"Oh, it wasn't a bear! It was–"

"Dennis!" Athena practically screeched. "Shouldn't you go let the dog out?"

Dennis blinked at her in bewilderment, "Which one?"

"Mr. President. She hasn't been out in hours and I'm not cleaning up her mess if she has another accident."

"Oh, sure, okay." He stood up and began calling out "Mr. President! Where are you? C'mon girl!"

Method frowned. The power of suggestion that her wrist computer had over Dennis was a two way street, apparently. A moment later, a chubby old beagle came waddling out of nowhere and stood obediently at his feet.

"C'mon girl, let's go." Dennis led the old hound away, her tail wagging merrily, and Method heard a sliding glass door open and shut in a nearby part of the house.

Athena glared at Method. "I think it's best if you leave now. We just buried a good friend today and we're not in the mood for getting the third degree."

"Mrs. Arden, I'm just hoping to prevent another terrible tragedy. The authorities tell me that the animal responsible for your friend's death is still at large. These creatures can be horribly dangerous once they develop a taste for human meat. Any information you may have on the matter could help us better understand what happened and possibly save another life–"

"You know *exactly* what happened and you and your friends don't plan on doing a damned thing about it, do you? I don't know what kind of a Jedi mind trick you pulled on my husband, but it won't work on me, sister. Now get the hell out of my house already!"

"Mrs. Arden, *Athena,* please–"

Athena shot off of the couch, making Chairman Meow jump away. "I said *get out.*"

Method felt a terrible pressure in her forehead. She wanted to tell Athena that she was her friend, that she was different from all the other ABC agents, but at that moment, she was no longer so sure that was really true. She actually found herself mumbling an apology as she hurried to the front door.

She heard the door slam behind her and Mr. President barking in response to the loud sound from the backyard. Her head was really pounding! As she walked back to her car, she felt something running out of her nose and down onto her top lip. She touched her face and was alarmed to see that she had a nose bleed.

"Jesus!" she hissed as she wiped away the blood. Apparently Athena Arden was a far more powerful psychic than Clark Kismet had reported.

As she settled behind the wheel, she knew that she really should just let all of this go.

She also knew that she couldn't.

"This isn't over yet," she swore. "Not by a long shot."

Part Three

Chapter Nineteen: Seventh Heaven

As soon as that terrible woman was out the door, Athena called Clark.

"Hello, Athena. I hope you're holding up okay. I'm sorry I couldn't attend the ceremony today, I'm trying to keep my name disconnected from the, er, incident. I did send a really big bouquet, though."

"That was you? I saw those flowers, they were nice. I think the family was a little confused about where they came from - you really went all out! Listen, this isn't a social call though. I've just had a strange visit from the you-know-who."

"Really? We shouldn't discuss this over the phone. Do you think you and Dennis can meet me at my store soon?"

Athena's eyes went wide. She hadn't even considered that they were monitoring her phone calls, but of course they probably were.

"Definitely! We both took the rest of the day off. We'll be there in a few."

"Great, see you then."

Dennis walked back into the house with Mr. President happily trailing behind him. "Where did that lady go?"

"You mean the lady that was with the ABC?" Athena asked him sourly.

"Shit! She was with the ABC?"

"Yes! That's what I was trying to tell you, but you let her in anyway!"

"Oh man, I remember now. I'm sorry, I don't know what was wrong with me."

"It's alright. I figured she was doing some spooky MIB shit to you that didn't work on me for some reason. But it's probably not safe to talk about this right now. C'mon we're gonna take a little trip," she whispered to him. Now that all his faculties had been restored, Dennis was smart enough to realize that the fewer questions he asked while inside the house, the better. He simply nodded his understanding and followed her out the door.

***

Agent Method was still sitting behind the wheel of her company car when she saw the Ardens pull out of their driveway and pass her.

"Where are you off to in such a hurry?" she wondered aloud, since she actually hadn't been listening in on their conversations. She'd been too busy trying to get her still-bleeding nose under control - but that little problem was now temporarily set aside in light of this latest development. She pulled out of her parking spot and followed them.

She wasn't particularly concerned about losing their trail. When she'd been walking up their driveway to ring the doorbell she'd slipped a tiny tracking device onto their car, almost as an afterthought. It was the sort of thing that ABC agents typically carried in their pockets, along with the equally minuscule, yet potent listening device she'd surreptitiously dropped into the cushion of the armchair she'd sat in once inside the house.

She followed them onto the Garden State Parkway, where they got off several exits south of Barnegat, then traveled for awhile down one of the narrower state roads through a small town that Method recognized - this was where Clark Kismet's occult shop (or "shoppe" as he insisted on styling it), Seventh Heaven, was located.

"Of course, she would go running off to him, wouldn't she?" she said, continuing her external monologue.

She wasn't disappointed. Sure enough they came to a stop in front of Seventh Heaven, parking behind an old purple conversion van with the logo for the store and a rather tacky picture of a wizard riding a unicorn emblazoned on its side. She glided to a stop in front of the building next door, Larry's Discount World O' Linoleum.

"Holy shit, I can't believe he's still keeping that old monstrosity running!"

Thanks to the microphones built into her car, she could hear Dennis make that remark as he strained to get out of Athena's car.

"He's probably using magic to keep it working. Remember how it was bigger on the inside than the outside?" Athena added as she walked up the trio of short concrete steps that led up to the front door.

"Yup, just like Doctor Who's TARDIS! It was pretty trippy, I thought I was seeing things." Dennis smiled at the memory as he followed her into the store.

As soon as the door shut behind him, Agent Method was greeted with nothing but silence. A look of consternation seized her face. She messed with the controls for the microphone array built into the car's console, boosting the power to maximum. Still nothing. She switched the direction of the mics to spy on the building across the street instead, and could hear the people inside as clearly as if she were standing next to them. She pointed the mics at Seventh Heaven again, and got nothing. She sighed loudly. He must be using some kind of spell to protect the place from her devices. She wished that Agent Ember were there to cast a counterspell, but she wasn't, nor would she approve of any of this.

Method sighed once more and tried to look on the bright side: at least her nose had stopped bleeding during the drive. While she waited for the Ardens to come out, she looked at her wrist computer. She pulled up the file on Clark Kismet for the umpteenth time, hoping that staring at it again would somehow bring on a fresh revelation she'd overlooked.

Magic users were an odd and eccentric bunch to begin with, but even amongst such a group, Clark Kismet had always stood out as particularly peculiar. For one thing, nobody knew exactly where he'd come from. It didn't help that he often gave contradictory accounts on the subject. Some stories claimed that he wasn't even human, but was really an extra dimensional being who made himself appear to be human so he could blend in. According to this school of thought, he'd been exiled from his home dimension for getting into an epic fight with a rival sorcerer that had nearly destroyed their capital city. In the end, both he and his nemesis were forcibly ejected from their native dimension. In another version of the story, he was lost in time and space after participating in a massive fight to save the cosmos. Set adrift in the multiverse, he eventually ended up in our world, in (from his perspective) the past.

The only thing that was known for certain was that he first showed up in ABC's records in the early 19th century, when he came to the attention of the Inquisition. His mastery of magic so frightened and impressed them that they made him a member of the Temple of the Old Gods during a period when they were notoriously snobbish about recruiting outsiders. It was said that he'd taught them new things that they'd never fathomed about the nature of magic. During his long years with the organization, he'd held just about every office in the group, except for the most important one - that of Pontifex Maximus, the supreme leader of the Temple of the Old Gods. He could've easily taken that job, but he didn't seem interested in it. His most recent apprentice, Wendy Sommardahl, did eventually rise to that office though.

Apparently, he'd been friends with one of Athena's ancestors, the witch Marlena Anderson who had acted as the Guardian of The Scar for a whopping eighty-eight years. Some accounts said that he'd been hopelessly in love with her, but she only had eyes for a certain pirate captain. Some of the nastier rumors said that Kismet even had something to do with the captain losing his head. Unable to bear being around the object of his unrequited love, he was the one who sent her away to the wilds of South Jersey to act as the Guardian. He'd kept an eye on her family line ever since. Some people said it was because he was fulfilling a promise he'd made to her, but others claimed that he was hoping she'd someday reincarnate as one of her descendants so he could attempt wooing her again. Whatever his true motivation, it was why he'd retired to this Godsforsaken place.

And he was apparently lying about how powerful Athena was - and likely her brother too.

In more recent history, Kismet had had a big role in persuading the various Guilds of secret societies (who had remained neutral throughout the Second World War) into finally taking action against the Third Reich when he'd proved that they had acquired dangerous new weapons from an alternate universe. Shortly afterwards, he'd suggested that a new group should be created to coordinate covering up the actions of the Guilds when they were forced to intervene in mundane affairs. That group became the ABC, and he'd ensured that his friend, the now legendary Sara Berry, was installed as its first Director.

This was why everyone at her job seemed to be so alternately in awe of and terrified by him. For whatever reason, she didn't share that sentiment. She thought that most of the stories about him were just that - stories. She believed that he was something of a charlatan who had done a great job of crafting an air of mystery around himself, but there was little hard evidence to substantiate his overblown reputation. If anything, he was a washed up old has-been, running a dinky little occult shop in an even dinkier little town. She didn't see what the big deal was about him. Sure, he was unusually long lived, even by wizard standards - but that didn't mean he was really from another dimension. It probably just meant he was dabbling in forbidden magic to extend his life and maintain the illusion of youth. Everyone else was just too frightened of him to bust him for it.

She closed the file in disgust and glared at the storefront. She'd gained no new insights by reviewing the data. What she'd give to know what was going on inside of Seventh Heaven right now!

As soon as Athena and Dennis entered the store, they were greeted by a pleasant looking young woman with short platinum blonde hair, dressed in a somewhat punk rock style, complete with big shiny Doc Marten boots, torn fishnets, jean shorts and an off the shoulder top. Athena thought she looked like a refugee from an eighties movie. She was using a feather duster to clean a large crystal ball on a shelf that was overcrowded with books and all manner of strange tchotchkes. She paused mid-dusting to smile at them.

"Welcome to Seventh Heaven! Let me know if there's anything I can help you find."

"Thanks, Is Clark around?" Athena inquired.

"Who's asking?" a voice asked from the other end of the store. Athena looked over to see a handsome young man who looked like he was in his late teens or early twenties sitting with his feet up on top of the counter. He was tall and sporting an impressive black pompadour, wearing a tight fitting plain red t-shirt. His well-toned arms were covered in tattoos. If the girl looked like a refugee from the eighties, this guy looked like one from the fifties - well, with the exception of all those tats. He was reading an old comic book, which he set down as he took his feet off the counter and leaned towards them.

She rolled her eyes at the kid's tough guy act. "Just tell him that Athena and Dennis are here to see him."

Saying her name brought about a complete change in the boy's demeanor. He grinned broadly. "Not *the* Athena?"

"Well, sadly I'm no Ancient Greek Goddess, but yeah, my name is definitely Athena." She didn't understand his reaction.

"It's just that he mentions you all the time lately. I didn't think I'd ever get to really meet you.," the boy explained. "My name is Midge and that's Jasmine."

"You can just call me Jazz. So you're the ghost hunter, huh? Pretty cool." Jasmine looked at her with a renewed appreciation.

"Sorry if I came across as sort of an asshole, I was just afraid you were maybe with the ABC."

Dennis looked surprised. "You know about them?"

Jazz laughed. "Sure, Clark tells us everything!"

"Well, not *everything*," Midge corrected her.

"Maybe not, but definitely too much!"

"Yeah, I guess he is the king of oversharing," Midge agreed, then cocked his head up to the ceiling and shouted at the top of his lungs, "HEY CLARK! ATHENA AND DENNIS ARE HERE!"

Athena winced and plugged her ears with her fingers. She couldn't stand people shouting like that. As a librarian, loud people were her natural enemies, plus she'd heard enough shouting to last her a lifetime before her parents divorced.

Jazz gave her an apologetic look. "Sorry, he always does that."

They heard the sound of a door opening from someplace above them accompanied by Clark's voice, "Yes, yes I know. Send them up here!"

"You heard the man." Midge pointed to a flight of steps to his right.

Athena and Dennis climbed up the long, creaky flight of wooden steps and through a door that Clark had left open. The upper level was Clark's private apartment, and the living room didn't really look very different from the store below in that it was filled with shelves crammed with books and other odd items. The main thing that distinguished it from the ground floor was the presence of a big antique Victorian sofa covered in red velvet, with a matching armchair next to a fireplace. Sitting atop the mantle were a variety of photos, and even a few tiny painted portraits.

Clark was standing near one of the shelves hunting for something when they walked in. "Aha! There it is!" he exclaimed as he pulled a small polished stone from the shelf. He smiled and twirled around to face his guests. "Welcome to my humble abode! Come in, have a seat!"

Athena did a double take as she regarded the wizard. He was looking very much more like what she was used to, his beard had been shaved off and his long hair trimmed down considerably. He was dressed in proper wizard robes now too, purple trimmed in yellow with a pattern of stars, moons and ringed planets printed all over it. A floppy hat that drooped down over his eyes completed the eccentric ensemble. He looked almost exactly the same as he had when they'd first met twenty-two years earlier, except he was lacking the stupid mullet he'd worn back then.

Dennis beat her to the punch: "Wow, you've totally changed your look."

Clark actually blushed slightly. "I never really meant to change it to begin with, I was just far too absorbed in pursuing certain *other* matters to take proper care of myself, but the tragedy with Tyler has served as something of a wakeup call for me. I can't go on keeping my head buried in the sand like I have been. If it wasn't for those two kids downstairs this place would've gone out of business long ago. It's as much their store as it is mine at this point. But enough about me! I understand you had a visit from the ABC recently? Tell me all about that."

They did, recounting all the events you've already read about. When they'd finished their story, Clark looked pensive, and stroked his now clean-shaven chin.

"Hmmm. It's quite odd that there was only one agent who came by. They typically work in pairs when interrogating members of the public. That's why Midge feared you were with the ABC."

Athena snorted. "C'mon! Do we really look like a couple of those stiffs?" Then she looked down at herself. She was still wearing the same black, sleeveless dress she'd worn to the funeral. Dennis was wearing a black suit, sans the jacket, and he'd loosened his black tie. They did indeed look like a pair of Men in Black.

"Well shit, I guess we do!"

Clark grinned and carried o., "Also, you mustn't be too cross with poor old Dennis for letting her in, she was using a device that makes people open to suggestion. It's standard equipment for all agents. I suspect that your psychic abilities shielded you from it. The important thing is that she didn't really get any information out of you. Here, take this." He handed her the round polished stone she'd seen him take off the shelf.

The light green rock failed to impress her. "What is it? I've already got a paperweight."

"Remember how I told you that we mages use a magic item called a sphere to communicate? Well, that's a spare sphere I had, it's about 700 years old. Got it off of an evil sorceress who called herself the Queen of Wyrms. She was as beautiful as she was deadly." That peculiar wistful look that Clark sometimes got when discussing the past touched his face again for a moment, as if he was briefly lost in a memory.

He shook himself out of his reminiscence abruptly. "It's easy to use. Simply hold it in the palm of your hand and think about me, like you did when you summoned me with my calling card back in the woods."

"I'm not sure I can ever muster up that same level of intensity again, but I'll give it a try," Athena said doubtfully. She closed her eyes and cleared her mind, thinking only of Clark. When she opened them again, to her surprise, the sphere was hovering in mid air at her eye level.

"Holy shit! How'd I do that?"

Clark smiled slyly. "It's meant to be a kind of hands-free technology." He pulled a blue sphere from a hidden pocket in his robe. "When someone is trying to contact you, the sphere will grow warm in your pocket. Not hot enough to burn you, but warm enough to get your attention. It's quite a pleasant sensation, actually. You might also suddenly find yourself thinking of the person trying to contact you."

He held his sphere up against Athena's arm so she could feel its warmth.

"That *is nice.*" It reminded her of a heating pad she had back at home.

"To answer it, you just think about doing so, and *viola!*" As he said the words, his sphere shot into the air. Athena was shocked to see that his face was somehow projected onto her sphere. It almost looked like his head was inside of it.

"Hello, Athena," he said. She heard the words not only from the wizard standing across from her, but also from the sphere itself and even inside her head!

"Um, hi," she replied hesitantly.

"Oh, that is so COOL!" Dennis couldn't hide his enthusiasm. "Look honey, you're inside his little rock too!"

Clark strode over to stand shoulder to shoulder with Athena to show her.

"Thousands of years ago, before recorded history, your clever ancestors invented what's still the most secure form of communication on the planet. The ABC can't listen in when we talk using these." She heard what he was saying in triplicate and it was a bit overwhelming.

"Awesome, how do we end this prehistoric FaceTime call?"

"Just think about it."

She did, and the sphere fell back down into her still-outstretched hand.

"Ah! See how you instinctively knew to keep your hand open to catch it? You're a natural at this, I've always known it!"

Clark's excitement was infectious and now it was her turn to blush at the compliment. Blushing always made her feel self conscious; since she was so pale, it was particularly obvious.

"Keep it close to you at all times," the wizard urged her. She was wearing a dress, so she didn't have any pockets. Instead she put it in her ubiquitous little purse.

"And this, too." Clark pulled something else out of his pocket and handed it to her. It was a polished bronze dial slightly larger than a silver dollar. Strange symbols were etched into its surface and a pretty piece of turquoise sat in its center.

"What's this one do?" she asked.

"It's a baffler."

"It sure is living up to its name, because I'm totally baffled!"

"Keep it in your home. That agent almost certainly planted bugs when she was there. They're so tiny that you'll never find them, they're almost nanoscale. This will scramble them, and any other listening devices they may train on your house. As an added benefit, it will also improve your Wifi signal - although I have no idea why!" The wizard frowned in befuddlement.

"Truly baffling," Athena agreed, adding it to the contents of her purse and seizing the opportunity to add a stick of gum to the contents of her mouth.

"When you're not around the baffler, try to keep what happened last week out of all your conversations, and for Gods' sake don't ever text or email about it!" he warned.

Athena rolled her eyes. "Geez Clark, we're not total idiots, ya know."

"Yes, quite. I'm sorry to imply otherwise."

"Hey! Who's this in all these pictures? I didn't know you had a kid," Dennis said from over near the fireplace where he'd been examining the numerous framed photos crowding the mantelpiece.

Athena joined her husband and scanned the pictures. Many of them showed a red headed girl, through many stages of development from a child to a woman in her fifties. In some of the later photos, she was with a beautiful black woman and a mousy, brown haired little girl.

"Oh that's my last apprentice, Wendy. I raised Wendy from the time she was around eight years old. Her family had left the Temple of the Old Gods centuries ago, rightfully upset by their draconian practices at the time. They weren't around when a remarkable woman named Esmeralda Hazleton reformed the organization into a much more benevolent one, so they weren't very happy when Wendy's gifts manifested at a young age."

He pointed at the other woman in the pictures with Wendy. "That's her wife, April. I officiated the wedding," he revealed proudly. "And that's their daughter, Celine." His long, bony finger tapped on a picture of the kid with the brown hair.

"Wendy and her family are the closest thing I have to one of my own in this world, although I really only see them around the holidays nowadays. Even in retirement, Wendy keeps terribly busy. Too busy to bother very much with me. She founded the TOTOG Foundation to search for artifacts from before the Great Magic War and still sits on the board."

"The TOTOG Foundation?" Athena scrunched up her face in concentration as realization dawned on her. "Don't tell me TOTOG actually stands for 'Temple of the Old Gods!'" She'd always been a whiz with acronyms.

"It does. One of our principles is to hide in plain sight."

"Weren't they the ones that funded that archeological expedition to Deercrest Lake?" Dennis wondered aloud. "If you raised that girl like a daughter, shouldn't she have known that The Boy was there?"

All the color drained from Clark's face. "I'm afraid that she didn't. It happened a year or so before she moved in with me and I was too ashamed of it all to ever tell her anything about it. Only the ABC ever knew, and from what I've gathered, when the TOTOG Foundation asked to excavate on that land, the ABC assumed that they knew what they were walking into and could handle it, so they granted permission. I've kept far too many secrets all these years and it's only now that I'm starting to understand the cost. The deadly cost. I'm done with secrets. So you see, those deaths are really my fault too."

Athena was moved by the deep sadness in the wizard's voice. She placed a hand on his shoulder. "You couldn't have known."

He smiled faintly at the gesture and pointed to an old portrait in an equally old looking silver oval of a frame. It showed a pretty woman with long, golden blonde tresses. There was a hazy, ethereal quality to her; she was so radiant that she almost seemed to be glowing.

"That's your ancestor, Marlena."

Athena studied the painting more intently. She saw little resemblance to herself, although perhaps there was a bit of something around the eyes. The longer she stared at the picture, the more she felt a connection to this long-dead woman. "She was beautiful."

"Indeed she was! No portrait could ever capture her true beauty, her inner light. She was very precious to me. She was the one who first found me when I arrived in your world. She persuaded the Inquisition to stop hunting me and make me a member. A few years later I was running the group! I may not be here at all today if it hadn't been for her kindness. I owe her a debt which I can never repay."

There's that look again, Athena thought, *getting lost in the past, better snap him back to reality!*

"The ABC's visit wasn't the only reason why I wanted to talk to you today, Clark," she began.

"Oh?"

"Yeah, I've been doing a lot of thinking this past week and I might've come up with an idea for dealing with the creature. But I dunno…it's stupid. Maybe I shouldn't mention it."

"No, go on honey, it's not dumb!" Dennis encouraged her.

"Yes, I'm all ears," Clark quipped, flicking one of his earlobes. His ears were indeed quite large.

"Well, what if we made a really deep hole in the ground and just buried it? That way it would still be on the land, but it couldn't hurt anyone. I mean, I know you feel sorry for it, but something has to be done. I don't think it's quite as innocent as you think it is, either. I swear that thing was laughing at us when we were trying to fight back. I think it's starting to really enjoy what it does."

Clark did his little chin-stroking routine again before speaking. "It's not the worst idea, but there's a few holes in your plan -if you'll pardon the pun."

"Like what?"

"For one thing, the hole would have to be extremely deep to ensure that he can never claw his way out again. It is possible to create such a deep hole with magic, but it's very time consuming and will require all of my attention, so I won't be able to renew the magical barrier that would protect us from the monster if it should expire before I'm done."

"Hey, why not make the hole right on the opposite side of the standing stones so he can't attack us while we make it, then knock the stones down and lure him into the pit?" Dennis suggested.

"That's an excellent idea, but he won't go into the pit voluntarily. He's stupid, but not *that* stupid. He has an animal's cunning. He's also drawn to magic. He'll sense us when we're making the hole and watch us as we're doing it unless we make it some distance away from the megaliths. Even then, we'll have to lure him towards it once the stones are knocked down and that's going to be quite dangerous for whoever is acting as bait. There's only me to protect us. If he gets too close to the person he's chasing and I have to zap him to save them it'll be difficult to get him to come back out of hiding again so long as he knows I'm still around."

"It's a pity that the real Jersey Devil can't just fly down, scoop him up and drop him inside!" joked Athena.

"What a wonderful idea! We could probably do exactly that! Summer is their mating season! I could easily summon a wyvern. I could show you how to control it. They have very thick, scaly hides, he'd have trouble biting through it!"

'Whoa, hold on there! I was just kidding around! Do you really think I could do something like that?"

"I'm sure you could do it, after all, it's in your blood. You likely inherited Marlena's affinity for animals."

Athena thought about how many fur babies she had and found herself nodding in agreement.

"Hot damn! I can't believe I'm finally going to see what the real Jersey Devil looks like!" Dennis marveled at his luck. But then he remembered the chain of tragedies that had brought them to this point and his joy was dampened.

"It's settled then. I'll contact you on the sphere as soon as I've wrangled one up and I'll train you in how to control it."

There was much discussion after that about trying to coordinate this with Dennis' work schedule (difficult), and Athena's (easy), but I'm not going to bore you with all that. Suffice it to say that once the details had been hammered out, the Ardens thanked Clark for the magical doodads he'd bestowed upon them and took their leave of Seventh Heaven.

Back in her car, Agent Method noted the Ardens leaving the occult shop. She considered following them back to their home as she had planned, but she'd spent the entire time they'd been inside simmering in anger over not knowing what was happening and being powerless to eavesdrop. She wasn't used to not being able to spy on normies whenever she wanted to, although her still-throbbing head served as an unpleasant reminder that Athena Arden was anything but a normie.

Her fury was so great that she made the extremely irrational decision to abandon her plan to continue trailing the Ardens and instead confront Clark Kismet directly. She'd done a pretty good job of convincing herself that he wasn't "all that" - nothing she couldn't handle on her own. She was a very passionate and confident young woman, some of the qualities her husband loved the most about her, but such impulses didn't always serve her best.

This would prove to be one of those occasions.

She walked through the door and at first things played out very similarly to how they had when Dennis and Athena had walked in. Jasmine was still waging her private war against the decades of dust that plagued the store, and Midge was still sitting with his feet up on the counter, only this time he was reading a completely different comic book.

"Welcome to Seventh Heaven! Let me know if you need help finding anything."

"I need to speak with Clark Kismet," she told Jazz.

"Who's asking?" Midge belligerently bellowed from behind the counter, despite the app on Method's wrist computer being dialed up to the maximum setting. This should've been her first clue that things wouldn't go according to plan.

Clark had still been puttering around downstairs after seeing the Ardens off, determined to take a more active interest in the running of his store along with all the other things he'd been neglecting lately. He poked his head out the storeroom, saw the redheaded woman dressed all in black and immediately knew who she was.

Without hesitation, Clark chanted in his strange baby talk wizard language and cast a spell to immobilize her.

"What the fuck?"

Well, it immobilized everything but her mouth.

Clark sauntered over to her in triumph and walked a complete circle around her, looking her up and down before coming to a stop right in front of her.

"You didn't really think you could just walk in here without any consequences, did you?" he tutted. "Wait, don't answer that. Let's do something about that lying tongue of yours. American Bear Committee indeed!"

"It was 'commission,'" Method replied feebly. She could barely move her mouth.

"Oh, whatever! My friends aren't morons, y'know!" Clark barked back, then cast another spell which made it impossible to speak anything but the truth.

"Where's your partner?" Clark inquired.

"Still recovering from being attacked by that monster in the woods."

Clark's face fell slightly, "I'm genuinely sorry to hear that. Why didn't they assign a new partner to you in the meantime?"

"They don't want me pursuing this investigation. I was warned to stay out of it."

"Aha! I knew it! You're a busybody! Why did you disobey orders?"

"Because I'm interested in knowing the truth, doing my job correctly, and I'm not scared of you. You're a fool! Did you really think you could stop the killings just by buying those apartments? You have no idea how many hikers have died in those woods!"

"That's because nobody will ever tell me what's going on anymore!" Clark protested.

"No, it's because you don't *want* to know! We've emailed you plenty of reports, they don't show that you've ever even opened them!"

"Bah! Email! An infernal invention, nothing but a way to give you even more junk mail! I never check it!"

"That's true, Clark hates e-mail," Midge affirmed laughingly. He and Jazz seemed only vaguely interested in the confrontation unfolding in the store. This was all disturbingly routine to them.

"No, can't any of you see? He simply doesn't care about anyone but himself! It's all just a big act! He might not even be human!"

"That's not true!" Clark protested, "I do care!"

"What are you going to do with me?" Method was finally starting to realize how vulnerable she was, and that maybe antagonizing the person who had her completely at his mercy wasn't the best strategy.

"I *should* report your insubordination to your superiors. Where are you operating out of these days? Still using that old complex under Ong's Hat?"

"Yes."

"Unfortunately, reporting you would draw exactly the kind of attention that I'm trying to avoid...and a part of me admires your dedication to your duty."

A compliment was the last thing she'd expected from him. She was beginning to wonder if she was wrong about him.

Clark quickly chanted another spell, then spoke to her in plain English. "You're going to forget all about investigating the JSPS like you were told to do. In fact, you're not going to recall anything about your visit here, or to Athena's house. You're going to go home, relax and enjoy a nice bottle of your favorite wine."

"I don't like wine."

"Well, you do now! Get yourself a nice Chardonnay on the way home!" He snapped his fingers and Agent Method could suddenly move again. She looked around for a moment with a perplexed look on her face, then rushed out the door.

Clark looked at his young friends apologetically. "I'm really trying to get out of the habit of doing that, but some people make it so difficult!"

Inside her car, Agent Method pulled away from Seventh Heaven. She had no idea where she was right now or how she got there, but all of the sudden, she wanted nothing more than to go back home and have herself a nice Chardonnay. She'd definitely have to stop by the liquor store on her way back and pick up some.

What was weird was that she normally hated wine, she was really more of a beer person, but none of that seemed to matter right now....

Chapter Twenty: How to Train Your Wyvern

In her office at the library, Athena watched the video for the gazillionth time, and tried not to cry. The video in question was a tribute to Tyler that Dennis had put together using various clips from old JSPS investigations over the years. It was sort of a "greatest hits" of Tyler compilation, consisting of lots of behind the scenes moments of him clowning around or just being Tyler. Athena was ashamed to admit that she'd forgotten how funny he could be sometimes, because he was also often such a pain in the ass - which unfortunately became his most memorable trait for many people. The family had loved the video, and so had Tyler's girlfriend. Athena hadn't even known he'd *had* a girlfriend until they met at the funeral. It made her feel strange to realize how long you could know someone, yet never *really* know them. She felt funny receiving the positive messages about the video from Tyler's family and girlfriend since she still felt like if it hadn't been for her, he'd still be alive. Thankfully, they didn't seem to blame her, which likely would've been way too much for her to bear. She had to hand it to Dennis, he had done one hell of a job putting the video together, although combing through all the old clips of Tyler to select the best ones had really done a number on the poor guy emotionally.

She was glad that they'd decided to honor their fallen friend in this way on their website instead of posting any footage from that final investigation. Even though the video they'd captured included some of the best evidence they'd ever recorded, sharing it with the world felt incredibly disrespectful.

She knew that her brother Mark couldn't stop kicking himself over the fact that he hadn't had the presence of mind to pull out his phone and snap any pictures of The Boy while they'd had him trapped. He was still obsessed with exonerating Becca Greene, but Clark had assured him it wouldn't have mattered if he had taken pictures or shot any video, the ABC wouldn't have allowed the truth to come out either way.

As her mind continued to drift over the events of that weekend she couldn't help but wonder if Tyler's skeptical spirit had stubbornly stayed behind to join the other ghosts that haunted those woods, or if he'd moved on. The thought that his spirit might be trapped there bothered her tremendously. It was something she'd have to check into, perhaps with Clark's help, once they made the place safe to visit again.

She didn't know if it was the video, or the idea of Tyler's ghost haunting the Pine Barrens, but she lost her battle with her tear ducts.

As she wiped the tears from her eyes, she wondered if this was the end for the JSPS. Nobody was much in the mood for a ghost hunt lately, herself included. And she couldn't really blame them. They'd found the paranormal and it had claimed one of them for its own.

Her dark ruminations were interrupted by a warm sensation coming from her pants pocket. She knew what that meant, and rose to lock the door to her office (nearly tripping over the many boxes on the floor in her haste) before taking out the sphere. As she settled back into her seat, she willed herself to answer the call and was pleased to see the stone fly up in front of her face.

"Sweet." She smiled. The novelty of it all wasn't even close to wearing off yet.

Clark's countenance appeared inside the sphere. "Salutations, my dear! Today is the day! The veil is particularly thin this evening and I shouldn't have much trouble peeling back the Band-Aid that covers The Scar long enough to coax a wyvern out."

Athena blinked in surprise. "Oh? I thought you were gonna call me when you already had one under control?"

"I was, but I thought you might enjoy seeing this part of the process."

It didn't take her long to consider the offer. "Sure, sounds interesting. I can cross seeing a mythological creature flying out of another dimension off my bucket list."

"Excellent! I'm already in an isolated part of the woods where we should be able to conduct our business in peace. I'm going to place the directions directly into your mind; you'll be able to access them whenever you need to just by thinking about it."

She was taken aback. "You can really do that? Even from where you are? I'll be honest, that's a little spooky." She was really starting to warm up to Clark, but she still wasn't sure she was comfortable with the idea of him (or anyone else for that matter) just implanting information into her brain like that.

Clark just laughed off her concerns. "Don't concern yourself with it. I'm not *that* powerful - normally. Our spheres strengthen the link between us and make such things possible."

She couldn't help but frown a little. "Well, okay, go ahead then. I guess it beats using Google Maps."

"The important thing is that it's untraceable, unlike when you look up directions on your phone."

Athena was alarmed at the speed with which the information appeared in her mind. As soon as she'd given her consent, she could access it.

"I was right, that *is* spooky!"

'You'll get used to it."

"I'm still not sure I want to!"

Clark ignored her hesitancy and plowed on. "Oh, and bring your baffler, but leave it in your car. They've likely put tracking devices on your vehicles."

"But I thought you took care of that crazy ABC lady?" Clark's call to regale her with the tale of how he'd bested Agent Method a few days earlier had been her first real chance to test out using the sphere.

"I did, and she wasn't crazy, just extremely dedicated. Under different circumstances that would be quite admirable."

"We Earthlings have a special word for people who are a little too dedicated, it's 'fanatic' and it's not an admirable quality."

"Well either way, one can never be too careful. Her bosses could always change their minds about keeping out of this and send someone else. Best not to make things too easy for them if they do."

Athena couldn't argue with his logic, so she didn't try to.

"You already know that Dennis wants to see the wyvern, but he's not the only one. I told Miranda and Mark about our plan and they both want to see what the creature that inspired all the stories about the Jersey Devil looks like up close and personal. Is that okay?"

Clark sighed. "I suppose so. Just don't bring that reporter fellow. I don't trust him. I was quite tempted to erase his memories."

"Hey, mess with Lars' mind and you'll have to answer to me! Don't worry about him, he's okay. We go way back. I know he can be a little hard to read, even for people like us, but I think I've finally got him all figured out. Honestly, I think he's more interested in satisfying his own morbid curiosity than getting a scoop. Besides, he's seen firsthand what the ABC did to Becca Greene, he's not stupid enough to risk pissing them off by trying to print a story about any of this that gets too close to the truth. But if it makes you feel better, I'll continue to keep him out of it. He's not *real* JSPS anyway, more like honorary JSPS."

"It would make me feel better. Oh! Make sure you all come in the same car so the baffler will protect all of you."

Athena groaned. If they were all going to go in the same vehicle, they'd have to take Dennis' work van, which didn't have any seats in the back. She knew Miranda wouldn't mind, she rode in it all the time on investigations, but she could practically hear Mark whining about how sitting on the floor was hurting his ass already. Sometimes her brother could be such a primadonna! On top of that, she thought Clark was being a little paranoid about the ABC continuing to harass them now that she knew that Agent Method had been acting on her own.

"I am *not* being paranoid! I know a lot more about how to deal with these kinds of people than you do, at some point you're going to have to decide to trust me."

"I *do* trust you, but it's a little tough when you can just read my thoughts like that!"

"Well, that's fair I suppose. As I said earlier, these spheres amplify our telepathic abilities while they're in use and my old Inquisitorial habits die hard, I guess. I do apologize, although I must confess that some of your thoughts are so strong that they're almost impossible to miss!"

She laughed. "I'll take that as a compliment."

"It could get you in real trouble if you run across another powerful telepath someday. I'll have to show you how to put up some effective mental defenses sometime, it's not very hard."

"It's a date."

"Well, let's try and get through *this* date first. Get your friends together and join me. I don't have much to do out here in the meantime aside from communing with nature."

"Commune away! I'll see you soon."

"See you!"

And with that, the sphere fell neatly into her hand with a satisfying plop. Athena wasted no time in texting Dennis, Mark and Miranda, using the code phrase she'd come up with earlier: "the crow flies tonight," followed by a request to meet at her house. She unlocked her office door, gathered up her things and told her assistant Ana that she was heading out a little early and she'd have to close up the library by herself.

About forty minutes later, Dennis was parking his van on yet another sandy trail deep in the Pine Barrens somewhere off of Route 72, not very far from where Brenda had her encounter. Mark was the first one out of the back of the van, and was vigorously massaging his aching butt cheeks in a way that made Miranda blush.

Athena raised an eyebrow at his theatricality. "Jeez, is that really necessary? The ride was uncomfortable, we get it already!"

He cast a sideways glance at her backside. "We're not all blessed with such a generous amount of natural cushioning, sis!"

"It's not my fault that you got all the bony ass genes in the family!" she joked back.

"Can we please find something else to talk about? Like how the hell we find Clark out here?" Dennis pleaded. All this derriere discussion was obviously making him uncomfortable. Or perhaps what was really bothering him was how strange it felt to be out in the woods like this again so soon after what happened with Tyler.

Athena was surprised at how much it was affecting her, too. Even though she knew they were miles away from where The Boy was and further north, she still felt oddly exposed.

"He's down this trail." She pointed down a narrow path to the right and led the way.

After a short trek along the trail, they came to a big clearing in the forest where Clark was sitting on a fallen tree, crocheting a pair of mittens. He was dressed in his full wizard regalia again, purple robes and all. A blue cooler sat near his feet. He looked up as he heard them approach.

"Ah! There you are! Thank goodness I found this in my pocket." He held up the half completed mittens. "I was making them for Celine for Yule last year and misplaced them, turns out they were in this robe all along! It's kept me busy while I've been waiting."

"Sorry we took so long, it's not easy to get four people who've all got jobs and crazy lives together so quickly," Athena apologized.

Clark stood up and shoved the mittens and crochet needles in his pocket. "Think nothing of it! It's a pleasant enough evening for a spot of knitting in nature! I was rather enjoying myself."

"Clark?" Miranda asked a little shyly.

"Yes?"

"Not to be a party pooper, but I've been wondering how necessary all of this actually is. Do you really need to make a super deep hole and use a dragon to drop him into it? Couldn't you just use your magic to, I dunno, levitate him into a steel cage or something?"

"I've actually entertained similar ideas. My fear is that no mere cage will be able to hold him indefinitely. This creature cannot die, is unnaturally strong and you've all seen how crazed it can become. I fear that in time, it would break its way out of even the toughest cage. Besides, this way is simply more fun!"

"But if he's really so strong that you think he can bust out of a steel cage, won't he dig himself out of the hole someday too, no matter how deep you make it?" Dennis asked.

"I have a solution for that too! I'm going to place a special enchantment on the hole that I've recently come up with myself. I like to call it 'one step forward, two steps back.'"

"Because opposites attract!" Mark sang tunelessly. Everyone looked at him blankly.

"What? Doesn't anyone else remember that Paula Abdul song?"

"Sure, but we were reacting more to your terrible singing!" Athena teased. Mark stuck his tongue out at her sassily.

"I got the idea when that song came on the radio at Seventh Heaven the other day! You see, for every foot that the creature digs himself out, the hole will become *two feet* deeper! It'll be impossible for him to ever escape!" Clark beamed broadly, obviously impressed by his own cleverness.

"Sweet, but I thought you brought us here to show us a wyvern?" Athena reminded him impatiently. She had learned that sometimes you had to help keep Clark focused on the task at hand.

"Yes, yes, of course."

"Where is this Scar of yours? Everything looks pretty normal out here to me," Miranda said.

"The Scar? It's usually invisible to those who don't have the eyes to see it. It starts around this area and runs all the way up the east coast into New England. Once I pry it open a bit, even you won't be able to miss it. I just hope I can compel a wyvern to come through before the opening attracts the attention of the current Guardian. Since it's mating season there should be some hanging around nearby just waiting for it to naturally open up."

"Aren't there any already on this side of The Scar?" Mark asked.

"Probably, but they're notoriously hard to find. Trust me, this is much easier."

"Check this out, you're gonna love it!" Clark raised his hands and began chanting. He gesticulated wildly at the sky over their heads. It all looked rather silly, to be honest. The others exchanged puzzled glances before they noticed a glowing band of light appearing in the distance overhead. The bright yellow band expanded, both lengthening and widening. They could see a bloody, crimson sky on the other side of the ever expanding crack in reality. Clark's chanting intensified in volume and an unnaturally powerful wind stirred the pine trees, blowing the hat right off his head. The wizard closed his eyes and began swaying back and forth.

Dennis pointed the camera he'd brought towards the phenomenon, only to make a disappointed face when he couldn't get it to power on, which was strange since he was certain it had been fully charged when he'd grabbed it before leaving the house. He tried to use his phone camera instead, only to discover that device was dead too. He recalled how Brenda had lost all power when she had her encounter with the Jersey Devil, and deduced that The Scar must somehow be responsible for the unexpected power loss.

Suddenly, something dark flew through The Scar.

"Did you guys see that?" Athena shoute., "I think we've got one!"

The ghost of a smile danced around the edges of Clark's mouth at her words. He started rotating his hands and humming loudly. As he did so, The Scar closed up.

"Where did the wyvern go?" Athena demanded of the wizard.

His eyes were still closed, but he opened one of them long enough to glare at her. "Shhh!" he hissed back, "I'm still trying to establish contact with him!"

No sooner were the words out of his mouth than a great, dark shape whizzed right overtop them, making everyone but Clark scream and duck for cover.

"Calm yourselves!" Clark's voice sounded supernaturally loud and commanding. "You're frightening him!"

"*We're* frightening *him?*" Mark laughed incredulously from where he was, still half crouched down.

"Yes! He's coming back for another pass. Now everyone please remain still. He won't hurt you, I promise. I'm going to see if I can persuade him to land."

Athena heard the beating of the massive wings before she saw them, but when she turned her head to look, her breath was instantly taken away. Gliding towards the clearing was the wyvern, its leathery, bat-like wings fully extended. She estimated that they must be about twenty feet wide altogether. Its legs were pointed forward, big black talons outstretched. She could see now that it was a rusty, almost brownish shade of red, like the color of a leaf in the fall. It was covered in scales, with a bright ring of what looked like feathers dancing around the bottom of its long neck, almost like what you'd see on a buzzard. Its head was long and narrow, with large nostrils and small ears. A pair of appropriately devilish-looking horns curled out of either side of the skull. A long tail that was split into three spikes trailed behind it.

The beast landed right in front of Clark, stirring up a small cloud of dust and pine needles as it did so. It sniffed the mage, who now opened both his eyes and beamed at it. He reached out and patted it on the nose, only inches from his face.

"There, there. You're a good boy, aren't you?" he whispered, scratching under the creatures' chin. The wyvern made a strange hooting sound of contentment and folded his wings against his body.

Clark looked over at the others, whose mouths were all hanging agape. "We've reached an understanding. Well, don't just stand there lollygagging! Come over and say hello!"

The others were hesitant, except for Athena, who immediately felt a peculiar kinship with the creature. She practically ran over and joined Clark in scratching under its chin. She exchanged a smile with the sorcerer.

"He likes that doesn't he?"

"Oh yes, he's agreed to hang out with us for a bit in exchange for a few chin rubs. His little foreclaws can't quite reach that spot, which he finds terribly irritating."

As if in response to Clark's words, the beast flexed those claws. There were three on each stubby arm, along with what appeared to be an underdeveloped opposable thumb.

Dennis tried his camera again, and, pleased to find it working, he began shooting some footage of the spectacle. "For most of my life I've been wondering if this thing was real, or if I'd ever get to see it for myself. And now here I am." He was surprised to hear himself choking up, he lowered the camera and with one trembling hand joined Athena and Clark in scratching its chin. It hooted again in joy. Dennis grinned at his wife, and she smiled back.

Mark was the next one to join in the chin scratching festivities, eventually followed by Miranda. Soon they were all laughing and grinning like a bunch of children on Christmas morning.

"Ha! He's loving all this attention. I think you've all got yourselves a new BFF!" Clark announced.

"I know we do, I can *feel* it!" Athena replied.

Clark raised an eyebrow at her. "Can you really? Hold onto that feeling, and go deeper with it. What do you see?"

Athena closed her eyes, calling upon all the meditation techniques she'd taught herself over the years to try and deal with her staggering list of anxieties. She cleared her mind of everything but the emotions she was picking up from the wyvern, much like what she did when she was on a ghost hunt and trying to connect with the spirits she was sensing. As Clark had urged her, she held onto those feelings and probed deeper, her awareness rushing towards them, *into* them....

Her eyes snapped open and she gasped. She was seeing double! With her natural vision she was seeing the wyvern and all her friends gathered around it, but at the same time she was seeing herself in blurry black and white, with the background behind her in much sharper detail. She could also hear all the little scuttling sounds of the birds and squirrels in the woods around her, and smell the familiar scent of her husband's Old Spice deodorant fighting with Miranda's perfume, Mark's nice aftershave and Clark's obnoxious cologne. She was uncomfortably aware of her own odors.

"Ohh, this is weird, this is trippy! Am I experiencing what he's experiencing?"

Before Clark could answer, she found herself laughing. "Damn, this dude is horny! Literally and figuratively! He's wondering where all the nice lady Jersey Devils are on this side of The Scar, isn't he?"

"You've got the gift! Just like Marlena! I knew it!" None of them had ever heard Clark sound so ecstatic before. "Mark, you try it now!"

"Try what?"

"Open your mind to what the wyvern is feeling. Think of nothing else, don't doubt whatever you begin to feel."

Mark grimaced skeptically. "I'm not really any good at all this meditation shit. Athena's tried to teach me, but it's hard to focus, y'know?"

"Hush! You've got this, baby brother."

"Do, or do not, there is no try," Dennis added. Clark looked askance at him. "Couldn't resist." He shrugged back.

Mark was amazed to discover that he felt like he could tell what the thing was feeling, especially when he was touching it. He laid his open hand against its neck and new sensations flooded his mind.

"OMG! I'm seeing double! And hearing double and, ugh, smelling double! Clark, we really need to talk about your choice of cologne."

Clark sniffed indignantly. "It was a gift, I'm obligated to use it. I'm glad that you've both inherited the gift. Now let's all step back and give him a bit of space."

They all did as Clark suggested. "Now Athena, ask him to fly up, circle around us and land again. Just picture him doing it in your mind and gently push that image back to him."

"Uh, okay." She felt unsure of herself, but pushed the feeling down as best she could.

No sooner had she imagined the wyvern doing the maneuver than she was both seeing it happen in real time and experiencing it from his perspective.

"Whoa! Now I'm married to Daenerys from *Game of Thrones*!" Dennis exclaimed.

"I'm afraid our friend here isn't quite big enough to ride on the back of for very long, but it's a fair enough comparison," Clark replied.

"Can it breathe fire?" Miranda wondered aloud.

"Indeed he can! Recall that these animals were originally created to be weapons of war. Let's see if we can create a little pyrotechnics without setting the whole Pine Barrens ablaze. Mark, picture him pointing his head to the sky and shooting flames from his mouth."

"I think I need to be touching him for it to work," he answered dubiously. He was no longer sharing the wyvern's sensations since he'd broken physical contact with him.

"Try it anyway," the wizard suggested.

Mark closed his eyes and took a deep breath, but nothing happened.

"Don't feel bad, m'boy. I think you're trying too hard. It might just take a bit more practice for you. Now you try it, Athena."

She did, and was immediately rewarded with the sight of a hot plume of flames shooting up into the humid summer air. She could feel the heat of it on her arms even from several dozen feet away.

"Hot damn! And I do mean hot!" She laughed, and asked her new friend to stop before he fried any birds unlucky enough to be passing overhead. He obeyed and then she began to smell a fishy smell and was overcome with an overwhelming mix of curiosity and hunger. The wyvern was now craning its long neck down towards the blue cooler Clark had brought with him.

"Hey, we're hungry! Give us some of those fish you've been hoarding already!" she called over to the mage.

"'*We're* hungry?' Yes, well, our new friend here has certainly earned his reward." Clark flipped open the cooler, and had to jump back as the wyvern poked its snout inside, knocking it over and spilling ice cubes and several trout onto the ground. He snatched them up greedily in a few gulps.

"He needs a name. How about 'Daniel' after Daniel Leeds?" Athena suggested.

"Yes, that's a capital idea," Clark agreed as the newly-dubbed Daniel finished his meal and looked expectantly at the wizard with his big cat-like eyes. Athena hadn't been prepared for how cute those eyes were, she was quite smitten with them. Clark spread out his hands. "I'm afraid that's all I brought." Daniel hooted in disappointment.

"Well, I think that's enough for today. Let's all say goodbye to Daniel for the time being, I'm sure he's eager to start looking for some female companionship. Now that I've mentally bonded with him, I should be able to summon him back here when we need him. Let's try practicing with him a few more times this week before we go after The Boy this upcoming weekend, shall we?"

"Oh, do we really have to say goodbye so soon?" Athena was visibly pouting. She still felt the connection with Daniel, and was continuing to experience everything as he was. It was definitely an exceedingly bizarre feeling, but she had quickly gotten used to it and was completely fascinated with it now. It felt right, somehow.

"I'm afraid so. Surely you can feel how eager he is to, erm, do what comes naturally. The longer we keep him waiting the less agreeable to our company he'll become."

"Does the next training session include me? I'd like to have some more time with him too," Mark said eagerly. He was obviously feeling the same rush Athena was at this newfound power.

"I don't see why not. It's probably a smart idea to have someone else who can control Daniel with us in case Athena should become distracted. I'll likely be too busy making the hole to be of much help in that area."

"No way! I don't want you coming with us next weekend. I don't want you anywhere near The Boy again. It's way too dangerous, we barely escaped with our lives last time! Dad's gonna kill me if anything happens to you."

But I'd kill myself first, she thought darkly.

"What? You can't stop me from coming, I'm not a kid anymore! I want to see that thing pay for what it did to Tyler just as much as you do! I have a right to be there!" he shot back hotly.

Daniel shifted uncomfortably, snorting several times and flapping his wings. Clark held up his hands to silence the warring siblings.

"On second thought, perhaps Athena is right. What we're planning on doing is very dangerous and the less people we have to worry about keeping safe, the better. However, I *do* believe that you've got lots of untapped potential, Mark. I don't see why you can't at least attend our training sessions and sharpen your skills."

The arrangement didn't really satisfy anyone but the person who'd suggested it, but that's often how compromise goes. They both reluctantly agreed.

Clark clapped his hands loudly and Daniel abruptly took flight. Within moments he was naught but a dark speck disappearing on the horizon. Athena sadly watched her new friend fly away. The direct connection she had formed with him slipped further away with each beat of his enormous wings until it had faded from her awareness completely, only to be replaced by a deep sense of loss. It was as if she'd just lost a small part of herself that she never even knew existed until today. She actually knew what it felt like to be a wyvern now, a proud and powerful force of nature, completely free of all the myriad petty anxieties which constantly plagued her all too human mind.

She couldn't wait to feel like that once more.

Chapter Twenty-One:
The Day of Reckoning Approaches

"Hey, wake up!" the voice called to her. Agent Method groggily opened her eyes to see her husband Tristan looking down at her with concern.

"Another nightmare?" he asked superfluously. He knew damned well that it was. She'd been having them all week.

She sat up on the beach towel where she'd fallen asleep enjoying the sensation of the sun on her skin. "Yeah."

"Having recurring nightmares is supposed to be my job, okay?" he kidded her. He had been plagued by the same strange dream for years now, she was usually the one comforting him. This sudden role reversal was difficult for him to get used to, he was worried about her. "Is it anything you can talk about?"

"Unfortunately not. Work related."

"Huh. Even after almost two weeks off, you still can't get that job out of your mind." She could hear the disappointment in his voice and it killed her. How she wished she could share that part of her life with him! Perhaps someday, if all this secrecy didn't tear their marriage apart first.

As much as she enjoyed sunning herself, she was also quite worried about burning. She had a very fair complexion and even with a high SPF lotion she had a tendency to turn into a lobster if she indulged herself for too long.

"I wanna go back home soon," she announced.

"Alright, but let me take one last dip. Care to join me?"

She smiled up at him. "That's okay, I'll just stay here and start packing up our stuff."

He shrugged. "Suit yourself."

She watched him navigate through the maze of towels, umbrellas and folding chairs on the crowded Long Beach Island beach and wade into the pounding surf.

She sighed. It was impossible for her to fully enjoy herself. He was right, even on her "staycation" she just couldn't get her job out of her mind. In the past few days she'd been hiking in state parks, gambling in Atlantic City and screaming her head off at Six Flags Great Adventure, doing all the things she usually took for granted because she was a local, but nothing worked. Her job even haunted her dreams.

She kept on having the same dream about going to the house of that woman, Athena Arden, and getting into some kind of an argument with her, but she could never recall exactly what it was about. Then the woman zapped her with her psychic powers. It wasn't like her to have nightmares; despite all the weird shit she'd seen over the years, she always slept like a baby. The ABC counselors had taught her some very effective methods of dealing with such stresses, but lately all those techniques had been failing her.

Her theory was that she kept dreaming about Athena because of her guilt over just giving up so easily on pursuing the case of that so-called 'bear attack' a few weeks ago. She'd been sorely tempted to go against Agent Ember's orders and continue to investigate it on her own, but instead she'd caved and just taken two weeks vacation to clear her head. The vacation had done nothing to clear her mind, in fact it felt unusually foggy.

She was beginning to suspect that there was more to her nightmares than guilt. Something more sinister. Sometimes recurring nightmares were caused by having one's memories magically altered. It wasn't just the dreams, some of her memories from last weekend were really hazy. Everything was clear up until that Saturday when she bought that bottle of wine, which was also weird. She didn't usually have strong cravings, especially for wine! She'd split the bottle with Tristan when she got home, which definitely gave her a nice buzz, but she didn't get trashed. She certainly hadn't drank enough to fuck up her memory like this. She could barely recall anything from the earlier part of the day *before* she started drinking. She didn't remember why she'd been dressed for work or driving around in her company car on her day off. It was all very curious. Worst of all, she started to get a migraine if she thought about it for too long.

Which was also a symptom of having your memories magically edited.

She stood up and began collapsing the umbrella that protected her from the worst of the sun's attempts to fry her.

Who would do such a thing to her? The ABC wasn't above editing the memories of their own personnel in extreme circumstances, but it had never been done to her before. Well, as far as she knew. Her supervisor,

Agent Ember, was an expert in memory manipulation. It was how she got her code name - because she only left you with the embers of your memories. The idea that Ember might've tampered with her mind enraged her because she'd worked with her for years, even thought of her as a friend. It felt like a personal betrayal, but she knew that Ember had gotten as far as she had because she was a company woman. If Ember was ordered to erase her memory, she might grumble about it a little, but ultimately she'd obey.

But why would anyone give such an order to begin with? What had she been involved in? As she folded up the pair of chairs they'd bought and struggled to get them back in their bags a new idea suddenly hit her. She could check the trip data in her company car. If the ABC was behind this, they'd probably already wiped it, or substituted it for false data, but she still felt like she should check. There was always the possibility that someone else had messed with her mind, some unknown enemy who could be a threat to the ABC itself. It was worth a look. She was desperate to get some idea where she'd been last Saturday before everything started getting fuzzy.

She *had* to know! She couldn't wait to get back home and check on it.

Daniel whooshed straight up into the sky, going higher, higher, until he dived back down towards the ground at an alarming speed. Athena and Clark instinctively ducked as he swooped over them, picking up Clark's cooler with the talons on his feet. The wyvern then zipped back up into the air, executed three perfect barrel rolls and came in for a landing. He dropped the cooler in front of Clark right before alighting on the ground. He nudged the top of it with his snout, trying to pry the top open, then hooted plaintively, fixing the wizard with those adorably big eyes of his.

Clark chuckled. "Alright, alright! You've made your point! A maneuver as impressive as that deserves to be rewarded!" The mage snapped open the cooler. He'd had to invest in a new one that wasn't quite so easy for the beast to pry open. He pulled out a fish, but before he could even hand it over, Daniel had already slurped it away from him.

"Hey, where's my fish? I'm the one who was doing the driving!" Mark teased.

"Yes, you're doing quite well. However, I don't recommend consuming raw fish. I'll get you a gift card to Red Lobster if you like."

"I was just kidding, man."

"I knew that," Clark said so defensively that Athena didn't have to be psychic to know that he didn't.

"If you thought that was cool, check this out!" Athena wasn't about to be shown up by her kid brother.

Daniel shot up into the air again, knocking the hat off of Clark's head again, as he did almost every time he took off.

This time, Daniel did everything Mark had just asked him to do, with the addition of creating a ring of fire in mid air and flying through it before it disappeared. The obedient wyvern returned to the ground and was promptly rewarded with another fish by Clark.

"I would like to remind you, Athena, that we *are* trying to maintain a low profile. It's bad enough that we're doing this in broad daylight, but making burning rings in the air?" He clicked his tongue in disapproval. Athena favored him with one of her patented eye rolls.

"Show off!" Mark accused, but his smile betrayed the playful nature of the remark.

"Hey, if you've got it, ya might as well flaunt it!" Athena winked back.

"Honestly, you two are more juvenile than Midge and Jasmine sometimes!" Clark observed as he dusted off his hat and replaced it on his head. "Nevertheless you've both made extraordinary progress in such a short time. We're more than ready for the big day tomorrow."

"What time should we meet up?" Athena wanted to know.

Clark stroked his chin before answering. "I'm thinking around noon. I'll share my exact location with you via the sphere when I arrive. Be sure to tell the others."

"'The others?' I thought only you and Athena were going?" Mark's surprise, tinged with a hint of outrage was evident in his tone.

"Clark!" Athena growled.

"Sorry!"

Athena had to wonder if he really was. She suspected that most of his absentmindedness was frighteningly deliberate. She knew that he wanted Mark with them as a backup for herself, and had only forbidden him from coming to placate her. She didn't think the wizard was above stirring the pot a little to get what he wanted. She didn't plan on playing into his hands. She planned on sticking to her guns regarding Mark.

"This is outrageous! Miranda's got a husband and a kid at home and you're letting her come?"

"Hey, she's my bestie, she's always got my back. I couldn't talk her out of it. She wants to see this thing resolved as much as the rest of us do," Athena replied lamely.

"And Dennis?"

"Isn't about to let his wife face a man-eating monster without him. Ah, so gallant! I knew there was a reason I let that guy marry me."

"And what's he gonna do if things go to hell in a hand basket? Toss his camera at it? Feed it another pair of nunchucks? I can control Daniel too, *and* I have a gun!"

"Yeah, fat lot of help that was the last time!" She regretted the words as soon as they had flown out of her mouth. She didn't want her brother to think she was blaming him for Tyler's death. She blamed herself enough for the both of them.

Mark looked so angry that for a moment Clark almost thought he'd strike his sister.

Daniel was pacing back and forth during the entire exchange, then lifted his head and let out an utterly heartbreaking sound that none of them had ever heard him make before.

"Stop this bickering now!" Clark bellowed. "You're agitating Daniel! This has already been settled. Athena believes she'll be too distracted worrying about you to do her job effectively and I want her on her A-game tomorrow!"

"Sure, and having her husband and best friend in danger won't be distracting at all?"

"Dennis is like my big, walking security blanket, I find his presence comforting. Ditto for Mira."

"It doesn't make any sense! You guys *need* me!"

"I told you already, this is not open to debate," Clark said in a low tone that brokered no further argument.

"Y'know, I didn't want any part of this to begin with. First you go out of your way to involve me, then you try to shut me out completely. I just wish you'd be a little more consistent, sis," Mark said sulkily.

Next, he looked Clark in the eye. "And you! You haven't done a damned thing to help Rebecca Greene yet! The first person who tried to warn us about all of this is still rotting in jail right now."

"Patience. One thing at a time, Mark. I *do* have a plan for that, but it rests upon our success in dealing with The Boy."

"Whatever!" Mark threw his hands in the air and walked off down the trail towards where they'd parked their cars - alone.

Clark scratched Daniel under his chin to calm him down and cocked his head towards Athena. "You should probably go after him."

"Nah, that'll only make things worse. He'll get over it, he just needs time." She joined Clark in petting her new friend.

Clark shrugged. "You know him better than I do."

As soon as she'd helped carry all the stuff they'd bought with them to the beach inside, Agent Method found a reason to go to her company car. In this case it was the old "I think I left something inside" excuse.

Tristan was so tired and hungry that he barely acknowledged her as he trudged towards the fridge to see what he could put together for them.

As soon as she slid inside her work vehicle, Method activated the car's computer system. She scrolled through the trip history until she got to last Saturday. Assuming that the information it was displaying hadn't been tampered with (which was a *big* assumption) she'd spent part of the day at a graveyard, then been parked near Athena Arden's house, then traveled to Clark Kismet's occult store. It seemed pretty obvious what had happened, if the data was correct.

That damned wizard had done this to her! She'd obviously disobeyed orders and been following Athena and her friends around while she was supposed to be off duty. Frankly, this sounded much more like her than the idea that she'd given up on the investigation so easily.

Or perhaps this was what someone wanted her to believe rather than what had actually happened? Was this whole thing some sort of a strange test from her superiors, perhaps to see how resistant she was to this kind of mental manipulation? If so, would she be rewarded or punished by them if she took up the investigation again?

She sighed. There was only one way to know for sure. Only one way to ever find out what had been done to her. Her path was clear now: she had to resume her surveillance of the JSPS. But not tonight. Tristan was making dinner and she was fresh out of lies. She'd have to spend the night figuring out what to tell him so she could get away long enough to find out the truth.

Just one more day. One more day and she might finally have the answers she longed for.

Chapter Twenty-Two: Jeopardy

Agent Method had told her husband she was going to go to the gym and then meet up with a friend for lunch. In reality, the only gym she belonged to was the one in the ABC base beneath Ong's Hat, but he didn't know that. She could've just told him that something had come up and her job had called her back into work earlier than scheduled, but she didn't want him to think she was doing anything work related just in case someone from work really did come around looking for her, or decided to interrogate him concerning her whereabouts. He didn't think it strange that she was taking her work car, she rarely used her personal vehicle unless she was going on a long trip. This was mainly because the ABC reimbursed her for her mileage when she used their car, if you used it to run a few errands around town nobody ever really bothered to question it.

So that is how she came to be dressed in her sweatpants and a tank top while sitting in her company car parked down the street from the Arden residence on a sunny Saturday morning, sipping her cold Starbucks from her favorite travel mug, the one with a picture of Snoopy on it. Right now she looked more like a fitness model than a member of an extra governmental secret police force. The only remnant of her usual trademark look was her ever present sunglasses. She was trying not to get too annoyed by the fact that her car wasn't picking up any sounds from inside the house. Despite the earliness of the hour, she knew that they were up because she'd seen Miranda Drake Robinson pull up to the house and go inside ten minutes earlier. She thought she'd seen the top of Dennis Arden's head barely poking over the top of the tall backyard fence an hour before that, probably letting the dogs out to do their business. Apparently Kismet had bewitched their house to prevent her spying on them.

She had been distraught to discover that she couldn't even tap into their cellphones. Whatever spell he was using must be powerful. She had been able to get into Miranda's phone up until she got too close to the house. She hadn't learned much from it, although there were a few cryptically worded texts during the past week or so, including one that stated that "today was the day" and she should show up at their house before noon.

Obviously, they were up to something today. Something big, but what?

The hours crawled by for Method as the clock edged closer towards noon. She wondered how much of her recurring dream was true. Had she really already confronted Athena Arden only to find herself under attack by her psychic powers? It seemed absurd on the surface, there was nothing in Clark Kismet's reports to imply that she was much more than moderately gifted. Assuming, of course, that the wizard's reports were honest. If Athena really had used her powers on her, and then Kismet had sent her into a week-long mental fog, then perhaps this wasn't the wisest course of action? Things hadn't ended for her so well last time. She'd actually drunk Chardonnay. She *hated* Chardonnay.

But she couldn't let it go. She had to know what was happening. She had to know what they'd done to her.

Finally, she saw some activity from the house. She put on her binocular headset and zoomed in to see the Ardens, followed by Miranda, leaving the house and getting into the van parked in the driveway. Wearing the headset gave her an idea.

"I'm an idiot!" she swore as she recalled that these binoculars recorded what they saw, there might be files from last week that could shed some light on her missing memories. She pressed some buttons on the side of the headset and accessed a menu. There was indeed a file from a week earlier. She played back a little of it and saw that it was from the graveyard. She fast forwarded through it, but there was nothing there but even more boring funeral footage.

"Oh well, that would've been too easy, wouldn't it?" She pulled off the headset as the van registered to Dennis Arden's HVAC business backed out of the driveway and drove past her. She waited a few moments before following them. She didn't want to lose them. She hadn't bothered to sneak a tracer onto the van, she was certain that Kismet would've already put countermeasures in place to render any such devices useless. She was going to have to do this the old fashioned way, which was actually kind of exciting for her - not having to rely so much on the ABC's slew of high tech gadgets. Her pulse quickened and she had to admit that she was beginning to enjoy this.

She followed them at a distance for about thirty minutes, all the way down to Leeds Point. "Well, well, returning to the scene of the crime, are we?" she mumbled to herself. "What are you fools up to?" She was beginning to wonder if this was going to turn into an impromptu rescue operation if these people got too close to where the creature stalked.

The van turned off the main road and onto a familiar trail of white, sandy soil. She recognized it as the dirt road which led to the old camp at Deercrest Lake. She drove past the spot, then turned back around. She didn't try to drive down the same trail, it would attract too much attention. Instead, she parked on the side of the road near the start of the path. She was going to have to catch up to them on foot if she was going to remain undetected. She slipped her pistol holster over her shoulder and strapped her wrist computer to her arm. Finally, she put on an olive drab windbreaker to conceal it all and left the car behind to chase her quarry.

When Athena, Dennis and Miranda arrived at the remnants of Camp Massingw, Clark was already waiting for them with Daniel by his side. Today the wizard had traded in his trademark purple robes and floppy hat for an equally purple suit that was also covered in stars and moons. He wore a derby with a single yellow crescent moon in its center, this new hat still tended to slip down over his eyes, just like the other one did. Athena and the others had seen him dressed like this once before, when they'd first met decades earlier.

"Wow! This place has a totally different vibe to it than the last time we were here," Athena noted as she approached the wizard and the wyvern.

"Yeah, even I can tell. It doesn't feel like some angry ghost is about to try and take my head off with a door like before," Miranda added.

"I got bored while I was waiting, so I cleansed the place as well as I could. I've managed to get most of the poor souls that were still hanging around this place to move on. Hardly any of the original thirteen victims are left here now. It's yet another thing I should've taken care of years ago. I didn't realize how many of them had gotten stuck here," he explained, a note of regret in his voice.

Athena greeted Daniel with a grin. The wyvern lowered his head to allow her to scratch behind his ears, and blinked his big, cat eyes at her as he hooted in pleasure. Athena looked over at Clark.

"It's really amazing how different this place feels now. Do you think you could show me how to help spirits cross over like that some day?"

"I would be happy to. It would definitely be a more productive use of your talents than trying to record them. C'mon, I've identified a spot nearby that I think would be a good place to begin making the pit where we'll trap the creature." He led the way and they all followed after him, even Daniel who had to tuck his wings in extra close to his body to fit on the trail.

Miranda pushed her way past the others until she was walking shoulder to shoulder with the wizard. "Clark, I've been thinking about your 'two steps forwards one step back' spell and I'm worried that I've found a problem with it."

He chuckled. "My dear, you seem to do nothing but try to find holes in our plans! Perhaps you should be in charge of making the pit since you have such an affinity for holes?"

"Seriously though, if it gets too deep, couldn't it put the monster so far away from the surface that it's no longer considered to be in this land? Didn't you say that if it was removed from the land it could trigger a natural disaster? Well what's the difference between driving it 30 miles away from here or burying it 30 miles beneath here? Isn't the result the same? At some point 'here' stops being 'here.'"

"That's actually a very good point, I'm impressed. However, I've already taken it into account. There is a limit to how deep the hole can ever get from his efforts to dig himself out. It will always keep him well within the range that should prevent such a cataclysm."

"*Should*?" Mira asked skeptically.

"*Will,*" he sighed. "Trust me, I've been over it a dozen times. It's foolproof."

"Good. I don't want all the real estate I've been selling to suddenly end up in a giant sinkhole or something."

"Gods forbid I should ever mess with anyone's property values!"

"Hey Clark," Dennis said, "We're getting really close to where I first spotted cameras up on top of some of the trees. Can you do something with your magic to stop the ABC from spying on us?"

"You brought that baffler with you like I asked, didn't you?"

Athena patted her ever-present purse. "Of course, it's right here."

"It'll scramble the cameras if we get close enough for them to detect us. Hopefully, we'll have concluded our business here before they send anyone out to see what's wrong with them." He stopped suddenly at a spot where the trail widened out.

Athena could see that several of the pine trees all around them looked as if they'd been recently knocked over by some tremendous force and realized that Clark must've made this clearing himself earlier on.

"And here we are. I thought you might like to watch me do this, but I must ask that you don't make much noise. It's going to take lots of concentration for me to create such a deep pit. The Boy can't reach us here, but he'll definitely sense sorcery of this magnitude being used so close to his stomping grounds. Athena, you should probably take Daniel aloft soon and see if you can get a bead on The Boy's location."

Athena gave him a neat military salute that would've made any drill sergeant envious.

"Where are you gonna stash all the dirt from the hole while you're making it?" Dennis asked. "I mean if it's going to be a really, really deep hole, we're talking about an epic amount of dirt and rock aren't we?"

"That's easy. I'll be temporarily shunting it into a pocket dimension, then I'll put it all back when it's time to fill it back in."

"Oh! A pocket dimension! I know all about those! Like where Optimus Prime's trailer disappears to when he transforms? Or where the extra mass goes when Megatron transforms down into a little gun?"

"My dear Dennis, I have no idea what you're blathering about!"

Athena laughed. "Just agree with him, it's what I always do!"

"Now if we're done discussing all the delicate mechanics of magical pit making, I'd like to get on with it already!" Clark said a little huffily.

"By all means, start digging." Athena bowed.

Clark bowed back to her, cleared his throat, hummed a few bars of something, then began his unearthly, childish-sounding chants. His hands were surrounded by an amber glow, and a circle of the ground before him began to churn as though someone was stirring it up with some invisible giant blender. Then this swirling mass of earth began to get lower and lower as Clark's invocations grew louder and louder. In no time at all, a large crater had formed in front of the mage, and it was getting increasingly harder to see the bottom of it as it continued to sink ever deeper.

"Whoa!" Miranda exclaimed, then covered her mouth when Clark gave her a dirty look.

Clark paused just long enough to tip his hat at Athena. She took that to be her signal to get Daniel up into the air, so she closed her eyes, took a deep breath and stretched out to meet the mind of her bestial buddy. The wyvern spread his leathery wings majestically, the early afternoon sun shining through their membranes, and took to the skies.

As she jogged along the trail, still doggedly following the tire tracks from Dennis Arden's van, Agent Method abruptly came to a dead stop. She looked up, watching in awestruck wonder as a dark red shape erupted from the treetops to soar off into the sky somewhere up ahead of her.

She knew what it was immediately. She'd seen videos and photos of such creatures before, in the ABC database, yet she'd never run across one in the wild before.

To come across something so rare, so beautiful and spectacular in such a normally dismal place of terror and death! It was overwhelming!

"God, I love my job!" she breathed as she watched it bank away from her, flying off in the opposite direction.

At that moment, it was totally true. Despite all the horrors, endless bureaucracy, deceptions and incompetence she'd encountered in her career, *this* was why she'd joined the ABC, to experience truly magical things like this, things that most people would never come across in their entire lives. She still hadn't lost her capacity to be amazed by such spectacles, and it was at these times that she felt the most alive, like she was inextricably connected to something far grander than herself. It was the biggest reason why she didn't just throw in the towel and quit.

She allowed herself to bask in the glorious glow of her seemingly random sighting for a few more seconds, then with some effort, snapped herself back to reality.

She still had a job to do.

Athena and Daniel were as one being when she kept her eyes closed to her immediate surroundings. She was thrilled as she felt the warm summer air slipping past Daniel's body, she watched the treetops far below her as she urged Daniel to wing his way over to the part of the woods where the only real devil in these woods held his bloody court. Through Daniel's eyes, she spotted the gleaming white tops of one of the megaliths. She gently suggested that he fly a little lower so she could try to find the cursed being that they called The Boy. It felt good to be the one doing the hunting again.

"Athena!" Dennis was calling her name from what now felt like it was a million miles away. She reluctantly opened her eyes and was so shocked to discover him standing right next to her that she almost jumped backwards.

"The pit is done, we're gonna go knock down one of those little Stonehenge thingies now," Dennis explained.

She blinked and saw that there was now indeed a massive, dark hole in the ground only a few feet from where she stood, like a gaping open wound in the earth itself.

"Damn, that was quick! I totally missed it." She was disappointed. Clark had been right, it had been neat to see how he did it.

"It took at least fifteen minutes," Dennis clarified.

"Jeez, I guess I really lose myself when I'm so deeply connected to Daniel, it only felt like maybe five to me." She could still see what Daniel was seeing, but it was superimposed over her field of vision, which was quite disorienting. She had to steady herself against Dennis to keep from toppling over. She imagined herself falling into the pit and gulped.

"Have you located our target yet?" Clark inquired.

"Nothing yet. We just crossed over into his territory, we'll keep searching."

"Good. As soon as you spot him, try to catch him," Clark commanded, then led them up the trail in the direction of the nearest megalith.

Shortly after they had left the pit and were out of sight, seemingly swallowed up by the forest itself, Agent Method came running up to the scene. She nearly toppled headlong into the pit - she'd been spending more of her time looking up as she ran rather than down, in the hopes of catching another glimpse of the wyvern. She stopped just short of its edge, knocking a few clumps of dirt into the darkness below. She never heard any of it hit the bottom. Her eyes widened behind her shades as she peered down into its inky depths.

"Damn, that's one deep hole!" she whistled. Where did it come from? You'd need some heavy duty excavating equipment to make something like that, but she didn't even see so much as a single shovel lying around. An even better question was where had all the dirt from inside the hole disappeared to?

A new suspicion began to form in her mind. She pulled back the sleeve of her windbreaker to reveal her wrist computer and used it to scan the pit. As she had anticipated, it revealed a residue of magical energy; in fact the readings were off the scale. It had taken a great deal of power to make this pit, and judging by how much of that energy was still permeating the area, it had been created very recently.

"Kismet!" she snarled the word. It had to be his work. She hadn't spotted any other vehicles nearby other than Dennis' van, but the wizard's store was well within teleportation range of this place.

What are these people up to? she wondered. Was the wyvern connected to this, or had her sighting just been a bizarre coincidence? She decided to find a hiding spot nearby and see if they'd return rather than trying to catch up with them. If Kismet was with them, she'd have to be extra careful.

Athena, Dennis, and Miranda looked on as Clark levitated the stone that connected the two megalithic columns, which he had informed them was called a capstone. The massive rock must've weighed several tons, but Clark was able to make it float like a feather effortlessly. They watched as he gently set it down beside one of the columns that was still standing.

"I had these things custom made and flown here all the way from Wales, it cost me a small fortune," he said with a twinge of regret. "We're vulnerable now. I need all of you to stand over here right next to me - *quickly!*"

They all scrambled over to stand around Clark. He performed an incantation which created a shimmering shield of transparent emerald energy that sizzled as it pulsated around them in a ring shape. Its top extended about two feet above Clark's head.

"I don't sense him nearby, but better safe than sorry," Clark commented.

The others nodded numbly. Despite the fact that they should be safe enclosed by Clark's shield as they moved back down the trail in the direction of the pit, none of them truly felt that way. They were all too scarred by their ordeal from the last time they were in those woods to feel very secure. Even with a wizard as powerful as Clark mere inches away, a man who could make a seemingly bottomless pit with words and move huge rocks around with a wave of his hand, none of them felt at ease. Athena kept imagining the loathsome creature perching up near the top of one of the taller trees, poised to leap down into their protective sanctuary as they passed by.

"Steady on, Athena, I told you I'm not sensing him in our immediate vicinity. Clear your mind and concentrate on using Daniel to find him." She felt the words inside her head as clearly as she heard them, and for once felt more comforted by them than angered over the uninvited intrusion of her mind. She did as Clark suggested, closing her eyes and letting Dennis guide her walking body. He held her hand and gave it a reassuring squeeze. She smiled broadly, drawing strength from his touch.

Now she was fully with Daniel again, swooping just over the treetops and occasionally landing on the trails and looking around. It was during one of these landings that she *smelled* the creature through Daniel's sensitive nose. The fetid stench of rancid flesh was unmistakable, the thing was somewhere upwind of Daniel. She asked Daniel to scan the forest all around him with his eyes, and he twisted his lengthy neck around as he searched, but his long range vision was rather weak and revealed nothing, though she could hear a crashing and snapping of branches through her wyvern's ears. She urged Daniel back up into the air, asking him to circle low over the area near where he'd just been standing.

On his second pass over the spot, she saw a sudden, furtive movement below.

"I see it! I see it! That's it! Go get it!" she cried out excitedly. Dennis squeezed her hand again in encouragement, while Miranda let out a big breath she'd been holding and smiled. Clark simply pursed his lips grimly and quickened his pace towards the pit.

Through Daniel's eyes, Athena could now see the hideous thing once more. It looked even worse than she remembered with its twisted, disproportionate limbs, and ever bubbling and rippling masses of flesh. Dark splotches painted its malformed face, which she was seeing in black and white. She assumed that this was blood. Tyler's blood! How much of his life blood was mingled with that of the things' other victims on that filthy mockery of a face? The thought enraged her. Daniel must've picked up on her feelings because he bellowed out a challenging howl as he speeded towards The Boy.

The Boy wasn't running away, it was running *towards* Daniel and leaping at him, only to come crashing back down, then repeat the maneuver. Every time it jumped up into the air, it greedily snapped its jaws. The crazed thing actually wanted to make a meal out of Daniel! She was amazed that it wasn't intimidated by the larger creature. How dumb or desperate was this thing?

She had Daniel spread his talons wide and plough into the creature, snatching it up by its lumpy shoulders and lifting it off the ground. The Boy struggled mightily, thrashing around and kicking uselessly out into empty space. Daniel hooted in triumph. Athena stumbled as she walked, she could really smell the thing now, as if it was right beside her, and it was making her queasy. She could feel its hot drool landing on Daniel's talons, and its skin moving beneath them.

"We've got it now!" she reported.

"Excellent! Bring him to us," Clark ordered, finally allowing himself a small smirk of satisfaction.

"Roger that," Athena replied, in full military mode now. She asked Daniel to turn around and move in the same direction they were walking. In the skies behind them, the wyvern made a wide arc in the air.

"Roger? Who's Roger?" They couldn't tell if Clark was genuinely confused or was just making a lame joke.

Athena would've rolled her eyes if they weren't still closed.

As Daniel sped back towards their neck of the woods, The Boy's movements became ever more spastic. He clawed at Daniel's talons with feral abandon, but even though his fingers were strong and his nails long, Daniel only felt mild discomfort from these efforts. The wyvern did have to squeeze those talons even tighter though, in order to maintain his grip on the struggling monster.

The Boy began rocking back and forth and stretching and craning his neck towards the strong talons that held him fast. Eventually, he succeeded in biting Daniel, chomping down with a terrible ferocity. Daniel screeched in pain. On the trail below, Athena screamed and fell against Dennis.

"What's wrong?" an alarmed Dennis demanded as he helped her back up, but she had no time to answer.

Daniel dropped The Boy. The thing careened into the ground with a cacophony of crunching bones, yet was back up in an instant and hurriedly loping away.

Apparently, it had decided that this meal wasn't worth the trouble.

Athena fought through waves of throbbing pain that wasn't her own to convince Daniel to turn around and go back after the monster. It wasn't easy, and she couldn't blame him. He was literally once bitten and twice shy. She felt guilty asking him to do it, but it had to be done. In the end, she won the brief battle of wills and was able to persuade the reluctant wyvern to go back after the retreating form of The Boy before it could disappear back into the woods. This time, she had Daniel kick at it as it barreled towards him, knocking the creature into a tree. The monster picked itself back up, only to have Daniel swat it back down to the ground again with a lightning quick flick of his forked tail. Next, Athena had Daniel fly up into the air only to land back down right on top of the creature's stomach, knocking the wind out of it. She had him repeat this move two more times before picking it up again, this time grabbing it around the waist rather than the shoulders before taking flight again.

With the situation finally under control again, Athena gave her update to the others, who had stopped walking and were standing around her with worried expressions that she couldn't see, but could feel. "We lost it for a minute, but we got it back. It's one feisty little fucker, I'll give it that! It took a bite out of my Daniel's toe!"

"Damn! Poor Daniel," Miranda exclaimed.

"Ah, we'll be okay. Twas only a flesh wound." Athena couldn't resist quoting *Monty Python and the Holy Grail.* Likewise, Dennis couldn't help but catch the reference and snicker.

"Good work, Athena. I know you won't lose him a second time," Clark replied, and started them moving forward again.

They all arrived at the pit before Daniel did, who still had to contend with a wildly struggling monster interrupting his normally smooth flying. As they neared the hole, the green shield flickered a few times, then disappeared.

"It's alright. We shouldn't need it any longer. I trust that Athena has everything well in hand. I believe in her," Clark said proudly.

Athena visibly blushed at his words. Alas, the moment wasn't to last long. No sooner had Clark spoken those fateful words than many things happened all at once. A perfect storm of 'what can go wrong will go wrong' had been brewing and now it was about to rain down on them all.

Athena still had her eyes closed, and was confused to hear a nearby rustling of bushes, followed by a gasp from Miranda. She felt Dennis being suddenly pulled away from her. She snapped open her eyes to see that awful woman from the ABC pointing a silvery gun at them with one hand. With the other hand, she'd grabbed hold of Dennis' arm and yanked him towards her with surprising strength. In a flash, she had an arm around his neck, choking him, and her ray gun now pointed straight at his head.

"I need some answers now, or lover boy gets it!" she snarled.

"How dare you!" Clark bellowed, blue lightning crackling threateningly around his outstretched hands.

"Let go of him, you *bitch*!" Athena shouted at Agent Method.

She thought she saw the woman rock backwards on her feet for a moment as if she'd been pushed by an invisible hand. A trickle of blood drizzled from one of her nostrils. Yet she kept her grip firmly on Dennis and her gun trained on his temple.

Just then, Daniel came flying overhead, and with her attention entirely focused on the threat to her husband, Athena forgot all about the monstrous Boy held in his talons. She'd been reinforcing Daniel's will to keep his grip on the violently struggling creature and without her help, he dropped it too soon.

The creature landed on its feet this time, mere feet from the edge of the pit that had been created to entomb it forever. It hissed at them, baring its broken, blackened, jagged teeth, then lunged after Miranda with uncanny speed. She screamed in terror.

Mark came running from somewhere off to the side at top speed and tackled the monster to the ground seconds before it could reach Miranda with its outstretched claw-like hands.

Yes, Mark. You didn't really think he'd stay away, did you?

Mark and the bestial Boy struggled for a few tense moments in the dirt, nearly rolling into the yawning depths of the pit at one point, but the creature quickly gained the upper hand, savagely smacking Mark across the head with its arm. Mark seemed to pass out, and The Boy effortlessly tossed his limp form over its shoulder. It ran off towards the woods carrying him, instantly disappearing into the dense tangle of vegetation.

Blue bolts of lightning sizzled after the monster, joined by beams of exotic energy from Agent Method's pistol.

But it was no good. The horrible, monstrous thing was already gone - and now it had Mark.

Chapter Twenty-Three: Final Jeopardy

Athena ran to where Dennis was scrambling to get to his feet after Agent Method had tossed him aside to fire upon The Boy in futility.

"Are you alright?"

"Yeah," he heaved the words out as he supported himself against a tree.

Athena whirled around to face the ABC agent. "You!"

"I wasn't really going to shoot him - I swear! I just wanted my memories back! I just wanted to know what you've been up to!"

"You wanna know what we've been up to? I'll tell you! We were about two seconds away from getting rid of that Goddamned thing forever when you came along and fucked it all up!" she screamed at her. Athena's fury was so palpable that it drove Method to her knees before her.

"And now it's got my brother!"

The agent threw her head back, grimacing in agony. More blood gushed from her nose.

"Athena!" Clark thundered. His voice reverberated in her head. "Calm yourself! Mark is still alive! I can feel him, and you can too if you concentrate! There's still time to save him! Use Daniel!"

Athena immediately snapped out of it, as if someone had just splashed her face with a bucket of cold water. She was shocked by what she had just done. She had no idea that she even had that kind of power, and was frightened by it. But there was no time to deal with that right now. Clark was right, she *could* feel Mark out there. He was hurting, but alive. She looked up to see Daniel circling the sky directly above them, and closed her eyes to reconnect with him. She could use her ability to zero in on her brother's presence to lead him straight to The Boy this time.

Daniel whooshed off in the direction where The Boy had carried Mark, once more knocking Clark's hat from his head.

The Boy was barreling through the woods with supernatural speed. It wasn't on any of the trails, but blazing a trail through the underbrush, paying no mind to the branches and thorns that constantly snatched and tore at its skin. It carried Mark's still unconscious form on its back, occasionally casting a fearful look over its shoulder. It was almost to its lair. Almost to safety.

Finally, it reached a chicken coop with white paint peeling from its rotting timbers, blasting through the open doorway with Mark. As soon as it was within the dark interior, it threw him onto a wooden table like a rag doll. The pain of that impact woke Mark up just long enough to see The Boy leap onto the table. It looked over him, its stinking breath filled his nostrils. He had just enough time to scream before he felt those disgusting teeth sinking into his shoulder.

Just then, a red blur smashed through the ceiling of the chicken coop, sending splinters and dust flying everywhere. The Boy's head snapped around to face his nemesis, his mouth hanging open stupidly, a dollop of Mark's flesh falling out his twisted mouth. Daniel kicked The Boy off the table with his powerful legs, sending the monster flying through the wall of the coop and rolling back out onto the ground in front of the now-collapsing building. Daniel blasted through what was left of the ceiling and up into the air. The wyvern let loose with a column of blue flame directed at The Boy. The burning creature howled in pain, the acrid smell of its charring body filled Daniel's large nostrils as he continued to pour it on.

The creature continued to burn for a few minutes, thrashing and rolling around in an effort to extinguish the flames. Finally, it keeled over onto one side. It was still twitching, and its flesh was struggling to cover its now exposed and smoldering bones and tendons with new tissue. Daniel beat his wings over it rapidly, putting out the remaining flames, then scooped up the monster and took to the air once again.

About halfway to the pit, the creature had recovered about as much as it ever could. It looked much the same as it had before it was fried by Daniel's flames, except for now it was completely naked, all of its loose and ragged clothing having burned off. It began struggling again, twisting its body around to scratch and bite at Daniel's talons.

"Don't drop him again, not yet! You're nearly there! We can do it! Just hang in there a little longer!" Athena urged him aloud, feeling each fresh scratch and bite the creature managed to land as if her own body was under assault. She swooned from the pain of it, and again Dennis was there to catch her and hold her as always. She gritted her teeth. Sweat ran down the side of her beet-red face. They were so close now, she could see herself and the others through Daniel's eyes, blurry shapes arranged around a dark hole in the earth.

As if sensing how deeply it was endangered, The Boy bit down even more ferociously than ever before, tearing out a big chunk of meat from Daniel's foot. Daniel made that same terrible, haunting sound he'd made when Mark and Athena had been quarreling. Athena grabbed onto Dennis' arm so desperately that she was cutting off his circulation. He rubbed her back and whispered encouragement to her. Daniel responded to this latest attack by digging his claws even deeper into the monster. Blood erupted from The Boy's body, raining down on Athena and her companions as Daniel circled over the pit.

"Now!" Athena hollered.

They all watched with grim satisfaction as The Boy streaked down into the pit.

"Woo hoo!" Miranda cheered, "You did it! You really did it!"

Clark was immediately by its side, chanting intently. A glowing hole opened up in the air right over it and a blur of dirt and rock poured into the hole, like a seemingly never ending geyser in reverse. Everyone choked on the dust from it, except for Clark, who kept up his chanting and waved his luminous hands around frantically. Finally, the torrent of earth ceased and the tear in the fabric of reality itself sealed shut. Clark grew quiet. He looked down upon the freshly buried hole with solemnity, doffing his hat and muttering what sounded like a prayer.

"I'm sorry it's come to this. Sorry I couldn't find a better way," he whispered.

Athena ran over to him and tugged on his sleeve. "We don't have time for this! Mark's hurt really badly! He's losing lots of blood. You've got to teleport over to him and do your healing thing on him!"

"Where is he?"

"It was like an old chicken coop. Hurry!"

"Yes, I know the place. Everyone! Link hands!"

Agent Method had been sitting up against a tree, rubbing her temple and wiping the blood from above her lip. Clark met her eyes. "You too, get over here!"

She got to her feet and took Athena's outstretched hand with a bit of trepidation. Then there was some arcane chanting, followed by an intense flash of light and they were gone.

They reappeared only a moment later inside the coop, right next to the table. Mark was moaning in pain; a long roof beam had fallen across his legs, pinning him to the table. Clark wasted no time in levitating it off of him, sending it hurtling out of the large, freshly-made hole in the wall.

"Oh my God! Look at all the blood!" Athena cried, "Is he going to be alright?"

"Yes, I think we've arrived just in the nick of time." Clark waved his hands over Mark's wound and sang his unusual words. As he did so both his hands and the wound glowed until the wound had sealed itself shut. Clark smiled down at him. "You should be feeling alright now."

Mark rubbed his shoulder. "Good as new! Thanks, Clark."

He sat up and swung his legs over the edge of the table, but before he could get up, Athena was all over him, hugging him despite the blood that was getting all over her clothes.

"Geez! I'm happy to see you too!" His words were muffled by her body.

She pushed herself off of him, "What the hell are you doing here you idiot?" she sobbed.

"Hey, it's a good thing I decided to show up, or it might've been Miranda who was lying here bleeding out. I got here just as big red over there was holding Dennis hostage. I was gonna try and sneak up behind her when it started raining monsters," he explained as he got himself off the table.

"Yeah, thanks for saving me, Mark," Miranda said.

"Anytime." He grinned at her.

Dennis glanced around the cramped space and noticed a pile of bones littering one corner. Some of them looked human.

"Let's get the hell out of here." The others all muttered in agreement and walked out through the new hole in the wall.

As soon as they were outside again, Athena turned to Clark. "Holy shit! How could I forget? Daniel! He got hurt too, you need to heal him too!"

"Certainly. Bring him to us."

"Don't look now, but he's already found us," Mark said, pointing up.

The wyvern landed in front of them. He whimpered pathetically as his wounded foot made contact with the ground. Athena ran to him and began stroking the end of his snout. "My poor boy! You're gonna be okay, I promise."

Clark glided over to the wounded wyvern and repeated his healing spell on the bleeding feet of the beast until they were fully restored. Daniel hooted in appreciation.

"You've done very well, I'm sorry I don't have any fish for you. Gods know you've definitely earned them today!" Clark said as he scratched Daniel beneath his chin. Clark faced the others. "I think it's time for us to say goodbye to our heroic friend here, he's served his purpose, he should return home now."

"Does he really have to go?" Athena pleaded.

"I'm afraid he doesn't belong here - well, not all the time. He's meant to be able to migrate freely between our two worlds whenever The Scar opens up. And mating season is about over now. We must release him to let him live his own life again. All wild things deserve to be free."

The wizard stepped back and stood beside Agent Method. They looked on as the others surrounded Daniel, petting him and saying their goodbyes. Athena wrapped her arms around his long neck and closed her eyes, reveling in their special connection one last time. Tears rolled down her face and Daniel leaned down to nuzzle the top of her head affectionately.

"I'll never forget you. Thank you, for everything," she managed to get out, her voice choking with heartbreak.

Daniel hooted, spread his wings wide and was soon naught but a dot disappearing over the treetops. As she watched his diminishing form, Athena felt as if a piece of her had just been torn out. Dennis put an arm around her waist and Mark squeezed her shoulder. She might've lost her wyvern, but at least she still had her men - and her bestie!

"Is it really over?" Agent Method asked Clark.

"Yes, that unholy marriage of undead flesh and a nature spirit is now buried beneath tons of earth and rock along with other magical protections to keep him in place. It is finally over - well, except for one thing." He touched one of his slender fingers to her forehead. "Remember!" He intoned. She felt as if her head would burst for a moment as all her lost memories came flooding back into her mind.

"Thanks, I guess."

"No need. I'm merely returning what I had no right to steal," he said regretfully. "Perhaps now that I've taken care of our mutual problem with the monster, the ABC won't mind doing a little something for me?"

His words reminded her of the unfortunate reality which awaited her. And she shuddered at the thought of all the paperwork in her near future. "Sure, what are you looking to get in exchange?"

"That unfortunate woman, Rebecca Greene. She must be set free as soon as possible and properly compensated for what you've done to her life. Find someone else to blame all of this on, someone who actually deserves to be punished."

Method thought about it for a moment. "I'll be happy to relay that message. A wizard of your stature still commands lots of respect in our circles, I'm sure they'll take your recommendations seriously. In fact, you should've just come to us right away instead of trying to take this on all by yourself."

"I didn't take it on all by myself. I had plenty of help from my friends." He smiled broadly as he looked at Athena, Dennis, Mark and Miranda.

"Anyway, how could I possibly trust an organization that frames innocent women for its own failures? My dear old friend Sara would be ashamed of the whole lot of you! We never intended the ABC to degenerate into what it has become! I'd heard rumors of what's happened to the ABC lately, but I didn't want to believe it. There've been far too many unpleasant truths I've been trying to ignore, but all that stops now. Just make sure that they understand that I'll be very upset if they don't honor my request. Very upset indeed, and they *don't* want that."

"No need to resort to threats, it's beneath you. I'll make sure they understand how serious you are about it. The ABC isn't completely hopeless, we still have a few good men and women in it. Perhaps all we need is somebody with the courage of Esmeralda Hazleton to take on all the corruption?"

"Ah, good old Esmeralda. The Great Reformer of the Temple of the Old Gods. She was a personal friend of mine, you know?"

Method actually giggled. "Of course she was."

"I'm impressed that you know so much about the history of my people."

"I enjoyed reading about her in the *Magna Historian Mundi*," she confessed.

"I enjoyed those books too. Yes, maybe you're right and not all of you ABC agents are quite so bad after all." He winked at her, then ambled over to where the others had gathered and were talking amongst themselves excitedly.

"Nice work everyone! Hmm! Apparently I'm not the only one who approves." He tilted his head off to the side. The others all looked in the direction Clark indicated and saw Tyler standing at the edge of the clearing. He gave them all a smile, a big thumbs up, then did a little air guitar before fading away.

"Did you all just see that?" Dennis asked in amazement. "Full body apparition! Way to go, Tyler!"

"He wouldn't have believed it unless he saw it himself," Athena laughed.

"No need to worry about his troubled soul any longer, he's at peace now," Clark informed them authoritatively.

"Yeah, that's right. I can feel it," Athena agreed.

"So can I," Mark added.

The wizard wrapped his long arms around them and grinned at his new friends - his new *family*. "Now, who's in the mood for a little Greek?"

Epilogue: The Bonus Round

A week and a day passed by. Athena Anderson Arden sat at her dining room table, sipping her morning coffee. She nibbled at what was left of the breakfast Dennis had cooked for her before he decided to take Mr. President out for a walk. She looked at the headline on the latest Sunday edition of the Asbury Park Press with satisfaction. "REBECCA GREENE EXONERATED" it screamed in a rare front page story written by Lars Ericson. The picture showed the woman she'd met weeks earlier smiling as she was walking down the steps of a courthouse.

The ABC had pinned the deaths of the archeologists and his students on someone who Agent Method (or Krystal Graham as she now knew her), had assured them was a real, bona fide serial killer. The man had been eager to confess to murders that he hadn't really committed since having a higher body count appealed to his sick ego. The disappearance of Dustin McCloskey had also been blamed on him, something which happened *after* Becca Greene was already in custody, further proving her innocence. Lars had been happy to regurgitate the story the ABC had woven for him, he didn't get exclusive scoops like this one very often.

Through the bay window of her living room window Athena saw Clark's van screech to a halt in front of her house. He'd indicated that he wanted to talk to her in person this morning, which was the only reason she was dressed in anything other than her pajamas this early on a Sunday. She wondered why the wizard bothered to drive anywhere instead of just teleporting as she watched him climb out. She decided that he must just liked to drive sometimes. There were many things about the wizard that didn't really make any sense to her, but she kind of liked it that way. She gulped down what was left of her coffee and rose to open the door for him as she saw him making his way up the walkway.

"Good morning, Clark!" she called cheerily as she swung open the front door.

"Good morning, Athena!" he replied. He was dressed in his business suit again, and he tipped his derby in her direction. "Won't you invite me in?"

"I dunno, you're not a vampire *and* a wizard are you?"

"Goodness no! The last of those was killed back in '05!"

"1905?"

"2005."

"That recent, huh?" As usual, she wasn't sure how serious the mage actually was.

"Well, I guess it's safe to let you in." She stepped aside to allow him through. "Ya want some coffee?"

"No thanks, I'm really more of a tea drinker."

"Jeez, you're really trying to reinforce all those British stereotypes, huh?"

"British? Who's British?" He looked puzzled.

"Oh, so you're just a massive poseur. Makes sense."

Athena threw herself onto her sofa and Clark sat in the armchair facing it.

"So what's up?"

"I assume you already know that I asked your brother to become my apprentice and he accepted."

She did indeed. She wasn't sure she completely approved. But recent events had helped her come to grips with the fact that her little brother was a grown man now, and she had to let him make his own decisions.

"Yeah, so?"

"I just wanted you to know that despite the fact that I'll be training him, my offer to you still stands as well. I know that you plan on carrying on with the JSPS. You have to understand by now that even if you ever did obtain completely convincing evidence of the paranormal, the ABC would never let you release it publicly, at least not without making you look like a complete fool. If you're going to carry on, why not do something truly worthwhile with it? I could show you how to help restless spirits move onto what awaits them beyond the veil of death, just like I did back at the camp."

"Oh." She leaned back in her seat and looked past the wizard, at the birds doing cartwheels in the sky outside her window, and thought of Daniel. She considered her next words carefully before opening her mouth to respond.

"Your people, this Temple of the Old Gods, they used to burn other witches, right? Why? Because they're a bunch of control freaks who can't stand the idea of a little competition? I know you say they stopped doing that ages ago, but they still had no problem destroying Daniel Leeds' reputation, making sure that his family name was forever linked in everybody's minds with a monster. That's really not any better in my book. The fact of the matter is that I could never be comfortable joining up with a group with such an incredibly fucked up past. I know you didn't have much of a choice in the matter when you joined. The Inquisition was hunting you, so it was either join up or let them lock you away, but I *do* have a choice and my decision still is not to join them."

She saw the genuinely hurt look on Clark's face and wondered if she'd gone too far, perhaps she shouldn't have phrased it so harshly?

"Perhaps if I took you to meet my old apprentice Wendy and some of the others, you'd understand how different everything is now?" the wizard sputtered.

She held up a hand. "There's no need. I didn't finish. I didn't say that I don't want to learn how to use my abilities better, I do, I'd especially love to learn it from you."

"Oh?" He smiled, obviously flattered by her words - then it faded. "But there's a catch isn't there?"

"You know me too well. Yes. I'm willing to be your student or whatever, but I don't want to join the Temple of the Old Gods - *ever*. Keep my name off the books."

Clark was silent for a moment as he considered what she'd said. "A secret apprentice? It's highly unorthodox and completely against the rules! I do wish you'd reconsider. I'm not sure you fully understand what you're turning down. We share our wealth with all our members, you'd never have to work in that little library ever again...."

"Hey! I really like working in that library! You tried to tempt me with the money aspect twenty-two years ago too, remember? It didn't work then and it won't work now. I can't be bought. It's not about the money, it never has been. This is about being able to keep my friends and family safe. Maybe if I'd been able to really use my powers correctly, Tyler would still be with us today. And like you said, I'd like to know how to help troubled spirits finally move on. To make the JSPS into something that really matters."

And I need to learn how to make sure I don't accidentally hurt someone the way I did with Krystal, she thought.

He sighed a sigh of surrender. "You're really serious about this aren't you?"

"You're the one who's always rummaging around in my head without my permission, so you tell me. Yes, it's my final offer."

"I'm the one making the offers here!" he cried out in exasperation.

Then he laughed, and in a more gentle tone he said, "You know, you really are the most infuriating woman! But then again, so was Marlena. I suppose that's part of why I liked her so much. I've been waiting twenty-two years to show you the wonders of the universe, so Gods help me, if this is what it takes then I accept."

"I'll take that as a yes."

"Your brother was a lot easier. As soon as I hinted about the money he was all in."

"My little brother just doesn't want to get a real job. Kids these days, no work ethic, y'know?"

"Yes, I'm certain that he wasn't at all enticed by the idea of learning how to do magic or control mythical beasts. There's nothing remotely cool about any of that," Clark replied sarcastically.

"So, do you think you can really handle teaching two crazy Andersons at once?" she grinned mischievously at him.

"It looks like I'm going to have to figure out a way to, doesn't it?"

She leaned over and patted him on the hand. "You're a clever guy. I know you'll work it out."

"I suppose I should thank you," the wizard said hesitantly.

"For what?"

"I'd lost my way these past few years, lost my purpose. I'm not from here, Athena. I'm from another world, another time, another universe entirely. In the past few years I've felt like my work here is done and I've become obsessed with trying to find a way back home. I've been neglecting my store, my employees, and even my own health. Just spending twenty-four hours a day trying to figure out a way to get back to a world where they probably don't even know that I'm still alive. But all of this business that we've been wrapped up in, it's made me realize that I still do have a purpose here, and important responsibilities. I can still make a difference. I don't need to find my way back home now, this place *is* my real home."

Athena was so touched by his words that she was uncharacteristically speechless for a moment, but it didn't last.

"I'm glad you've got your mojo back, but I just remembered that I have something a little more substantial for you to thank me for." She got up from the sofa and pulled something off the top of a nearby bookshelf. It looked like a folded up piece of clothing because that's exactly what it was. She unfurled it so Clark could see.

"A JSPS t-shirt?"

"I thought you looked so cute in Mark's that you deserved one of your own. Congratulations! You're officially part of the team now."

Clark took the shirt from her and folded it up again in his lap. "It's just what I've always wanted," he replied with a wry smile, then looked at her with a more serious expression on his face.

"Are you really going to be okay? It sounds as if you're still blaming yourself for Tyler's death."

"It's hard *not* to. Even though he gave me a thumbs up for what we did back there, I can't shake the belief that he'd still be with us today if I hadn't been such a stubborn ass. Self forgiveness doesn't come so easily."

"I know what you mean, I often blame myself for all of the deaths too. You know, the Guilds have special counselors especially for people like us. There's even one in the area. In the past I suppose I've been too proud to utilize them, but I think perhaps it's time to start acknowledging some of my own limitations."

"It's really difficult for me. My whole life I've struggled with my anxieties. In some ways they've gotten better as I've gotten older and in other ways they've gotten worse. I've always been skeptical about drugs and therapists and all that, I've always tried to manage it all on my own, but since we lost Tyler it's become even harder. The only thing that's really given me any peace lately was when I was in Daniel's head. Being one with someone with such an uncomplicated life, a creature of pure instinct...It was...*transcendent*. I'm really gonna miss that wyvern."

"You could summon him again sometimes, make him your familiar. It should be easy for you now that you two have bonded. I can show you how. I think he'd like that too, although Mark might become a little jealous."

She was floored. She really believed that she'd seen the last of her scaly friend. "What? Really?"

"On one condition, that you agree to see the counselor. I don't want my new apprentice to be operating at anything less than 100 per cent!"

"You don't have to attach any strings to it, I was gonna agree to go anyway. I'm tired of fighting this battle on my own. And it's not fair to put as much of it on Dennis' shoulders as I do. If I'm not at my best, then how can I really be there for anybody else when they need me? I want to be better. Life's too short not to make the most of it, y'know?"

"Hmm. Life's too short. Perhaps for some of us." As he said it, for a moment Athena imagined she could see the weight of all his years pressing in on him, and then it was gone as if it had never been there. He stood up and moved towards the front door. "Your training begins at Seventh Heaven tomorrow after you get off from work. I'll see you then."

He let himself out the door and Athena watched him climb into his ridiculous old van and drive away.

She smiled, excited by the prospect of seeing Daniel again, and all the strange and wonderful things she'd learn from Clark. Excited for the peace of mind which had so long eluded her, yet now seemed tantalizingly within her grasp. Yes, all her tomorrows were starting to look so bright that she just might have to get herself a new pair of shades....

The End

Athena and the JSPS will return in "Night of the Mothman"